The Princes' Revolt

The Princes' Revolt

Book 17 in the Anarchy Series
By
Griff Hosker

The Princes' Revolt

Published by Sword Books Ltd 2018

Copyright © Griff Hosker First Edition

The author has asserted their moral right under the Copyright, Designs and Patents Act, 1988, to be identified as the author of this work.

All Rights reserved. No part of this publication may be reproduced, copied, stored in a retrieval system, or transmitted, in any form or by any means, without the prior written consent of the copyright holder, nor be otherwise circulated in any form of binding or cover other than that in which it is published and without a similar condition being imposed on the subsequent purchaser.
A CIP catalogue record for this title is available from the British Library.
Thanks to Design for Writers for the cover and logo.

Dedicated to three perfect grandchildren: Thomas, Samuel and Isabelle

Contents

The Princes' Revolt i
Prologue 1
Chapter 1 3
Chapter 2 18
Chapter 3 35
Chapter 4 53
Chapter 5 68
Chapter 6 82
Chapter 7 93
Chapter 8 103
Chapter 9 115
Chapter 10 126
Chapter 11 140
Chapter 12 155
Chapter 13 166
Chapter 14 180
Chapter 15 190
Chapter 16 198
Chapter 17 210
Epilogue 218
Glossary 220
Historical Notes 223
Other books by Griff Hosker 232

The Princes' Revolt

Part One
William, Earl of Cleveland

Prologue

My father, the Warlord, had spent less than a year with us after we had defeated William of Scotland. His left arm had been hurt in the fight and he had been slow to recover. That was not a surprise. He had been a warrior for more than fifty years. He was old. We both knew that he would never be the warrior he had once been. I wondered why he rode to war at all. I had thought that the death of the Empress Matilda would have made him look at his family more. He seemed obsessed with serving King Henry. I could not fathom the reason for that. I, too, was loyal. I was of an age with the King. I was just a few years older and I had ridden with him in Normandy. I was loyal to him yet for my father service to King Henry seemed paramount. It went beyond fealty.

Once he had healed he had gone with the King to Normandy. King Louis sought to take the Vexin and my father was one of the few warriors feared throughout France and the other countries which bordered King Henry's Empire. He was there to advise the King and to intimidate and frighten the French. His service to the King kept him apart from us. He returned every few months and seemed happy, even relieved, to be back in Stockton but then a missive would come and he would be forced to leave. He was constantly at the King's beck and call.

He missed many events while he was away. Samuel, my son, became a knight. He had shown great skills as a squire and it was an easy decision to give him his spurs. He was desperate to be just like his grandfather, the Warlord. Each visit from my father was a joy to the young knight. My daughter, Ruth now grown into a young woman, also looked forward to his visits. His work for the King meant he missed the change in her too.

When we received the news that he was to return home again I decided to it into a real celebration. I sent messages to all his knights. Like my family they missed him. I think the one who missed him the most was me. I had not seen much of him when I had been growing up. He had been trying to save England from King Stephen. Then I had been absent. I confess that I was a bad son for a while. I shut out my father. He never saw my first family. I think that when they died and I went on crusade part of the atonement was for what I had done to my father. Now it was he who was absent. I needed him.

I did not need his military advice. I had skills myself and besides since we had defeated King William of Scotland, then the border was quiet. Our main work was to scour the land of bandits and brigands. We were still vigilant for the Scottish cattle raiders who still travelled great distances to steal our animals and enslave our people but we had not lost a man in the four years since William had been defeated. I knew that my son, Samuel and his squire Thomas, yearned for some action. The only battle Samuel had experienced had been the one against the Scots and it had whetted his appetite. My wife, Rebekah, thought the peace we had enjoyed a good thing. The town and people had all prospered.

The only cloud in an otherwise perfectly blue sky was the return of the Bishop of Durham, Hugh de Puiset. King Henry had made him travel to Rome in an attempt to rid himself of the Archbishop of Canterbury, Thomas Becket. From what my father had told me the King had hoped that the Bishop would sway the pontiff. He was wrong. The Bishop had been back for a year and already we saw that his people were suffering. Something would have to be done. That was for the future. First, we had to celebrate the return of the Warlord.

Chapter 1

My father did not return home by sea. He rode from York. He had with him just twelve men at arms and four archers. I saw his servants, Wilfred, Brian and Osbert. All three were old soldiers with wounds but they could still fight. The small escort was all the protection he needed. This was the Warlord, Earl Marshal of England riding through the land he had saved so many times that men had lost count. As they waited at the ferry I saw a banner I did not recognise and what looked like a new squire. My father waved as the ferry set off from the south bank of the river. Padraig, his squire, was with him and he was skilled enough to be knighted. Perhaps my father was training up a new one but I did not understand the banner. I did not see another knight. My wife was busy with Alice, my father's housekeeper, preparing for the arrival of the knight who had made Stockton the stronghold it was. Samuel stood next to me. He was as tall and as broad as I was. The grey in my hair and beard reminded me of my age but Samuel's presence did so even more.

The smile on my son's face showed that he was happy at the return of his grandfather, "I hope he stays longer this time. Each time he leaves I fear that I will never see him again."

"I feel the same but you cannot change my father. He has been this way since long before I was born. We just make the most of each visit."

"Padraig should be knighted! He is older than I am and has much more experience."

I nodded, "Perhaps he chooses not to be. He and my father have been together for more than ten years. I was not married as long to my first wife. It may be hard for both of them to part. That may be why he is here. I see that there is another squire with them."

Ethelred's son had ferried the Warlord personally. The esteem in which he was held was clearly demonstrated in the ferry's crew who could not do enough for him. I could only dream of such respect. I knew that I was a mere shadow of my father.

He stepped ashore and embraced me. I noticed that the left arm did not squeeze as tightly as the right. He whispered in my ear, "I have missed you, my son, your family and this castle. Would that I could stay here forever."

As we pulled apart I smiled, "You know you can! Any time!"

He nodded, "Affairs of state still demand my attention. If William Marshal was not another able lieutenant for the King then I could not even spare this visit." He gestured to Padraig, "And one of the purposes of my visit is to knight Padraig here in Stockton. I have been trying to do so for five years but I now have, for a short time, at least, another squire. This is Prince Richard. He is the King's second son."

That was the first time I had met the Prince. I had seen him as a child along with his brother Henry. They had both been less than five summers old. He had grown. His hair was redder now than it had been. I could see that he would be a handsome man. As the second son, he would not attain the throne but his looks and his father's power might ensure that his father made a favourable marriage for him. "You are welcome to my home Prince Richard."

"I have heard much about this mighty rock from my father. It is impressive." Even at that age, he showed us that he was a warrior and understood war.

I waved my arm. "Come, the river at this time of year can often bring on chills and fevers. Inside we have fires burning and Lady Rebekah has rooms awaiting you all."

I smiled as I saw the young Prince taking in the defences my father and I had built up over the years. We took it for granted but I knew that it kept the wolf from the door. Any army which wished to take the soft heartland of the vale of York would have to get by this bastion. When my wife and Alice discovered that we had a member of the royal family staying with us they became agitated. My father smiled, "Prince Richard is here as a squire just as his father was. I have him for a short time and I would not make his life soft."

Prince Richard nodded, "And I would be treated as any other squire or knight. My father told me being part of the Warlord's household made him a better king."

I wonder now, what might have happened had Prince Richard stayed longer with us and my father than he did. Events far in the future might have turned out differently. As Ralph of Bowness often said, "You know not what Fate has in store for you." He had thought to end his days in Constantinople but I had found him and brought him to England. It had proved mutually beneficial.

After they had washed and changed, for it was a long and grimy journey from York, I had wine, bread and cheese brought to the Great Hall. When our goblets were filled I raised mine, as host, "Here is to King Henry!"

"King Henry!"

Prince Richard added, "Good wine it reminds me of the wine my mother's vintner produces at Chinon!"

My father smiled, "It comes from my manor in Anjou; La Flèche. I confess that no matter where I travel, I never find a wine to compare with it."

"And, father, have your travels ceased for a while? Will Prince Richard be able to enjoy the hunting hereabouts?"

My father did not meet my eye. I sighed, "Then this is more than just a visit from the Warlord? You are here as Earl Marshal."

My father stiffened. My tone had not been the correct one and I regretted my words immediately. But, as they say in Normandy, '*the carrot is out of the ground.*' "You are right, William but we could have had a pleasant conversation before we turned to such matters."

"Of course. It is just that we all enjoy your company."

"I know and it pains me to make this such a short visit. I will tell you why I am here and you can make your own mind up. As you know there is money being raised for the crusade in the Holy Land."

I did and it pained me that money was being wasted in such a fashion., I had been a crusader and it was a war we could never win. We were fighting for Templars and silken robed knights. The coin that was being collected would be of better use in England and Normandy, reducing the number of beggars, improving the roads, lowering the taxes. It was an argument I could never win. "Aye. We have ours ready to go."

"And that is the problem. King Henry and King Louis have argued about how the money should be collected. There is war. Louis is now allied with the Bretons, the Scots and the Welsh."

Samuel, who often rode patrols as far as Barnard Castle said, "But there has been no sign of trouble on the border. The Scots have been quiet."

"That, my grandson, is about to change. I go to Wales to join the Marcher Knights. We will teach the Welsh the folly of allying with the French. The King goes to fight the French. Prince Henry will deal with the Bretons." He looked at me.

I knew what my task would be, "And I will lead the knights of the north."

"Exactly. Tomorrow I will knight Padraig and a day later I will take my men and we will go to Wales."

We drank in silence. "You are too old to be campaigning, father."

"I no longer fight. It is another reason to knight Padraig. He wishes to be a knight who fights for his king." I nodded, "Had Samuel not won his spurs I would have offered him the chance to be a second squire."

That was almost an insult but I let it go. "Sir John has a second son, Simon. He would have him as a squire. I intended to invite your old knights here tomorrow night anyway. This now gives me the chance to tell them of my plans and for you to examine young Simon."

"Perfect. Padraig will hold vigil in my church this night. It seems appropriate."

My wife and Ruth appeared, "Have you finished with affairs of state? Your granddaughter is eager to speak with you."

"Of course and forgive me, Rebekah. You must keep me on my guard. I am used to my ways and with no wife to remind me I forget how to behave."

I stood. "I have things to do." Samuel rose. "No, son, you stay with your grandfather." Ralph of Sadberge, my squire was waiting for me. "Send out riders to the knights of the valley and Sir John of Fissebourne. They and their families are invited to Stockton on the morrow for a feast."

"Aye lord."

I sought out William, my steward, and told him what I needed for the feast. He had been my father's steward and was now old and grey but he knew how to prepare a feast. His son John shouldered most of the work but William still liked me to speak directly with him. "I will see Alice, lord. It will be a feast to remember."

I then gathered my captains in the inner bailey. Ralph of Bowness, Ralph of Wales, Aelric, Roger of Bath and Wilfred were now, like me veterans. They worked well together and, to me, were better than any knights save those in the valley. "We go to war. The Scots are about to become annoying again. We will teach them the error of their ways."

The Princes' Revolt

Wilfred, who now had a bald pate which a priest would envy, nodded, "Good. My lads have been getting soft, sitting on their arses all day!"

"How many men will you need, lord?"

Ralph of Bowness, my ex-Varangian, was ever practical. Whatever I did not take would be all that he had to protect my town. "I will take half the men at arms and all of the archers. Just use the single men at arms; leave the married ones here."

"And where do we find the Scots this time, lord?"

"That I do not know. My father did not give me that information. I will send Aiden, Masood, Edgar and Edward to find them." With four scouts I could send two north and two west. The Scots would gather by the border. If they were coming from the north then they would muster at either Berwick or Jedburgh. If it was from the west then it would be Dumfries or Longtown. I went to the well of St. John where I knew I would find my scouts at this time of day.

They stood. They had been throwing dice. They believed the well would bring them luck, "Yes, my lord?"

"I need you to see if the Scots are planning some mischief."

Aiden was my most experienced scout. He nodded. "Do you know where they will begin their attack?"

"It could be anywhere."

"Masood and Edgar, you will head up to the wall and the Tweed. You are familiar with it. Edward and I will head west." He looked at me. "This may take seven or eight days, lord."

"If it takes less then we know they are close. Seven days give us time to raise the north." Even as I said it I knew that we could ill afford to be knighting Padraig. My father and I would be better used travelling to Durham and rousing the lethargic Bishop!

We learned more about the King and his family as we ate, that night, in my hall. It seemed he was on the cusp of having Henry, his son, crowned as joint king. Richard was silent as my father told us this and I saw the question in my son's eyes. Eventually, he could not resist asking it, "But why? He is young, is he not?" He looked at Prince Richard, "No offence meant, Prince Richard."

He shrugged, "None taken for I get nothing from this arrangement. I could have been given Normandy!"

He sounded a little petulant. My father rolled his eyes, "There is a logic to this, Samuel. It means the King can spend more time in

Normandy and his lands on the other side of the sea. William Marshal will have a solid hand on the young King's shoulder."

A sly look came upon Richard's face. He sipped his wine. "Of course, that is dependent upon the Archbishop of Canterbury performing the ceremony."

It all became clear to me at that moment. "And Thomas Becket is still in France!"

My father nodded, "That is why we came north. The Archbishop of York will travel to London. We have informed him of what is needed. Messages have been sent to two other bishops. When this unrest is dealt with then King Henry will have his son crowned. You and your knights will need to travel south and swear allegiance."

"And that is the reason we need to quieten the border. I understand now, father. This is like one of those puzzles we played with as children. You have to move three or four pieces to get at the piece you really need to move."

"And now you know why you were given those toys to play with."

When we had eaten Samuel, Prince Richard and the squires went to the church to spend some time with Padraig before he began his lonely vigil. For Richard, this was important for soon he would be knighted and he wanted to understand everything about the ceremony. For Richard knighthood was all. Samuel and Prince Richard got on well.

My father and I retired to my solar. It was his favourite place in the castle and Alice, anticipating our needs had lit a fire to take away the chill of the evening and placed wine and food there.

When we were settled into the two chairs my father said, "I know that you are unhappy about the short amount of time I spend here." He held up his hand for he could see that I was going to interrupt. "Let me speak. I wish to spend more time here. I am weary of travelling this land and spending time in other men's castles. All of the problems I have now are due to the appointment of Thomas Becket. The King's mother and his wife both advised against it and they were right. He squats like a toad in a French castle. He thwarts, by his absence, all that the King would do. The Pope conspires with both Louis and Becket to hurt our church as much as he can and that, in turn, leads to unrest on our borders."

I poured some more wine. "You said that William Marshall was more than capable. Why not sit back and allow him to do what you have done these past years?"

"As I said King Henry needs him to help his son rule England." He sipped the wine. "You know that we had to go to Ireland this year? De Clare had problems. We now have a High King, King Rory O'Connor. He may be able to control the island but I am not certain. I am more confident in your ability to quell the Scots. When we fought King William the last time he struck me as an overconfident king."

I nodded, "The problem with fighting the Scots, as you well know, is bringing them to a place where they can be fought. The castles to the north of us, despite the poor efforts by de Puiset, are too strong for the Scots to take. My fear is that the Scots will split into warbands and strike at the smaller places."

We spoke until we were both too weary to keep open our eyes. Who knew how many more evenings we would be able to sit and talk. Although the talk was of the campaign it revolved around our men. Knights like Sir Harold and Sir John were like brothers to him. "And how is Wulfric?"

"He will not go to war again. He wishes to but when you see him next, tomorrow night I hope, then you will see why." I could not help glancing at my father's left hand which he now kept covered whenever possible. "His wounds hurt him. He finds movement difficult and so he drinks more than is good for a man to take away the pain. He was always a well-built and powerful warrior. He has now lost that power. He is now just a big man."

My father nodded, sadly and raised his goblet, "Here is a toast to Dick and Wulfric. They were always, with Sir Edward, my rocks. Perhaps Dick was the lucky one. He died in battle."

Alice appeared in the doorway. She had her hands on her hips. "My lords, you two are the only ones left awake save poor Master Padraig. I wish to go to bed even if you do not!"

My father smiled, "You could go to bed, Alice. You do not need to worry about us."

She began to collect the goblets and platters. "The day that I cease to worry about you two will be when I am sleeping in the graveyard with my husband Alan! Come, it is almost cock crow!"

She was right and I had barely nodded off when I heard the hustle and bustle of the castle waking up. It would be a busy day. Padraig's knighting and the feast would keep us all occupied not to mention the preparations for the campaign. In many ways, it was not the ideal time to be going to war. It was coming on to autumn. Perhaps in the balmier lands of Normandy, it might be easier but here, in the north and on the edge of the kingdom, the weather could be as great an enemy as the Scots. Our one advantage was our herd of horses. We had enough so that all the men we took to war would be mounted. The archers would not fight from the backs of their horses but it was handy to know that we could get to the enemy quickly and, if needs be, leave just as quickly.

Samuel's knighthood had been a small affair. There had just been my household knights in attendance. Padraig's was also small and intimate. My church was a small one and it was cosier that way. When he had been dubbed my father gave him his spurs. He was now a knight. He had no squire and would still be dependent upon my father until he was given a manor. I discovered that he had already planned for that. My father had been given the manor of Reeth which was in the uplands by Richmond. It had been his plan to make that his home when he was no longer needed. That was an unlikely occurrence and so Padraig would reap the benefits of the taxes.

We returned to my hall for a small celebration. When the rest went inside I went to the gatehouse to see if any of my riders had returned. I saw Sir Gilles of Norton. He had with him his younger son, John. John was twelve summers' old. I smiled when I saw Gilles for he had been one of my father's squires when he was about young John's age. His elder son, Edward, was Gilles' squire. "Had you come just a little while earlier then you could have witnessed the knighting ceremony."

He nodded, "That is why we came earlier. My son will escort my wife for the feast but John here would be a squire and I wondered if Sir Padraig had one."

"He has not. This is a happy coincidence."

Gilles was ever honest. "No coincidence, lord. I have been seeking a lord for my son for some time. Had you not taken on Ralph then I would have offered him John. He is a good boy and he has worked with Edward since he was able to use a sword. He is bigger than most boys of his age."

"You do not need to convince me. Come let us go inside. There is a chill wind this morning."

As Ralph of Bowness would have said, it was wyrd. Padraig was more than happy to take on the young squire. I was not certain that his mother Mary would be as happy for her son would be leaving the next day with Padraig and my father. He would be going to war! Poor Gilles had to find the horse and provide for the journey south. He and John spent the afternoon preparing for the journey the next day. John of Fissebourne and his wife Edith would have an equally harsh parting. Their youngest son Simon was being honoured; he would be my father's squire. That meant they would see little of him. Such was the life of a knight.

During the afternoon more of my father's knights arrived, Sir Harold, Sir John, Sir Tristan, Sir Wulfric and Sir Henry. Sir Richard lived in the castle and Sir Gilles was already here. Sir James, Sir Phillip and Sir Hugh lived too far away. They would arrive but it would be after my father had gone. I think that Prince Richard felt that he had been slighted for all my father's knights gave a perfunctory greeting to the Prince and then gave all of their attention to the Warlord. This was his world and these were his knights. Prince Richard had known of my father's reputation but that was all. I now saw why King Henry had given him to my father. It was to make him less arrogant. It had worked for the King and Prince Richard would be a better man for the experience.

My wife entertained the wives of the knights. She enjoyed these meetings for she was able to speak with her equals. In the town, the ladies curtsied and bowed. She could not be herself. With Mary, Edith, Maud, Anne and the other ladies she could. She could talk about children and she could talk about clothes and wall hangings. Ruth, too, was able to engage in conversations which went beyond warfare. She was now a beautiful young woman. She was old enough to wed and these gatherings were a perfect place for romance to blossom. Sadly, most of the young men who would be attending the feast in the evening were either too young or already married. In a perfect world, she would marry a bachelor knight. That would suit them both. Sir Tristan's son, the recently knighted Sir Richard would have been perfect but he had married Sir Harold's eldest daughter, Maud.

It was good to have the castle filled. All of the knights and their ladies knew it well. It was like a second home for all of them. Alice and William had greeted them all like old friends for most had either been squires in the castle or, as I the case of Sir Wulfric, a man at arms. The last time we had all gathered together was on the occasion of Samuel's knighthood. There was much to talk about. Lady Maud was with child and so everyone went to congratulate the couple. I stood with my father. He was looking at his knights and there was a frown upon his face. I knew what was in his mind. He was looking at the bloated and corpulent lord of Thornaby.

"It is Sir Wulfric."

He nodded, "Aye it is. When did he get so old and...?"

"You could be kind and say unfit but it is more than that. His wounds mean he does not get to ride as often as he should. He no longer practises. He drinks to ease the pain and to help him to sleep. I am pleased you came, father, for I fear this may be the last occasion. Father Michael has looked at him and he fears he will not see the year out."

"You will not take him to war."

"No, that would be foolish and besides he still has a good mind and can control the valley from his castle in Thornaby."

He smiled at me, "Perhaps this will be my last campaign. I have fought for this valley and the north for more than fifty years yet I have barely seen it in times of peace. I yearn to do that. I would watch my grandchildren have children of their own!"

My wife arranged the seating. That was what she did. I did not get to sit with my father. I was seated by Samuel and Padraig. I dare say my wife meant for the best but I wanted to speak with my father for he would be leaving in the morning. Padraig noticed my distraction. "What is amiss, lord?"

"You leave in the morning. When will I see my father again? He is no longer a young man."

"He is hale and hearty."

"Padraig, he has seen more than sixty summers. There are no warriors left who are older than he."

He looked apologetically at me. He could do nothing about that. I turned to Samuel. He was staring at Sir Tristan's daughter, Eleanor. I smiled. I recognised the signs. He was smitten with the young beauty. He had not seen her for five years and in that time, she had blossomed into a beautiful young woman. I said nothing and I looked around the room. His eyes had alighted on the most beautiful of the girls who were there and I was pleased. In contrast to her brother and the beautiful Eleanor, Ruth looked disconsolate. All of the men in the hall were either married or boys. I could do nothing about her situation. My son, however, was a different matter. Life was too short to worry about conversations I might or might not have. I had not had enough with my father but my son was here and I could speak with him.

"You find young Eleanor attractive?"

He turned sharply as though I had caught him naked. "How did you know?"

I smiled, "Son, everyone knows. It is written on your face. Strike now. When we have finished eating and before she leaves, go and speak with her."

"What about?"

"Anything." I had seen young Eleanor looking at my son. "Trust me in this. She will be happy when you do so." I could see that he was not convinced but he nodded. I turned to Padraig, "And you, too, will need to cast your net for a bride. Time waits for no man!"

He laughed and when he spoke, I heard the lilt of the Hibernian in his voice. "Lord, I have just been knighted. Tomorrow I may get a squire; let that be enough for a while."

"You are right."

When the table had been cleared and the food removed Sir Tristan said, "Well Padraig go fetch your rote. Now that you are a knight you should be showing us that skill."

Poor Padraig looked mortified. I doubted that travelling with my father he would have had either the opportunity or the skill to master that particular musical instrument.

I said quietly to Samuel, "Now is your opportunity. Go fetch yours and you shall sing a ballad for Eleanor." He looked at me. "It will save Padraig the embarrassment of trying to sing without a rote." He nodded and slipped away. I said, "That is not fair Sir Tristan. Poor Sir Padraig has been travelling. My son has yet to show his grandfather his skill. He will sing a ballad for you. If that would do."

I saw young Eleanor's face light up and her father smiled, "Of course."

My son had a good voice but he was nervous. I saw Ruth squeeze his arm encouragingly as he passed the ladies to stand in the centre of the room. He concentrated on the rote. He adjusting the tuning. He did so to give himself time. He smiled and said, "I will sing a song of a knight longing for his lady. As Sir Wulfric's knowledge of Occitan is limited I will sing it in English as well as Occitan!" Everyone, including Sir Wulfric, laughed. English was the only language he spoke well.

Quan lo rosinhols escria
ab sa part la nueg e.l dia,
yeu suy ab ma bell'amia
jos la flor,

tro la gaita de la tor
escria: "Drutz, al levar!
Qu'ieu vey l'alba e.l jorn clar".

While the nightingale sings,
both night and day,
I am with my beautiful
beneath the flowers,
until our sentry from the tower
cries: "Lovers, get up!
for I clearly see the sunrise and the day".

He got no further than the first stanza before everyone applauded. I smiled at Rebekah. We knew our son was a true knight. I stood. "I pray you let Sir Samuel continue. This is an ordeal for him."

He continued with the whole song. There were many verses. Padraig whispered to me, "Thank you, lord. Will I have to learn this skill too?"

I nodded, "However, I believe that Prince Richard may be of service to you. Look."

The Prince was as wrapt as any in the words. I knew that he fancied himself as a singer of songs as well as a warrior. When my son had finished he was the first to go to him. When Eleanor sidled silently next to Samuel to speak with him then I knew that all would be well.

Rebekah came over and slipped her arm into mine, "Why William, I would never have had you for a matchmaker!"

I smiled and squeezed her hand, "My love I do not want to be like my father and only see my grandchildren every few years. The sooner Samuel marries then the sooner he can give us grandchildren."

"And Ruth?"

"Sir Hugh and Sir Philip arrive tomorrow. They have sons."

"Thomas is Sir Philip's son but he is just a squire and not ready to be knighted! He is the one of an age with Ruth."

"Be patient."

The two new squires, Simon and John had not attended the feast. They had much to do preparing for their new lives. I had given them both horses but, as they were leaving on the morrow they needed to acquaint themselves with their new master's horses and war gear. For them, the feast was a luxury they could not enjoy.

I saw that Samuel and Eleanor had slipped away. My father came to us, "I see that my grandson has a skill which you and I did not have, William."

"And that is a good thing. It means he has not had to spend as much time in war as we did. He will be a more rounded knight."

"And now I must take my leave. We have a long journey tomorrow. We ride for Chester. There the army I will lead gathers."

"Remember you are not a young man and you have a wound, father!"

He laughed, "Fear not; my days of fighting are over."

They left before dawn. His visit had been shorter than I would have expected and it made me, somehow, unhappy. My misery was short-lived for the knights who lived further away began to arrive. Sir Philip, Sir James, Sir Hugh and his son, Sir Ralph, all lived more than half a day away. Sir Philip could have reached us in time to greet my father but his castle, at Piercebridge, was an important one and, I suspected, he had awaited the arrival of Sir Hugh who was not only one of his nearest neighbours but a good friend. The youngest knight, Sir James, had been my father's squire and he had a cautious ride for his wife, Ada, was with child. His eldest son William came with him, riding a pony.

We gathered in the middle of the afternoon after they had all refreshed themselves in my Great Hall. Samuel and Eleanor had found time to walk along the river. It was good. We sat around the table and I spoke.

"Friends we have been charged by the Warlord to prevent the Scots from raiding our lands. They are allied with the French. We do not know their intentions but I am guessing that they are not peaceful." My men all laughed. "My scouts are seeking the Scots. Sir Hugh, Sir Ralph, you are the most westerly of my knights. Have you heard anything?"

Sir Hugh shook his head. I noticed that there were flecks of grey in his beard. He was getting older. His son, Ralph was the image of him. He and Samuel were great friends. They had been squires together and were as close as brothers. I idly wondered if he was wed. Sir Hugh said, "We have patrols to the west and the north of us. It has been quiet."

His son said, "My father thought it too quiet and I agree with him."

"What do you mean?"

"In the summer, when the nights are short and the weather clement, we have many annoying raids from small bands of Scots who come down the high divide to raid cattle and sheep. We are prepared for such raids and my father I and lead men on weekly patrols. This year we have seen none."

I liked Ralph. He had a mind and he had an opinion. I disliked those knights who just sat and did not tell you their thoughts.

"Sir John?"

"Durham is quiet but perhaps the Bishop knows more."

"Aye, you and I will ride on the morrow to speak with him. By the day after perhaps our scouts will have returned. As for the rest of you, how long will it take to bring your men here for the muster?"

"Do you wish the fyrd?"

I smiled, "No, Sir Harold; like my father, I would rather fight alongside fewer men of greater quality. With Sir Philip's archers and mine, we have enough bowmen to slow down the Scots."

Sir Wulfric growled, "And what of the Bishop? Will he get to sit on his backside doing nothing?"

"When I go with Sir John I will demand Durham knights." I looked at Sir Wulfric. He had drunk more than most at the feast. His eyes were red and he had been suffering from wind. He did not look well. "Sir Wulfric I would have you stay in the valley. With so many knights abroad, I need someone with a strong arm to protect my family."

He laughed, "And besides, Earl, you cannot have a fat old man who can barely ride five miles without needing to either pee or shit!"

I saw Sir Harold and Sir John smile, they knew the old warrior well. "You have served this valley valiantly Sir Wulfric. You deserve a time of rest."

He shook his head. "I should have died in battle with a sword in my hand. As it is…" he waved a hand, "I am an old man. Get on with your business lord. I have a visit I need to make."

When he had gone Sir Harold said, "It is good that he will stay here, lord. He is not the knight he was."

I nodded, "And I intend to use speed as our weapon. I do not want a ponderous and laboured march. When we know where they are, then we hit them hard. I have wasted too much time on Scots."

Sir Hugh poured himself some more wine, "And the ransoms are so paltry it is hardly worth the effort of collecting them."

"I would not bother with a ransom. If they surrender then all well and good but if not then slay them." I looked around and saw determination

The Princes' Revolt

written on their faces. "We meet here again in two days' time. That should be long enough for you to return and bring that which you need."

Sir Hugh said, "Lord, if it is possible I will wait at Barnard. It is a long ride here and I can make the north quicker from my castle if that is our destination. I can leave Ralph here. He will fetch me if it is the north."

I looked at Sir Ralph. He nodded, "That suits me, lord."

"Then it is settled. I want you to bring your best men and men who are all mounted!"

"Aye, lord!"

We sent a rider to Carlisle to tell the Constable my plans. I did not expect help from that quarter but they would be vigilant.

Chapter 2

I took with me Sir Morgan, who before he was knighted was Alf, my former squire and two men at arms when I rode with Sir John to Durham. We would speak with the Bishop and then stay at Fissebourne. Edith, Sir John's wife was tearful as we headed north. She kept wringing her hands. Her son had gone and gone quickly. I think Sir John was embarrassed about it. "It is not seemly to take on so. Our son is with the Warlord. It is an honour!"

I smiled, "I understand, Sir John. Mothers do not see young warriors. They see the helpless bairn they bore into this world." Edith nodded her gratitude. "Do not fret, Lady Edith. My father has promised that he will not draw his sword in anger. I promise you that your son will return unharmed and will be well trained. Your husband and I were both trained by my father and there is none better."

We escorted Sir John's family to Fissebourne and were then able to ride harder to Durham. Since the Bishop had been sent to Normandy by my father we had had no trouble accessing the castle and cathedral. We rode through the gates without hindrance and the sentries saluted. It had not always been that way. I had had to either fight or creep my way in. Leaving our squires and men at arms to watch the horses we strode to the Bishop's chambers. When my father had last been here there were Templars and traitors in the halls. This time I saw only priests. When, however, we saw the Bishop I saw that hatred still burned in his eyes. His mouth smiled but we were his enemies. He would bear a grudge. We would never be friends. I cared not. What could he do to us that would hurt? We had the ear of the King and my father was the second most powerful man in the land.

"Earl, this is unexpected. How can a humble Bishop be of service?"

I hated fawning and I hated lies. Yet I needed the Bishop and his knights. As yet the size of the Scottish army was unknown. I would not risk just my men. "We have intelligence that the Scots may be considering an invasion. They are allied with the French." My eyes bored into the Bishop. He had worked for the French before now.

"I am appalled. I thought there was peace."

His outrage was overplayed. He knew what the Scots were up to. "There was, but our king and King Louis have had a falling out over the Vexin. I need your knights."

"Of course, but do you know where they will attack?"

"No. I am awaiting the report of my scouts."

"Then I cannot in all conscience allow the Palatinate to be stripped of her defences." This was politics. He had a reason to hold men from me.

I smiled. I could play this game too. "I would not dream of doing so. You need not use the fyrd for this. They can defend your Palatinate. I need your knights and their mounted men at arms. I will expect them gathered here in four days' time. Sir John here will be my lieutenant and he will let you know where the Scottish attack will begin and he will lead your knights. Unless you wish to lead them yourself?"

The panic on his face made me smile. "No, Earl William, I am more than happy for Sir John to lead my knights. Was there anything else?" He was trying to be rid of me.

"Now that you are returned from Rome I would have you maintain a closer watch on the enemy. Your castle at Norham is perfectly placed to give warning of an attack across the Tweed. I would have you send me a report each month to let me know if the dispositions of the Scots have changed."

I saw him frown and chew his lip. He was working out if he could dispute with me and he realized he could not. He would have a victory but on his terms. "Of course, my lord. I am a loyal subject of King Henry. Your knights will be here four days hence"

"And how many knights will that be?"

"Eighty, Earl."

As Sir John and I rode back to Fissebourne he shook his head, "I feel that I need to bathe. That man makes my flesh crawl."

"I know but the King has decided that he can trust him. We can do little about it. At least we have his men now. Eighty is only part of his muster. He is not giving us all of his knights but I suspect it will be the ones he does not like and that makes them good men in my eyes."

We arrived at Stockton two days' later. My knights and their men at arms had already arrived and were camped around the north side of the castle. It was the area we used for common grazing. There was water as well as good grass. In the summer there were trees for shade. When we left the men of my town would reap the bounty of the horses which had been grazing on it. Our fields would be enriched and our crops improved. We wasted nothing.

I was greeted, almost as soon as I entered, by Sir Ralph of Barnard. "My lord I would like to speak with you."

"Cannot it wait, Sir Ralph? I am weary after the ride."

He stood and faced me. "No lord. It is important."

I sighed, "Very well then come to my solar." I was surprised that the rest of my family were not there to greet me. They normally were and then I realised that all would have much to occupy them. Alice had seen me arrive and anticipated my needs. She followed us up to the solar with goblets and a jug of wine. I gave her my cloak and riding gloves.

"Well Sir Ralph, what is so urgent?"

"I wish to have your permission to court your daughter, the Lady Ruth."

I was so taken aback that I was stuck for words. I took a drink of wine and studied the young man. I had known him all of his life but I had seen him infrequently. First, he had been the young boy who had helped Hugh's squire. Then, as he grew older, he had become a squire. When we had defeated King William of Scotland he had been knighted. Since then I had barely seen him for he was a warrior patrolling our western defences. Yet in all that time I had barely had a conversation with him and now he wished to marry my daughter.

"This is sudden."

He nodded and gave a shy smile, "I confess, lord, that I have little experience of courtly matters. My father and I are border knights yet as soon as I saw the Lady Ruth at the feast I knew that she was the lady for me."

"You have known Ruth since she was a child. What has changed?"

He blushed. He was right this was an area in which he was uncomfortable, "Lord she was a girl and now, well she is a woman."

"But how does she feel?"

His face fell, "Lord, if I thought that she would not return my affection I would not have asked your permission. In the last three days, we have spoken to each other often. Samuel escorted us along the river. I swear there was nothing untoward, lord. We just talked but… we have an understanding. She is also keen to marry but we need your permission."

The Princes' Revolt

I nodded. I had expected this at some time but I was not happy. I would be losing my little girl. However, Ralph was as fine a knight as I had ever met and he would make a good husband for my little girl. "Then you have my permission to court my daughter but as we will be fighting the Scots for a time I fear that you will see little of each other."

He looked relieved, "I know, lord. Thank you."

I now saw the reason for the absence of my wife and daughter. They were co-conspirators as I suspected was my son, Ralph's greatest friend.

As I left my solar and headed for the Great Hall they both emerged to greet me. "Well, father?"

The look on my daughter's face gave me the answer to the question I had asked of Sir Ralph. "Then you do wish to be Sir Ralph's wife?"

She threw her arms around me, "Of course I do! He is handsome, he is kind and he is funny!"

I glanced at my wife who nodded, "He is, William and they are both smitten."

"You know we go to fight the Scots?"

"But he will be at your side and he will be safe. Promise me that he will be safe, father!"

"That no man can do. But as the last man we lost was Sir Richard and that was more than five years ago I hope that you shall be able to enjoy a courtship with Sir Ralph."

She kissed me and raced off. My wife linked my arm, "And I believe that our son will be asking Sir Tristan for permission to court Lady Eleanor."

"Our world is changing."

"As it should. "She squeezed my arm and we headed for the Great Hall. "And your scouts have returned. I told them to wait in the Great Hall. I realised that once you spoke with them then poor Sir Ralph and Ruth would not receive a fair hearing."

"And you are right!" I hurried to the hall. My four scouts were there. "Well?"

Aiden had learned to read maps. My father had taught him and it made him a most invaluable gatherer of information. He unrolled the map of our land. "Masood and Edgar found nothing close to the wall and they came down the high divide towards Barnard. They found no sign of enemies there either. Edward and I headed north of Carlisle. We found the Scots. They have two armies. One is led by Lord Douglas. We recognised his banner. He is close by Gretna. There were more than a hundred banners. The other is at Langholm. That one is led by Lord Balliol. He has a hundred banners too."

I nodded and began to work out what my options were. My father had told me that the Earl of Chester had also been warned of the Scots intentions but he would have the Welsh to deal with too. His constable at Carlisle, Robert de Vaux, Baron of Gillesland, was a good man but he only had ten knights and forty men at arms to defend Carlisle Castle. If Lord Douglas attacked then he could simply bypass the castle and head south and east. He was the greater threat of the two. Lord Balliol was well placed to attack Barnard but that was a stronger castle.

"You have done well. Get some rest for we leave for the west in the morning."

Aiden nodded, "Aye lord but there is something else. We noted the numbers of banners but they have also brought the wild men of the isles and the highlands. We counted many campfires. They are here in great numbers."

Aiden knew war and he knew what these wild men could do. "Thank you for the warning." I turned to my squire. "Go to the stables I will join you there.

After sending a rider to Sir John to ask him to bring the knights of Durham to Barnard I held a council of war with my valley knights. Sir Harold shook his head, "I know why they come that way. It is not horse country."

"But we have the wall to slow them down." Sir James was ever the optimist.

"Let us not get ahead of ourselves. The wall may not even be necessary. They cannot cross the Esk until they reach Longtown. The Roman Bridge is the place we hold them."

"We fought there once before, with your father. Will the Scots not remember that?"

"Perhaps Sir Tristan and if they do then we will make more plans. We ride tomorrow and any who have yet to join can follow."

My knights all had questions. When I had spoken with them all I found myself left with Sir Padraigh. In times past Samuel would have been with him. He would have been eager to know more of my plans. As soon as the council was over he and Sir Ralph had left to be with their lady loves. I suppose I could not blame them. We were going to war and men died in war.

"How many men do you leave in Stockton, lord?"

"I have spoken with Ralph of Bowness. He says that we only need to leave the fifteen who are no longer young. He is confident that the men of the town could defend our walls if danger threatened."

"I am sorry that I bring but two men at arms and two archers."

"They are good men and besides we have the Durham knights with us. We will not have to bear the brunt of the fighting. You and your men are well mounted. Soon I will be able to give you a manor." He looked at me. "Sir Wulfric has no children. When he dies the castle will need a lord."

"And am I ready?"

"You had best decide that yourself but I believe so. Now go and make sure that the men at arms have all that they will need. I will go and see to the horses and Ralph my squire."

I had two warhorses: Lightning and Volva. Lightning was named for the blaze on his head which looked like a bolt of lightning. Volva had been named by Sir Morgan when he had been Alf, my squire, for she was a clever horse and Alf said that a volva was a clever Viking woman. I would take both. The palfrey I would take would be Goldie, so named for her golden colour. Her dam had been my father's horse, Skuld. Ralph was checking the reins and the saddle. A broken piece of tack could result in disaster on the battlefield.

"They are all three ready, lord."

"And your horses?"

"They are both keen to go to war."

I walked around my three horses to see for myself their condition. Their coats gleamed and they were well muscled. It had been too long since they had been to war. That would now change. "The spears are ready?"

"I will take them on my spare horse."

We left at dawn the next day. My people cheered us off. It was not a large number of men who left my castle. Sir Philip and Sir John, along with the Durham knights would meet us at Barnard. There were just eight knights. We had fifty men at arms and fifty archers. Eight servants came with the rouncys and the baggage. We would sleep in comfort at Barnard Castle and then there would be an uncomfortable night in the forests and moors close by Alston.

The Durham knights had not arrived and so we had plenty of room at Barnard Castle. As we ate with Sir Hugh and his family something was nagging at the back of my mind. "Sir Hugh, you know the land around here better than any."

"Any save my son. Ralph has led many patrols."

I turned to Sir Ralph, "How far is it to the wall?"

"Perhaps forty miles, lord."

I cut another slice of duck and chewed it absentmindedly.

Sir Hugh said, "Something bothers you, lord?"

"Why do the Scots split their forces? It makes no sense to me. We have always beaten them and I would have expected them to have the largest army that they could to face us."

"Perhaps they cannot feed all their army in one place. They may need grazing."

Sir Harold was right. He was ever practical. However, the Scots did not normally worry about grazing nor did they use as many horses as we did. I was not convinced. "I fear that this is a trap." I waved a hand around the hall. "Until my father won it this castle belonged to the Balliol family. Lord Balliol is not at Gretna. He is with the second army at Langholm. What if the one at Gretna, led by Douglas is to draw our forces thither?"

"What for?"

"Simple, Sir Gilles. It would leave the road to Barnard and my valley open."

Sir Hugh nodded, "My castle is strong and has never fallen. You know yourself that the Scots have tried many times."

"And if there was just your castellan and the garrison; what then?"

For the first time, Sir Hugh and his son understood the danger. The river which ran around the western side of the castle afforded protection. The bridge over the river was narrow but if they had the wild men of the islands then they could swim the river. It was a large castle and a hundred knights and their retinue could take it.

"Sir Hugh I would have you and your men at arms stay here. This castle needs to hold."

"That will leave you short of knights lord."

"Just two and that is a small price to pay for peace of mind."

"One knight lord. I will not stay here when you need knights. This is my first campaign and I would fight alongside Samuel." Sir Ralph's voice was full of determination and I understood it. He was courting my daughter. He would wish to be at my side.

The Princes' Revolt

I glanced at Sir Hugh who nodded. "Very well. And I will not wait for the men of Durham. I am anxious now. We will get to Longtown and hope that they have not yet crossed the bridge."

I waved for Sir Hugh to follow me. "You know that Sir Ralph has asked permission to court my daughter?"

"I do. It is an honour."

"Then let him know that he does not need to impress me on the battlefield. I would not have my daughter lose her knight before they are wed."

"Is that why you suggested we stay here?"

"No, Hugh. You will not let this castle fall. If I am wrong then I will send for you and your men at arms. If I am right then your presence here could save my valley."

"I have a good pair of scouts: Oswald and Cedric, they know this land well. I will send them to Langholm. They can keep watch on Balliol. I believe that you are right about Balliol. He does wish this castle to be returned to him but I have seen little evidence that King William is capable of such cunning."

"True but as we have seen before, Hugh, the French often send their knights to advise and this plan reeks of French intervention."

The weather was changing. It was partly the season: autumn was approaching but it was also the fact that we were higher. North of Barnard there was a ridge which ran from England to Scotland and divided the land between east and west. The road was Roman but it was a smaller one than that which led to Durham. The manor of Alston was vacant. It belonged to the Earl of Chester. When Scots had raided during the civil war the lord, Sir Alexander and his family had all been killed. Some said it was a blood feud with a Scottish lord but whatever the reason no one had wanted the manor. It was poor and it was run down. We camped there and kept a good watch. Aiden and his scouts left before dawn. They would scout the land through which we would travel. We were now on land which was beyond anyone's control. Bandits, brigands and local warlords controlled this land. Sir Hugh just watched for enemies. He did not have enough men to control it. Almost any that we met would be enemies.

It did not help us that we travelled through forests. Luckily, I had archers. My archers were woodsmen and they rode, not on the road, but they flanked us in the trees. It was a lonely wild place which had changed little since the time of the Romans and before. As we climbed towards

The Princes' Revolt

the wall then there were fewer trees and it felt less suffocating. I took heart from the fact that my scouts had not returned. They would only return if they found the enemy. When we passed through the village of Brampton some of the local farmers greeted us. They were English but I had no doubt that they would doff their caps if a Scottish lord passed through. They were practical and pragmatic men. I stopped and spoke to them.

"Earl, we thought you should know that there have been Scots scouting along the wall for the last month. They are the men of the lords who live north of the wall."

"And they have not raided?"

"No, lord. That is strange behaviour."

"What do you do when they raid?"

The headman shrugged, "Hide what we can and wait for them to leave. After King William was defeated then it was quiet and we prospered for a couple of years but this past year they have grown bolder."

That confirmed my suspicions. As we rode north I felt guilty. They had not raided my valley and yet both myself and the Earl of Chester, not to mention the Sheriff of Northumbria, had failed. I would see to it that we did not fail again. My father had an excuse for the depredations along the border. I did not.

We reached the bridge over the Esk and there were no Scots in sight. I sent the archers and half of the men at arms we had across the river. The servants began to erect our camp. I dismounted and leaving Ralph with the horses went with Sir Samuel to the largest house in the settlement.

A dour-looking man came out and bowed. "I am Angus son of Malcolm. I am the headman, lord. How may we serve you?"

In this part of the world you did not risk angering any lord. From the man's eyes, I could see that he hated us all but he had a village to think of. "We will not be here long but I should warn you, Angus, that there is an army at Gretna and your village may become a battlefield."

He looked due south. "We have kin just three miles south. We will go there." With that, he turned and went back into his house.

As we walked back to our horses I said, "Do you not think that strange, Harold?"

"Aye, lord. He could have gone west to where he would have the protection of Lord Douglas. Gretna is as close and he knows there is an army there. Did he fear that his own people were as great a threat as we? Why did he not go north? Does he fear Balliol too?"

By the time we reached our horses, Aiden and Edward had returned. "Lord, the Scots are still where they were but their numbers have increased a little. There are five more banners."

I wondered at that. Five more banners were little enough. It might add twenty men at most to the army. What were they waiting for? "Is there any sign of King William's banner?"

"No lord."

By the time the camp was erected and we had withdrawn most of our archers and men at arms across the river Masood and Edgar had returned. It was almost dark by the time they did so. "Lord Balliol has moved. He and his men are now camped at Booth Castle. There are another twenty banners with them."

That was worrying. Booth Castle was further south than Balliol's original camp. Had I been wrong? There was a road which ran north of the wall and would take them to the New Castle. It would eliminate Morthpath, Warkworth, Alnwick and Norham. Had I been outwitted? The Sheriff, like the Bishop, knew the threat but I had stripped the Palatinate of its knights. The Scots could cross the river anywhere and sweep down to my valley. I had a dilemma. I had too few men to do anything save to hold the bridge. Until the knights and retinue of Durham arrived then I was pinned in place.

I sent Ralph for some parchment, goose quill and ink. I did not tell him where to seek such items but, a short while later, he returned. I saw that the goose quill was freshly plucked and that the parchment had writing on one side. It was a list from the church. It was the names of men who had failed to provide service to the priest. The ink was still alive. He had, in a small leather pouch, a dozen beetles.

He smiled. "I will find something in which to put the ink. I pray it is not a long missive, my lord!" Ralph was resourceful. He would make the ink for me. It would not be a long letter. I needed to warn the Sherriff of the potential danger. He needed to rouse the men along the wall and block the crossings of the Tyne. I took out my dagger and sharpened the quill. I was not happy about writing in red but my predicament dictated my actions.

The next morning, I sent Edgar and Edward east to the New Castle. They would be there by the end of the day. We gave them two spare horses. Then we awaited the arrival of Sir John and the knights of Durham. I would not just wait for Lord Douglas to come.

"Sir Harold you stay here with Sir Phillip and the bulk of the archers and half of the men at arms. I will take the rest and we will go and speak with this Douglas."

Gone were the days when Sir Harold might have questioned my judgement. He nodded. "I will send Tomas ap Tomas and a few archers into the forests. We might as well have food and I will embed some stakes on the far side of the river." I was confident that we would have a secure bridgehead when we returned.

It was less than four miles to Gretna. The Scots must have known where we were and yet we had seen no sign of scouts. Samuel asked as we rode, "Do we go to provoke a fight, lord?"

I saw that Ralph was leaning forward to hear my words. "In truth, I know not. We have just ten banners here but my banner alone should intimidate this Douglas. When we cross the River Sark it will be like throwing down a gauntlet. I would have you look at the knights who are close to this Douglas. The Scots wear old fashioned armour. I would have you look to see if any look French." He nodded.

He rode next to Sir Ralph and it was good to hear them discussing the Scots and how we might defeat them. These two were the future. When they married they would be tied by marriage. They were now tied by war and were truly brothers in arms.

With Masood and Aiden ahead of us I feared no ambush. However, our numbers meant that we were spied before we reached Gretna. I heard horns as the Scottish camp was roused. I held up my hand and we stopped. The men at arms formed two blocks on either side of us. Henry Warbow and Tom the Fletcher dismounted and stood close to me. They would guard against any treachery. I had my helmet hanging from my cantle and my shield was hanging across my left leg. Lord Douglas would see that we were not here for war.

Thirty knights headed for us and I saw the rest forming up behind. The wild men of the islands and the levy were being herded into lines by the knights. I smiled. My father and I had a reputation for cunning and for tricks. The Scots would see just ten banners but they would assume we had more men close by. They would be wary.

I had met Lord Douglas after the failed invasion some years earlier. He had been one of the captured knights who had been ransomed. He was about my age. I knew that he had resented the ransom for it had impoverished his family. I had heard that he had had to raid the Hibernians to regain that which he had lost. For a noble knight like Lord Douglas that was nothing short of brigandage.

He stopped twenty paces from us. Like me, he had no helmet upon his head. I saw that he was flanked by the Mormaer of Dumfries. There were also two other knights I did not recognise. They looked to be French. "This is Scotland, Earl William. Why do you break the treaty that was made?"

"Why do you gather an army here close to Carlisle? This is not a peaceful gathering, is it? At best it looks like a chevauchée and at worst an invasion. I hear that King William has allied himself with the French. That is a dangerous thing to do. King Henry might choose to punish Scotland for such a rash act."

"Then why is he not here or his Warlord? Why is it the whelp he has sent?"

I felt the indignation ripple through the men behind me. I held up my hand. Words would not cause me any hurt. I waved my arm behind me. "I am here with my household knights to tell you to disperse this army. We have slaughtered enough Scots to weary of such exercise. There is little ransom to be had. You have two days to disperse or you will be punished."

Now it was the turn of the Scots to show indignation but they were more vocal. Lord Douglas' face darkened. He pointed a finger at me. "You have until dawn to quit your camp and crawl back into England. If you do not then we will drive you hence!" I watched as the two French knights leaned in to speak to Lord Douglas. They did not want this.

I turned and rode away without giving an answer. It was an insult to the Scots and was deliberate. Besides which I had made my ultimatum and they had given theirs. I wanted them to wonder if I would return to England or not. I said nothing to my men as we rode the few miles to our camp. I was planning my strategy.

I stopped just four hundred paces from the bridge. "Wilfred take the men at arms back to the camp. The men will be fighting tomorrow."

He understood what that implied, "Aye lord."

I pointed to the woods to the north of the road. "We will put my archers in there. Aelric is more than capable of evading the Scots if my plan fails. I turned and pointed to the stream which emptied into the Esk. "There we will put stakes." I dismounted and, leaving the road walked to the ground just to the south of the road. As soon as I did so my foot sank

The Princes' Revolt

up to my ankle. It was ground which had clay beneath the surface. It would hold the water. "Ralph, you are the lightest of us and wear no mail. See how far the bog extends."

My squire walked and I saw the mud sucking at his feet. The bog was forty paces wide. When he was on dry ground again then he waved.

"Where Ralph stands now we will wait with our knights and half our mounted men."

Sir Tristan said, "You do not hold them at the bridge? It worked last time."

"And last time they had fewer of these half-dressed savages. Did you not notice the numbers? They would swim across the river. We force them down the road. Our archers will drive them into the bog and there Sir Philip's archers will finish the job. I will draw them to me. When they cross the stream with their knights then we will hit them. If they threaten to overwhelm us then we pull back through our men at arms and archers and gather behind them. Familiarise yourself with the ground. I will go and explain to Sir Philip and Sir Harold my plan."

I included Wilfred and Aelric in my discussions.

"We will keep a reserve in the village. They will be knights. I intend to have Sir Samuel and Sir Ralph lead them."

"Have they the experience, lord?"

"No Aelric but I can trust them. I know not the knights from Durham. The knights of Durham have yet to arrive. I need two knights who will not flee if things go wrong. Both are clever. I will leave with them ten archers and twenty men at arms. Wilfred, choose twenty of our best men. If the Scots do not do as I expect then it will be up to them to extricate us from danger."

Sir Harold said, "You are asking a great deal from two young knights who have barely won their spurs."

I nodded, "I know and it weighs heavily upon me but I need all of my experienced men to face the Scottish knights. Aelric and Sir Philip have your archers embed stakes next to the river. Let us make it hard for them. Then you will need to make the woods safe for your archers, Aelric."

When my knights returned from their inspection of the ground I took Sir Ralph and Sir Samuel to one side. "You must wait and hold the bridge. You will not be given a command when to unleash your men. That will be your decision. You will not have many men but it will be sufficient for the task. If we are in danger of being flanked then it will be up to you and Aelric to enable the army to cross the bridge."

The Princes' Revolt

"That is a great responsibility."

I nodded, "If you feel you are not up to it Sir Ralph then speak and I will ask others. There is no shame in admitting that it is too great a task. That is what Sir Harold thought."

He coloured, "No lord. We are honoured that you trust us."

I smiled, "Sir Ralph when you marry my daughter I will be trusting you with more than this pathetic piece of bog in Scotland!"

Sir John and the Durham knights did not arrive until shortly before sunset. I could tell, from Sir John's face, that he was less than happy about the late arrival. He shook his head, "I am sorry Earl William! These are not warriors. They are pampered flowers! They rise late and stop frequently."

"It is not your fault and you are here. How many did you bring?"

"There are eighty knights and forty mounted men at arms."

It was not enough but it would have to do. I explained what I intended and how I perceived the battle unfolding. I then gathered the knights around me. They were not happy. I think they had expected to be staying in a hall. My household knights had bemused looks upon their faces as I addressed them.

"The knights of the Palatinate are being given a chance in this battle to show that they are worthy of the title knight. For myself, I have seen little or no evidence of any knightly virtue." I saw the shocked looks on their faces and I dared them to question my words. They did not. "Tomorrow the Scots will attack us. They have more men than we do but we will prevail. We will do so because all of you will obey my every command. The Bishop gave you to me to lead. I count that as an oath and I will treat harshly any man that I believe breaks that oath. You have all arrived late and that means that you will not be able to survey the battlefield. The knights will form the front rank and will bar the progress over the beck. My men at arms will form the second rank." I saw the knights exchange looks. That would not suit.

One of them, I recognised the livery as that of Middleham, said, "And what of the men at arms we brought?"

"They will fight dismounted behind us. My plan is simple. We draw the Scots to us and we drive them back. If we fail to do that at the beck then we withdraw behind the men at arms and archers. When they have bled enough we mount our second horses and make a charge." I looked around their faces. I do not know what they expected but it was not this. "I would get some rest for we will be in position by dawn."

The Princes' Revolt

My archers had hunted food and there was a stew for them to eat. I saw that the new knights were less than impressed with the fare. I cared not. I was fetched by a sentry late in the evening. It was Sir Hugh's man Cedric, "Lord, we have been to Langholm. The Scots are gone. They are heading west."

"For the New Castle?"

"No, lord, for our castle, Barnard Castle. I sent Oswald to warn Sir Hugh."

"Thank you. There is food."

He said, "With your permission, lord, when I have eaten and my horse is rested I will ride back. The castle is my home too."

The scout's attitude contrasted with that of the Durham knights. I had no doubt that there were some of the knights who were warriors but there were not enough. I went to Sir Harold and Sir John. They were my lieutenants. "I fear I was right. Balliol marches on Barnard. We have to fight this battle tomorrow, win and then go east to relieve the siege."

"Sir Hugh will hold."

I nodded, "But we have been outwitted."

"No, Earl, we have not for you predicted this. You are your father's son."

"That is good of you Harold but it does not feel that way to me."

I prayed that night for I knew we needed God's help. I had less than twenty knights on whom I could rely and the rest might try to flee at the first hint of trouble. I was well awake before cock crow and I made water before Ralph dressed me for battle. I sought out Samuel and Ralph. I was pleased that they had not needed rousing. Sir John and my other knights were busy rousing the Durham knights.

"If any knight tries to flee then stop them. You do so anyway you have to. They do not use the bridge."

Sir Ralph nodded, "Thank you for the trust, lord. We will not let you down."

"I know and the men at arms you command are my best men. Whatever you have to do then you will be backed up."

Aelric led the forty archers who would be in the woods. He said nothing but his grin and his wave told me that I had nothing to fear from him. He and his men would do their duty. Sir Philip's captain of archers, Peter of Derby, led the rest of our archers to their place. Wilfred had already taken the men at arms. I had heard raised voices and the smack of fist on flesh. If the men at arms were reluctant to fight then Wilfred was the one who would change their mind. Soon, the ones left in the camp were the knights and their squires. I mounted Volva. Ralph led Lightning across the bridge to wait with the other squires and the spare spears behind the archers. He handed my banner to John of Norton. He was a solid man at arms and he was reliable. My squire would need to be with the horses and the weapons. I mounted and said, "We ride!"

We made our way through the archers and the men at arms. Wilfred and the others shouted encouragement to us as we passed. When we reached the stakes, which were just four paces from the beck I had my knights ride up and down to churn up the ground. Then we moved back to the men at arms just a hundred paces from the water. My archers had the range. I dismounted and walked to the edge of the bog. Wilfred had echeloned his line so that it also faced that flank. We both knew that the fiercest fighting would be there.

"You are happy with what you need to do Wilfred of Stockton?"

"Aye lord. We are ready to hew wild men and slaughter knights!"

I returned to my horse and mounted. The sun was already a thin line of light in the east. We now awaited the Scots and the battle.

The Princes' Revolt

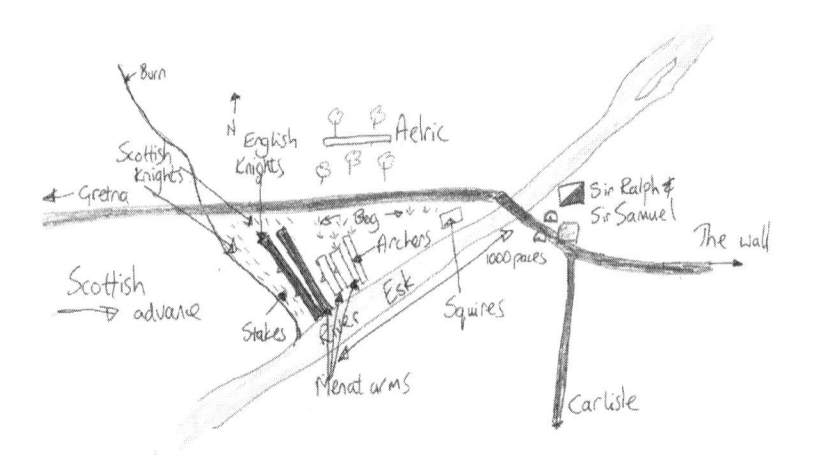

Chapter 3

We saw the Scottish scouts first. Mounted on hobelars they galloped from the village. As soon as they saw our banners they stopped. Aelric and my archers were too well trained to give away their position. The six men turned and rode back to Gretna. We all had our helmets hung from our cantles. We would have our heads enclosed in steel soon enough. Sir John said, "Quite a pleasant part of Scotland, this valley. Why does the King not take it and then Carlisle would have more protection? A castle at the bridge would guard the border."

"Perhaps he will. At the moment the Vexin is the problem. I am confident that we will take it one day."

We heard trumpets and horns from the direction of Gretna. The Scots were coming. They had seen our dispositions. They came at us using a broad front. They had the wild men of the islands on their right. In the centre, they had their knights and behind them what looked to me like their men at arms and the levy. I saw Lord Douglas halt and consult with his two Frenchmen. The stakes and the woods prevented his horsemen from charging. A horn sounded and his men at arms and the fyrd made their way through the horsemen. Already they were not doing as I had expected. Without the Frenchmen giving advice the Scots would have charged us. The men at arms would chop down the stakes and allow their knights to pour through. Even more alarming was the fact that the wild men came at the beck without any order, they just charged. Philip had just one hundred archers. They would have to split their arrows between the wild men and the men at arms.

I donned my helmet and waved for Ralph. The wild men had covered half a mile by the time he joined me. "I need the horn. Stay by me but when we contact the Scots then ride to the rear. These wild men have no concept of knights and squires."

"Aye lord." He sounded brave but I knew that he would be fearful. The Scottish and Hibernian warriors were half-naked savages, notoriously hard to kill. The French advice must have been to sacrifice them. Our archers had the range of the beck but they could not see it because we were there. We had a signal arranged. As soon as the Scots entered the stream my household knights all lowered their spears. To the Scots, it would appear as though we were going to charge but to my archers, it was the signal to rain death upon them. The men at arms, closer to the woods, were slower in their approach. Sir Philip and his archers would be able to send five or six flights towards the stream before they needed to divide their arrows.

As soon as the arrows hit the air was filled with feral screams and shouts of anger. The arrows kept coming and many Scots and Hibernians were killed and wounded. The handful who managed to evade the arrows then had to negotiate the stakes and finally the muddy ground. Our archers managed seven flights before they had to switch targets. I pointed my spear. "Charge!"

It was not really a charge for the Scots were just forty paces away but we struck them with a wall of spears and snapping horses. Had their full numbers made it across we might have struggled but, as it was, we used them as target practice. Without mail wherever we struck was a mortal wound. Even so, many of them did not die easily. They died hard. The third Scot I struck tore the spear from my hands as he died. I drew my sword but the Scots were now trying to tear the stakes from the ground. Many fell to arrows as they did so.

"Ralph, sound fall back!"

I backed Volva back the forty paces. It was as well that I did for one Scot had been feigning death and he leapt up with a curved sword. Volva lived up to her name and she swung around allowing me to swing my sword sideways into his skull. As we lined up again I saw a horse standing forlornly amongst the dead Scots. One of the knights of Durham had been killed.

"Ralph fetch that horse."

My squire galloped forward. He wisely slipped his shield around his back although the archers were now concentrating on the men close to the road. Aelric and his archers had not yet loosed an arrow. The longer they remained hidden the more success we would have. More than half of the stakes had been removed when Ralph returned with the horse. I pointed to the rear. He took the horse there. We could not allow the Scots to take our horses.

I watched the two Frenchmen speak with Lord Douglas and some men at arms were sent to bolster the resolve of the wild men and the Hibernians. Almost all of the stakes had been removed but at a great cost.

Sir John said, "Here they come lord. Now the Scottish knights think they have us."

Ralph returned with a fresh spear for me as the Scottish horns sounded and a hundred knights and twenty men at arms, not to mention eighty squires, charged obliquely at us. "Ralph sound wheel right!" The Scots were five hundred paces from us. They had kept well out of our archers' range. They were keeping a good line. We had time enough for the Scots were about to get a shock as the archers in the woods released their arrows. We managed to turn our line when they were two hundred paces from us and then Sir Philip's archers added the weight of their own arrows. With arrows falling on them from two directions the knights could not defend themselves.

"Forward! Sound the charge!"

My plan was a good plan. Despite the interference of the French knights we were still in a position to win and then fate, in the form of some of the knights of Durham, intervened. Twenty-three knights on the extreme right of our line turned and fled. They left a hole. It was too late to adjust our point of attack. Had not Aelric and Sir Philip's archers increased their rate of arrows then all would have been lost. They drew and released so quickly that it must have appeared we had twice the number of archers. In addition, the redoubtable and unflappable Wilfred just shifted a few men to face the new threat. He did so calmly and without hurry.

Lord Douglas and his French advisers had not led the attack. They were watching. It was now obvious to me that their plan was to hurt us so much that Barnard Castle would be left isolated and fall. I would not let that happen. Sir Hugh was one of my father's knights. Volva was up for a battle and I pulled my shield around a little more to my front as I pulled back my spear. Peering towards the advancing Scottish knights I saw the man I would spear. He had a yellow surcoat with a blue diagonal cross. A novice might have been tempted to go for the junction of the four arms of the cross. I aimed just above his thigh. If I struck when my spear was raised then I would hit his chest. If I hit when my spear was pointing downwards then it would be his thigh. I had fought in tourneys since the

The Princes' Revolt

time of Geoffrey of Anjou. I had forgotten more about jousting than the Scot I fought had learned. His spear, aimed at my chest rose as he struck and smacked off the side of my helmet. It made my ears ring but did not affect my strike. I hit him above the waist. My spear struck bone and the head was sheared from my spear's shaft but the Scot had a mortal wound. I threw the broken shaft ahead of me and then drew my sword.

I was lucky. I rode in the middle of a phalanx of my household knights and men at arms. I was well protected. The Durham knights whose peers had fled were struggling. If Wilfred and my dismounted men at arms had not been there then that might have been the end of the battle. As it was we were holding them.

My line of household knights had broken through their first rank. Those in the second were not as good as the ones we had felled. The spear which was thrust at me was easily blocked by my shield. A sword is a more accurate weapon in close combat and I swept it across the middle of the knight. I broke links and ripped through his gambeson. As I drew my blade towards me I saw blood. I was now the tip of an improvised wedge. We were driving deep into their lines. Aelric's archers were having a devasting effect. Their arrows were no longer being showered upon the enemy. Using the woods as cover each archer was acting as an individual and targeting knights whose backs were towards them.

The Durham knights, however, were suffering. The departure of their cowardly peers had isolated them. Their lack of skill became apparent and they died. As they died so my wedge became increasingly isolated. Had I not had my men at arms then I think we would have been defeated already. We were no longer moving forward for there was a press of knights and men at arms before us. Our skill was our salvation. We did not panic. Each knight and man at arms fought the man before him. Our horses fought too. The Scottish horse was not as good a beast. Even so I wondered if we would win and then I heard, from the east, the sound of my horn and a voice shouting, "Charge!" I heard the thunder of hooves.

There was no time for speculation for we were fighting for our lives. I saw Sir Gilles of Normanby's surcoat. There was blood and it was on his back. He was wounded. Sir Harold's horse had a wound. Whoever was coming to our rescue had to reach us soon or it would all be in vain. I blocked the blow from the Scottish sword with my own blade. I sensed, rather than saw, the sword which was thrust at my left side. I stopped it with my shield and, as I did so I lifted my foot from my stirrup and

The Princes' Revolt

kicked with my right leg at the knee of the Scot. It hurt and as he reeled I rammed my sword into his upper arm. I wheeled Volva just in time to block the blow from the second Scot. My horse snapped at his horse and when his horse whipped its head away from Volva's snapping jaws I brought my sword down onto his shoulder. It bit through the mail and into flesh.

Then there was a clash of steel and the sound of neighing horses as my son and Sir Ralph led mounted and mailed men into the side of the Scots attacking us. Allied to Aelric and his archers attacking from the rear it proved too much for Lord Douglas' army. The Scots tried to flee. In those few moments twenty men at arms and six knights died. As the others tried to flee I heard Scottish horns sound. They were retreating.

This was the moment when my decision would determine if we won or lost. "Knights and men of the valley. Get fresh horses. This is not over yet!"

I looked around and saw that Ralph was not riding to me with my spare horse. He was riding him. I saw then that the charge had been made of our squires, men at arms and a handful of the Durham knights who had fled. I waved him over and saw that his sword was bloody. "Well done Ralph. Give me Lightning. Take Volva to safety and then follow with Goldie."

"Aye lord. Sorry that I rode your warhorse but your son..."

I smiled at him, "Do not apologise. It was the right decision. Wilfred, Take charge here." Most of the Durham knights were in no condition to pursue. I led just thirty knights and twenty men at arms as we chased the Scots. I had much to thank my son and Sir Ralph for. That would have to wait. We galloped through Gretna ignoring the wounded and the camp followers who fled at our approach. We did not bother with the abandoned baggage. We would take those upon our return. Our horses were fresher than the Scots and we began to gain on them. We had no formation and we spread out in the fields next to the road. The men on foot were the first to die. Leaning from my saddle I swept my sword across the side of the head of the man at arms who had lost his horse. Then I spied Scottish knights. My surcoat was known and feared.

Four of them, seeing that I was hard on their heels reined in and shouted, "We yield Earl!"

I reined in and turned, "Sir Gilles of Norton and Ralph take these men back to Gretna."

"Aye lord."

My knights and men at arms had not waited. They continued the pursuit. I saw more Scottish knights yielding and, as I passed Sir Harold I saw one of the French knights. He turned to look back. That was always a mistake and his horse stumbled. He was thrown into the ditch at the side of the road. Aware that our horses were tiring and the capture of Scottish knights had thinned our numbers I held up my hand and shouted, "Hold and reform!" I turned and saw that Samuel was close by. "Find a horse for this knight. He may be the most valuable treasure we capture this day!"

"Aye father!" The joy of battle was on my son's face and I was proud of him.

I dismounted and walked over to the knight. I took off his helmet and removed his arming cap. He had fallen awkwardly. His leg was at a strange angle. It was obviously broken and he was unconscious and there was blood coming from his nose. I needed him alive. We had a couple of priests with us. They had come from the Palatinate. Perhaps they could be of more use than their knights had been.

Samuel walked over with the horse. "Help me to drape him over the saddle. We must get him to the healers." I wished now that I had brought Brother Peter with me but I had left him at Barnard.

Once he was secured my son held the reins and we headed back the five miles to our camp. "Why do you need this one alive, father?"

"For he is French and close to Lord Douglas. We may learn much from him. You and Sir Ralph did well. What happened?"

"Those cowards tried to flee the battle. We would not let them use the bridge for you had ordered us to hold. Some risked the river to escape. Three did not emerge but two rode east. Sir Ralph berated the others and said he would slay any who did not turn around and follow him. I went to the squires and ordered them to arm. It was little enough we could do but we thought if we sounded the horns and charged then the Scots might think we reinforced."

"It worked and today the two of you earned your spurs."

When we reached Gretna, I saw that Wilfred had seized the baggage, the food and the wounded knights. We saw them as they trudged towards our camp. We spurred our horses to overtake them. Wilfred was riding a horse with his spear pressed into the backs of four wounded Scottish knights. He grinned as he turned and saw me. "These buggers think they deserve special treatment because they are knights! They didn't surrender they were captured and will be treated accordingly."

One of them, with his arm in a sling turned and complained, "Your barbarian has no right to treat us thus. We are nobles."

I drew my sword, "Call him a barbarian again and I will teach you some manners. You were captured by Wilfred of Stockton and he can decide what happens to you! I would be pleasant to him, if I were you!"

On reaching the camp, I saw the healers were working on Gilles and the other wounded. Samuel and I took the knight from his horse and laid him on the ground. "Father, when you are done with those here is a Frenchman. I would have him made so that I may talk to him."

The priest looked up. I recognised him from my visit to Durham. "You have won a great and surprising victory, lord."

"It was not a surprise to me and would have been much easier if the knights the Bishop had sent had done their duty." There was anger in my voice but the priest just nodded as if he was not surprised.

Sir Samuel said, "I will go and see how the others are faring."

He finished bandaging Sir Gilles of Normanby and I helped him to his feet. It was Sir Gilles' left arm. "Tomorrow, Sir Gilles, I want you to escort the wounded and the prisoners to Carlisle. We have a siege to raise."

"I can fight with you, lord."

"You are wounded and I need someone I can trust to do this for me."

"Aye lord. Your son and Sir Ralph did well."

"They did."

He and his squire left us. The priest said of the Frenchman, "His leg is broken but that is not life-threatening. I am more concerned about his head."

"Do your best." I waved over Henry son of Will. He had been a wild man when in the Holy Land but since he had married and become a father he had settled down. He was reliable and he was tough. More importantly he could speak French. "Watch this one. I want to know when he can speak."

"Aye lord." He nodded to Samuel who was speaking with Sir Harold and Sir Ralph. "I hope that my son turns out to be a game 'un like Sir Samuel."

"Aye, I am lucky."

I wandered over to Sir Ralph and my son. They were talking with Sir Harold. "Make a note of the names of the men who fled and did not rally. I will see that they pay for their cowardice. We lost too many brave men this day."

Sir Ralph pointed to the squires. Many had been wounded and now sported bandages, "They all did well, lord. None of them even hesitated about following us. We will have true knights in the future."

"Sir Harold, I would have you go to speak with the knights of Durham who survived. Tell them that tomorrow we ride to Barnard Castle to raise the siege. I expect nothing less than total commitment from them."

"I suspect that you will probably get it now. I think they were shamed when the squires did what they would not and do not forget, lord, that there were over forty who did not flee. They fought the men of the isles and the Irish."

"You are right to chastise me. The beaker is half full and I see it as half empty. I am sending Sir Gilles, the wounded and the prisoners to Carlisle tomorrow. Make sure that any with a wound, no matter how small, should go to Carlisle. Sir Gilles will need all the help he can get and I would rather have fit men."

Sir Harold pointed to the cloak covered bodies of our dead, "And those men?"

"We have priests. We will bury them in the churchyard here."

While the archers scoured the battlefield for any who were still alive and to collect weapons, mail and treasure, the knights and men at arms buried our brothers who had died. Before we left, the next morning, I sent four of the squires we had captured with our ransom demands. It would be taken to Carlisle and Sir Gilles could return with it.

I went to the French knight. He was awake. "What is your name, Frenchman?" I spoke in French.

He stared at me. He was obviously in pain from his recently set leg. "Louis of Limoges."

"Do you wish to be ransomed?" My question was laden for if he said 'aye' then he would be accepting surrender and his parole would be given.

He nodded, "You are a clever general Earl William. I advised Lord Douglas to keep to the plan."

I knew that the priest had given him a draught to ease the pain and it had made him careless. I gambled, "It was a good plan too but Lord Balliol will now be under attack from the knights of Northumbria and the knights of York. Your plan has failed. Two armies have been defeated by our three."

It was not the truth. It was a ruse de guerre but Sir Louis showed his disappointment in his face. "How did you discover our plan?"

I stood without answering him. "Have this knight taken to Carlisle. He will be ransomed with the rest." As I went back to my knights I was confident that there would be no more surprises. There was just one army and it was Balliol's. I had feared that King William might attack the north of Northumbria but I knew now he would not.

The next morning, we headed east. It would not be a quick journey. It would take two days. Masood and Aiden rode to the castle to ascertain the position. Edward and Edgar had still to return.

The archers acted as scouts. Aelric and Sir Philip said that they felt like frauds. They had been protected during the fight by men at arms and the trees. None had been hurt. I told them that was as it should be for without them we would have lost. More than half the men who were killed in the battle fell to our archers. It was their victory.

Alston was exactly half way and we camped there. I found it hard to sleep. Once again, I found myself saddened that there was no lord here. King Henry was too preoccupied with Normandy and the Vexin. Had he made his own land more secure then he could have called upon more men to fight in Normandy. As I lay down to sleep that night I wondered how my father was faring. My disturbed sleep was also due to the ground. I found it hard to sleep on the ground these days. My father was twenty years older. I did not know how, or why, he did it. He had a great attachment to King Henry. I supposed it was because of the Empress. I knew that my father and she had been close. He was now the last knight of the Empress. That was a remarkable feat.

My four scouts returned when we were ten miles from Alston. Edward and Edgar had delivered my message and brought news that the Sheriff was sending forty knights with a hundred men at arms and crossbowmen. They would help us relieve the siege. Aiden and Masood brought us the news that the castle was surrounded but the Scots were unable to bring large numbers into the valley for the archers on the walls and the stone-throwers Sir Hugh had deployed made the passage of horsemen impossible. The bad news was that Balliol had almost a thousand men in addition to his knights.

As we travelled the last twenty miles I wracked my brains for a way to end the siege without losing too many of my men. It was when we stopped to water the horses that Aiden gave me the answer. "Lord, do you wish to fight a battle with the Scots in order to reach the castle?"

"Not if I can avoid it. We have lost too many men already."

"Then why not use the Wear valley. You can then approach the castle from the west. There are no horsemen there. The Scots have dug a ditch and are felling trees for a ram and stone throwers but there would be no mounted men to oppose you."

"But it is further."

"It would take an extra day."

I called over Sir John. "I plan to divide my forces. I will give you the knights and men at arms of the Palatinate. I will take your men at arms and archers. I will ride down the Wear valley. You need to camp close enough to the Scots for them to think it is my whole army. I will give you my banner to aid the deception."

"Do I attack?"

"No, you build counter siege lines. Have the men dig a ditch. You are there to stop the Scots escaping. I will attack the men at the western end of the castle and then we will sortie. You will hear our horns."

"If you think that I can do this lord."

"I do. I believe that the knights of the Palatinate will fight now."

And so we parted. I left the priests with Sir John and the baggage train. It meant we could travel quicker. The route we were taking was on a rough road. It had not been built by the Romans. It was not a well-cobbled surface and the rain began as we headed for Stanhope. It made the journey longer and harder. We did not arrive at this remote manor until evening. There was no castle but there was a hall and a lord of the manor. Sir John Fitzurse was a knight who had fought alongside my father at the Battle of the Standards. Unlike my father he was old. He made us welcome and had his servants provide food. When he heard of our battle and what we intended he insisted that we take his twelve men at arms and his six archers.

"I know that I am old and should have been put out of my misery but these eighteen are all good men. It would make me feel less useless if they fought alongside you. I hate the Scots. When your father and the Archbishop led us against the Scots it was one of the greatest days of my life." He shook his head, "King Stephen has much to answer for. In addition, they know roads which will bring you there quicker."

Sir Morgan smiled when he heard what the old knight had said. "There are men in the Varangian Guards who would say that we were meant to come here and to meet with Sir John. There is a thread which ties him to your father and thence to Sir Hugh. I believe in God lord but there are other powers in this world that I do not understand." He grinned, "Nor do I wish to. I just believe that they are neither good nor are they bad. They just are and we can do nothing about them."

Sir Harold shook his head, "Talking with you, Alf, makes my head hurt!"

My former squire shrugged. "It comes from being born in the east. Had Sir William not found me then I would have died years ago. My master would have had me punished for some minor offence and I would have struck him and then been executed. Every day that I look on the sun I feel glad to be alive. It could have been so different."

The next day the rain had stopped but, as we headed down trails little bigger than paths we found the going treacherous and our surcoats became so muddied that you could not tell one from the other. Sir John, however, was right. We made good time despite the weather and the conditions underfoot. When, not long after noon, Stephen of Stanhope told us that we were just five miles from the castle I sent out Masood and Aiden to scout. We prepared for battle. We had to strike quickly. My plan was simple. There were two gates to the castle: the town gate and the north gate. The Scots had invested the town. We would attack the Scots who were assaulting the north gate. It was the one direction they would least expect an attack. The fact that we would be attacking at dusk would also catch them by surprise. I knew that Sir John and the rest of my men would be camped on the other side of the Tees. Balliol would have moved men to counter that threat. Aelric and Sir Philip were aggrieved that it would be the horsemen who would mount the attack. That could not be helped. I gave them the task of following up and capturing, then destroying the siege engines.

We walked our horses through the trees until we were four hundred paces from the walls. It was late afternoon and the sun was already brighter in the west and we were in the gloom. Sir Hugh had cleared the trees to enable his defenders to keep an attacker away from the walls. There was an untidy sprawl of small camps and fires dotted around the periphery of the siege lines. The tents and the odd horse marked the knights. There were few of them. It was as Aiden had told us the majority of the Scottish knights were still on the other side of the river and were awaiting the taking of the castle which would allow them to use the bridge. I saw Scots walking back to their fires. The assault for the day was largely over. Even as we began to mount we heard the crack of a stone-thrower as Sir Hugh's men sent a huge rock towards the men we

The Princes' Revolt

could see building a ram. Even though the stone fell short it still struck a camp fire scattering burning embers and logs. I saw one man fall clutching his eyes. Orders were shouted and half of the men who had been retreating turned to face the stone thrower which cracked a second time. The others scrambled around for whatever shelter they could find. The half-built ram and stone-thrower were the only ones they could find.

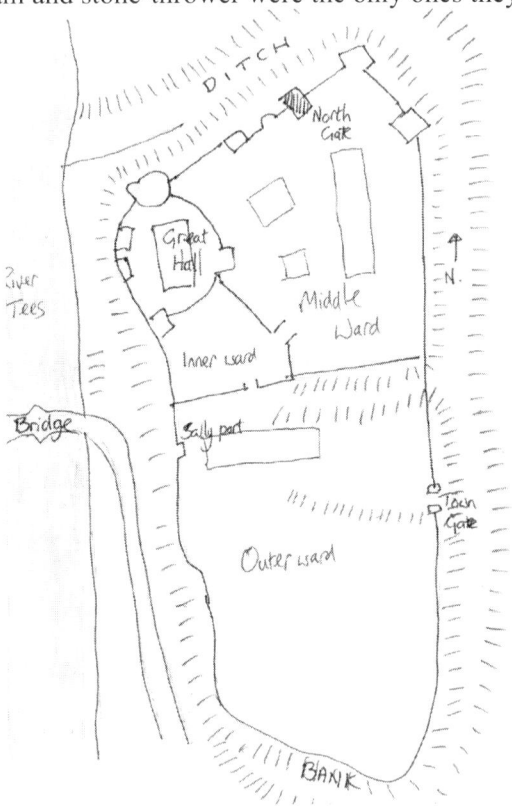

All eyes were on the walls and it was a perfect opportunity to strike. I raised my spear and dug my spurs into Lightning. Our squires would not fight this day. They would wait in the woods. If we succeeded then they would join us and if not, they would head back to Stanhope. The archers' horses were also left in the woods and they followed us to run across the open ground. There were few of us to charge their lines. We had less than sixty horsemen but we had something every commander and general dreams of; surprise.

There was no horn and no cheer. The sound of the cries from the camp hid us for the first hundred paces and then they heard us. Even though the ground was wet and soggy the thunder of sixty horses made the ground vibrate. They turned and saw, to their horror, a line of horsemen, mailed and with spears charging at them. There were shields and men holding them but they were closer to the walls and facing the bows and stone-throwers of the defenders.

Sir Ralph and Sir Samuel flanked me. My more experienced knights were spread out along my perilously thin line. The first Scot I killed fell not to my spear but to Lightning's hooves. He tripped as he ran from me and there was a crunch as his head was crushed. A Scottish knight grabbed his shield and shouted orders. We were not boot to boot and so I veered towards him. He tried to make himself as small a target as possible. I pulled back and punched at his middle. All that I could see was his shield. Lightning's speed and power allied to a perfect thrust struck him so hard that he was thrown backwards. His head hit the mail of two of his men at arms who were standing behind him. They fell too. Aelric, Sir Philip and his archers would capture the wounded.

I knew that we were seen from the walls for I saw hands waving. The stones would cease and Sir Hugh would have his archers ready to aid us. We were approaching the ditch and, as we had planned, I would lead half of the men to ride west while Sir Harold would lead the other half to ride east. Some of the men we charged now had shields but these were not knights nor were most of them men at arms. The majority of men we faced were the levy. They were mormaer's men who followed their lord to battle. The shields they had were crudely made willow boards to stop Sir Hugh's arrows. They were not meant to block the blow of a steel-tipped spear. I rammed my spear at one such board and my spearhead split the shield and struck the unarmoured chest of the man who held it. The Scots were fleeing and heading towards the town. I am sure that there were enough men in the town to have outnumbered us but panic is like the plague and the pestilence; it is contagious and it spread amongst those who had not yet seen us. All that they heard was the thunder of horses and all that they saw was a wall of horsemen. They did not know that it was a thin wall.

The main street of the town was wide and I headed down it. Wilfred led my men at arms down the smaller side streets. From the walls of the castle, Sir Hugh's archers directed their missiles at the fleeing Scots. The townsfolk who had had to endure the privations of the Scots joined in and they burst from their homes to fall upon the hapless Scots. The handful of knights knew that they could not outrun us and wished to avoid an arrow which did not discriminate between lord and peasant and towns people anxious for revenge. As we raised our weapons to slay them they yielded.

By the time we neared the bridge, only Samuel and Ralph remained at my side. We reined our exhausted horses in and surveyed the bridge. Th accuracy of the defender's bows could be clearly seen in the swathe of bodies clustered before and on the bridge. On the hill opposite, I saw the Scottish camp and Balliol and the majority of his knights. I could not see Sir Harold for there was no road from the north save the one we had taken. I took off my helmet and looked up at the two towers which rose from the walls. I spied Sir Hugh. He raised his hand and shouted, "I knew you would be here my lord."

I nodded, "And all is well within?"

"We were prepared."

"Good." We turned our horses and, as the sun began to set we headed towards the town gate. The first part of my plan had succeeded. Now we had to force the Scots to head back to Scotland. I was not certain that we had enough men left to defeat them in a pitched battle. We had killed the common men but not their knights. The bulk of them and their mounted men at arms remained at large on the other side of the river.

It was dark by the time we had collected all the Scottish dead and made a pyre of them and their siege engines. The wind was from the west and the fire, to the north of the castle, was one of burning wood and flesh. The smell was carried to the Scottish camp. My archers and men at arms used the Scottish camp. We were housed in the castle. The five knights who had surrendered were secured and we ate with Sir Hugh and his wife. We ate the animals the Scots had captured and butchered. When this was over there would be reparations and those who had lost would be compensated.

Sir Hugh told us what had happened. "We had warning of their attack and when they tried to cross the bridge our archers killed so many of their horses that they abandoned that attempt and instead built rafts to ferry their men across the river. We could do little about that but it meant their horsemen could not do as, I think, they had planned and ravage the valley. The attack on the walls began this morning. They spent the first day sending men across the river. How did the battle at Gretna go?"

I smiled, "We won. Thanks in no small part to our sons who led a charge to rout the enemy. They truly won their spurs."

The Princes' Revolt

Sir Hugh looked proudly at his son. His wife, Lady Anne, looked less happy. She was thinking of the word 'charge' and all that it implied. Sir Hugh said, "And what now?"

"Sir John has the knights and men of Durham blocking the road west. He will wait to hear our horns sound three times and then he will attack." I drank some of the ale which was before me. "Are the rafts the Scots used still in the river?"

"We had no means to destroy them so I am guessing that they are."

I smiled. "Then we use our enemies' own weapon against them. They will have men watching the bridge. They will expect an attack there. We send our archers across the river on rafts first and then the rest of our men. We attack through the woods and not the road. I will have the archers cross before dawn."

"Will they not be tired, lord?"

Sir Philip answered for me, "Sir Hugh we have been the passengers in this campaign thus far. We have watched Earl William, his knights and his men at arms do all the fighting and taking all of the risks. The archers are desperate to show that they too have the strength to fight the Scots." He stood. "I will go and begin."

Sir Hugh said, "And I will fight alongside my son, the lion of the north. Perhaps he can teach this old dog some new tricks."

Our squires took our weapons and mail. Swords were sharpened and mail was cleaned. They would have no horses to tend and they were eager for the battle. Gretna had whetted their appetite. They had fought their foes and won. The dead they had buried in the Scottish church by the river only steeled their resolve to do well.

I went with my knights to the chapel. All of us would pray to God that we would emerge victorious and that we would lose no more men. All men prayed before a battle. It was in the nature of war but praying in a house of God seemed to improve our chances of victory.

I slept well. I was in a bed! Ralph woke me before dawn so that I could dress and go to the river to see my archers slip across on the rafts. Aiden and Masood had gone first. They were deadly with their knives. The Scottish sentries would be silenced. After watching them slip across the river on the three Scottish rafts I returned to the middle ward. Wilfred and his men were all ready to go to the outer ward where they would leave by the sally port and try to force the bridge. Ralph had my shield and my helmet. My knights and the men at arms I would lead were waiting. Leaving by the town gate we went around the castle to the rafts.

The Princes' Revolt

The sun would be breaking soon but the huge bulk of the castle would delay the lightening of the sky. That suited us. We would be able to slip up through the undergrowth and attack the Scottish camp. Ralph had the horn. He would be at my side until I gave him the order to sound the horn.

We moved up through trees. The first Scot we found was close to a tree. His throat had been cut. He must have been a sentry and in the process of making water for the ground was wet. As we moved up the slope we saw more dead Scots. I knew that our luck could not hold and I was grateful that there was a line of archers before us. They would be at the edge of the trees and their bows would have the camp covered. I heard a shout from before us.

"Ralph, sound the horn three times." The night was shattered by the three strident notes. I drew my sword and swung my shield from around my back. I moved up the slope and saw the archers with drawn bows. Even as I approached they released and I heard the cries from their victims. To the west I heard a horn sound three times. It was Sir John. He had heard the signal and was preparing to charge. This was the moment for the knights of Durham to atone for the cowardice of a handful of knights.

The camp was in a state of confusion. Horns sounded all around them and arrows were coming from the woods. Wilfred would be leading my men at arms across the bridge. The Scots would be attacked on three sides. This would be a test of Lord Balliol and his strategy. With Samuel and Ralph by my side we burst into the camp. They were awake but not ready for war. Few had armour and men were scrambling around for weapons. I blocked a blow from a pole axe as I swept my sword sideways into a warrior who was trying to spear my son. This was an unknown country for the two young knights. This was not a tourney. This was a brutal battle where anything was allowed. You needed the reactions of a fox and the determination and guile of a wolf.

I saw a Scottish knight. He was mailed and ready for war. He ran towards me wielding a war axe. I balanced myself and made certain that my shield was angled so that anything less than a horizontal strike would slide down it. I held my sword behind me. It would disguise my intention. I noticed that he was bigger than I was. Unless he kept his feet wide then a swinging blow with an axe could unbalance him. Around me I heard the clash of metal on metal and the screams and cries as men died. Even as I approached the knight I saw an arrow fly from behind me and impale the Scot who was rushing to the knight's aid.

The Scottish knight saw the flight of the arrow and he rushed to close with me before a second one hit him. He swung too early. I was able to shift my weight and move inside the strike. It was the haft which hit my shield and not the edged blade of the weapon. I lunged with my sword not at his middle, his shield protected that, but his thigh. My sword came away bloody and as he cursed I stepped back and ducked as the axe swung over my head. The knight was angry and that is never the best way to fight.

"Cowardly trickster!"

As he shouted and raised his axe I spun around and brought my sword into his right side. It bit through to his ribs. As I pulled out the blade he crumpled in a heap.

Looking around for the next opponent I heard the thunder of hooves. Sir John was leading the knights of Durham into the camp. Although the Scots were being attacked by horses we still had many men left in the camp who were trying to use their numbers to overwhelm us. I saw that Lord Balliol had managed to mount the remainder of his knights and they rode to meet with Sir John. I heard a roar from my right and Wilfred led my men at arms up the road and into the camp. We had the opportunity to capture the camp and attack Lord Balliol and his mounted knights.

"Cleveland! To me!"

My knights and men at arms joined me as my archers formed a line behind us and started to shower arrows in a more organised way. Once they had cleared the ground before us I shouted, "Wedge!" This time I was flanked by Sir Harold and Sir Tristan. The rest of my men spread out behind us. "We run!"

I began to run. I knew that it would be harder for those behind but most had fought together for more than ten years. Our archers worked in pairs. One released while the other ran after us. Although it slowed down the number of arrows we sent it kept up the same rate of missiles. No one could stand before us. The odd man who survived the arrow storm was easily despatched. From ahead I heard the clash as the two bodies of knights met. It was the sound of neighing horses, screams, metal on wood, wood on metal and the screams of men impaled upon spears. I saw, ahead, the rear of the Scottish line.

Raising my sword, I shouted, "For God, King Henry and the Warlord!" I led my wedge of fifty men into the rear of the Scottish line.

The Princes' Revolt

The knights at the rear tried to turn their horses. That was never easy when in a line which was engaged. We had no time for chivalrous strokes and gentlemanly cuts. They were above us and had spears. I swung my sword sideways and hacked through the leg of the first Scot who turned. His spear struck my helmet as the leg was severed and he fell from his horse. My blade must have cut the horse for it reared. This was now a mêlée. Scots raised their spears to strike down at us and my men thrust upwards with their swords. The advantage we held was that we could attack the side without the shield and we could use our own shield for protection. I saw that Wilfred had put his shield over his back and he dragged a knight from his horse and skewered him as he lay on the ground.

We worked our way through the knights. Those at the front who were engaged with Sir John and his men could not turn. I spied Lord Balliol and his squire. Suddenly, as Samuel slew one knight who was close to the Scottish standard, Ralph leapt on to the body and into the saddle. He spurred the horse and hacked into the side of the standard-bearer. Balliol's squire tried to retrieve it but an arrow struck him in the head and he fell.

Ralph held on to the standard and shouted, "Yield, Lord Balliol! I have the standard!"

The Scottish lord looked around and spied me. He pointed his sword at me, "Trickster! I thought you led the charge!"

Just them an arrow flew and struck him in the right arm. He dropped the sword.

"Do you do as Sir Ralph demanded and yield, or will you and your men be butchered?"

He looked around, the blood dripping from the wound. He nodded, "We yield!"

I looked up at Sir Ralph who still held the standard, "And there is something to hang over the fire when you and my daughter have your own castle!"

**Part Two
The Warlord**

Chapter 4

My son had been more successful in Scotland than I had been in Wales. Perhaps I was getting too old for war or maybe the Welsh were just too cunning. Certainly, their mountains were no place for horses. It had taken us until Christmas to subdue them and to make a peace which would last. The reparations I had demanded were high but it was the hostages I escorted back to London which would ensure that they kept the peace. As Prince Richard and I rode back to London along the road the Romans had used to subdue the druids I used the time to speak at length to the young prince. His father had asked me to help mould the king. I liked him for he was courageous to the point of recklessness but he was also willing to learn. I did not know how his elder brother would be as king but Richard struck me as having the potential to be a king whom men would follow.

"What your father needs to do is to build castles at the mouth of the Clwyd and then guarding the Menaii straits. Without the wheat from Anglesey, the Welsh would starve."

He nodded, "They are wild warriors. That is a good idea. The castles would contain them. I would war against other knights."

"You do not choose your enemies. They choose you. You must fight all of them no matter how mean or lowly."

"And what of Thomas Becket? He is our enemy. Why does my father not have him killed?"

I laughed and shook my head, "Your father is already in dispute with the Pope. He cannot appoint bishops. I am not even certain he can have your brother crowned. The church in Rome can be like a nest of vipers. It is best to leave it alone."

"But my father is a good man. He even gives my brother the crown. Surely that must stand in his favour."

"It is good that you think this way. There have often been rebellious sons but a king's deeds and the reputation he has are two entirely different matters."

"My father has more power than the Pope."

"The Pope may rule a tiny city in Italy but every monarch and ruler in the west must accept his judgement. A king has to be anointed. The priest who does that also serves the Pope. There are some enemies you can fight and others you cannot."

We rode in silence for I had much to think on and my words had set in motion thoughts in Richard's head; he was clever. The hostages would be placed in the White Tower. The King did not use that as his home. He preferred Windsor. My share of the treasure we had taken was already on its way north under the care of Wilson of Bristol and his men at arms. I hoped that the speedy handover of the hostages would allow me to return to my family. The marriages of Samuel and Eleanor, as well as Ruth and Ralph of Barnard, would take place in April I wished to be there for that ceremony. I had missed my son's wedding. I would not miss my grandchildren's. The King had been successful in Normandy and he would be in London. It would be the perfect opportunity to ask for me to be released, at least for a while.

Prince Richard noticed my silence. "Your son did well in Scotland. In two battles he defeated the Scots. It took us longer to defeat the Welsh."

I was not certain if he was criticising me or praising my son. "My son led the finest knights, men at arms and archers in the land. We fought with an army cobbled together from many places. We know the land along the border with Scotland well. We have fought there many times. It is more forgiving than the Welsh land and we have good castles there but you are right. He did do well."

"And your grandson gained great honour."

The rider who had brought the letter from my son had been Davy of Ingleby. He had been at the battles, both of them, and he had recounted in every detail the two actions which made the names of Ralph and Samuel. The letter, penned by my son, gave details of the aftermath to which Davy of Ingleby was not privy. The knights of Durham who had fled had been found and tried. The Bishop of Durham could not defend them and they and their families were banished from the Palatinate. I

The Princes' Revolt

know that my son favoured a more draconian punishment, death, but the Bishop was lenient. I had no idea where they would go but it would not be in the north. My son had ensured the newly appointed lords of the manor were more acceptable to the valley. The coin which had been collected in ransoms and reparations was divided equally. Barnard Castle would be improved and other monies were given to my knights to strengthen their homes. When Ralph and Samuel were given manors then they would have the coin to make them strong and to furnish them as their wives would wish. I had ideas along those lines for King Henry. I would use my position to influence him.

I spoke to Richard of war. He was fascinated by my experiences and asked me about the battles I had fought to secure the crown for his father. When he discovered that William had been on crusade he was desperate to speak with him.

"Now there is a true enemy of Christendom. The followers of that blasphemous religion need to be wiped from the face of the earth so that Christ's home can belong to his people once more."

He had an idealistic view. It was an impractical one. "There are many thousands of them, you know. Even if we emptied all the lands of Europe of men to fight them they would still have many more men than we would."

He laughed, "Aye but they are savages and we are nobles." He pointed at the two men at arms and four archers who rode ahead of us. "Even those who are just ordinary warriors have more nobility than the highest born Turk!"

I did not think my son would agree but I would let William win that argument. "Before that day you must be knighted."

He looked at me, "Then you shall knight me."

"That cannot be. You are a prince. A king must knight you. Your own father was the only one who could knight young Prince Henry of Scotland before he was crowned King of Scotland. It will be your father's decision and you will have to wait until your brother, Henry wins his spurs."

"So he will get a crown and his spurs first and I will have nothing!" His petulance returned.

"That is the lot of the second son. You must learn patience."

"Is that why my father sent me with you, Earl Marshal; so that I may learn patience?"

The Princes' Revolt

"If he did then I have failed for you recklessly charged those Welshmen at Denbigh."

"They had no mail and I did. More importantly, Earl Marshal, they had no skill and I did. When I begin to fight in the tourney my brother had best watch out for I will be the greatest knight in Christendom."

"You cannot say that about yourself, Prince Richard. Others can but not you. A knight does not boast of his deeds. A knight's deeds do the boasting." When I spoke that day he was but thirteen summers' old. I saw him reflect on the words. He did not remain the same reflective youth as he became a man but that, I believe was the fault of others. The ride to London would be the last time that he would be in my charge.

King Henry was out hunting when we reached Windsor. We had royal guards and household knights to escort our hostages to the Tower where they would be housed. I was just grateful that I would have a comfortable bed that night and, hopefully, a bath.

Queen Eleanor came to greet me. Despite being over forty years of age, she was still a stunning woman. She came and kissed me on the cheek and linked my arm. Richard had disappeared as soon as we had entered the castle. "And how is my rumbustious son?"

I smiled, "He is wilder than his father was at the same age but he has a good heart and he is fearless."

"You will look after him. I am pleased that my husband chose you. I think he has chosen well for Henry too. William Marshal is a younger version of you."

"And how are you, my lady? You look as beautiful as ever."

"And you know how to flatter. That is disingenuous of me. You never flatter and always speak the truth. It is one of the many things I love about you. And so I thank you for your words. I confess it took me some time to recover from the birth of John. I had a difficult time." She waved a hand, "But you do not need to know that. He will be my last child." She led me to a small table with two chairs. "Henry has done much work here. You must have noticed the King's Gate as you came in?"

"I nodded, "It is a substantial gate and adds to the defence!"

She shook her head. "You knights and your preoccupation with defence! I want a home which is comfortable. The walls were crumbling! This is much more pleasant. I like to sit here for the light comes through the glass and yet it is away from the draughts. We do not have such draughts in Aquitaine. Chinon and Mirebeau are much cosier."

"Will you return there soon?"

"Perhaps. Henry is busy organizing the coronation. Archbishop Becket is a nuisance. He lives in France and yet his actions determine what we should do! I wish we were rid of him!"

"When is the coronation planned?"

"June. We have a few more months to wait. Once he is crowned then we can go back to Aquitaine. Henry can campaign in Normandy but I wish for warmth and the sun."

"You would be alone?"

She looked at me, "Alfraed, you of all people know my husband. His bastard, Geoffrey, is evidence of his liaison with that whore, Ykenai and I hear that he is casting his eyes over Ida de Tosny. I hope he keeps his secrets safer from his enemies than he does from me!" She patted my hand. "So long as I have Aquitaine then I am happy. I have done my duty and born him three sons who live. I have delivered my part of the bargain. His part is to keep my land safe from the greedy, grasping fingers of the French."

Henry's liaisons were not widely known but he could not hide the baby he had given the same name as the legitimate son his wife had borne him. I knew then that I had been lucky. Adela would never have spoken like that and my one indiscretion with Henry's mother had been just that; a brief moment of passion and then a lifetime of yearning.

I said nothing and the Queen must have thought she had said too much. "And how are your grandchildren? Their lives will be a little more normal than that of my children."

"I hope so for they live in a quiet backwater. They are both to be married in April."

She leaned over to kiss my cheek. "That is wonderful news. You must be so excited! They say that April weddings always last."

"Do they?"

"In Gascony they do. April? Then you will be able to be in London for the coronation. Your knights will need to swear allegiance to young Henry."

"My lady, I can ask you. Why the haste? With Becket causing problems and trouble on the borders it might make more sense to wait to crown young Henry. He is but fifteen."

"My husband and I disagree about many things but this is not one of them. This strengthens my husband's hand. He can concentrate on

Normandy, Anjou and the Vexin. William Marshal is a good man, is he not?"

"He is but…"

"My husband was not much older when he was named King. He has not done a poor job has he?"

I sighed. She was right but something about it felt wrong. "You are right. It is just that I see no reason to do this now. I suspect I am tired and I would like to spend more time with my family."

"And you shall. When Henry returns I shall tell him." I wondered how the King would take that. She recognised my look and she smiled. "I am the dutiful wife and queen in most things but when I give a command then it is obeyed. This is one command he will accede to. He owes you much. He owes me more."

I had always known her to be a strong woman. I had met her first when she was a child and she had impressed me then. I felt more hopeful about the prospect of returning home. I took my leave and went to my room where Simon, my squire, helped me to change. He was in awe of the castle although, in truth, I found it draughty and rather shoddily built. King Henry's improvements would make it a palace one day but that day was not yet. Simon had impressed me on campaign. He had not been called upon to fight but he had been there ready to help in any way that he could. He was diligent when it came to my weapons and mail. When we returned to the valley he would be able to practise those knightly skills which he would need.

I heard the King return. It was a noisy affair. He and his son were reunited and I knew that they would be discussing the campaign. I did not wish to intrude and so I took a short nap. I found it helped me to sleep better at night if I was able to sleep during the day. The Welsh campaign had robbed me of much sleep. When Simon and I descended for the feast to celebrate Prince Richard's return we were greeted warmly by both the King and Prince Richard. The other two princes were a little less effusive. In Geoffrey's case it was his sullen nature. He rarely spoke to anyone but with young Henry it was because he did not like me. I could not get to the bottom of the obvious dislike he felt. His eyes seemed to glare at me whenever I was in the room. I recognised one of the knights with the princes. He was Roger Le Breton. He had been a close friend of King Henry's young brother William who had died, some said, of a broken heart when Thomas Becket refused to allow him to marry his true love. When I saw the liveries of the other three I recognised them then. They were also household knights of the now-deceased Duke William: Sir Reginald Fitzurse, Sir Hugh de Morville, and Sir William de Tracy

"Warlord, I need to speak with you," King Henry looked pointedly at his sons, "alone." He led me to a small antechamber. There was a sentry there waiting. "See that we are not disturbed."

"Aye, Your Majesty."

Once alone he seemed to visibly relax. We were comfortable in each other's company. "First of all, I wish to thank you and your son. I hoped that the two of you would do that which others said was impossible and defeat the two threats to our borders. That you did so quickly astounded even me."

"We are both here to serve the realm."

"And you both serve me very well. I have things to say which you need to hear. They are for your ears only. There are few men in my lands that I can trust. You are one."

"You are too kind."

"I speak plainly. I have just come from Montmirail. I have a truce with the King of France." he waved a hand. "It will not last, of course but it buys me time. I need time to build alliances and for my sons to be able to manage their lands. Henry must be crowned. You will call in at York on the way to Stockton. I have letters for Archbishop of York, Roger de Pont L'Évêque."

"Of course."

"When you and your knights return south for the coronation then you will escort him. Since Becket fled then Roger is one of the few churchmen that I can trust. I have two other bishops who will also attend. Then we need Geoffrey to be married. Constance is too young and I need Brittany watched. That is a task for you."

"I thought I was to watch over Richard's progress."

"You were but that is superseded. When the coronation is over you will travel to Brittany with Geoffrey. Your presence will guarantee that Countess Margaret holds on to power until her daughter is of an age to be Duchess and marry my son."

"And what of Richard?"

"My brother's household knights, Richard le Breton, Sir Reginald Fitzurse, Sir Hugh de Morville, and Sir William de Tracy have sworn that they will be his mentors."

The Princes' Revolt

I nodded, "They are good knights." He smiled. "But Your Majesty, I would like to spend more time with my family."

He smiled as though he was the most generous of men, "You have between now and June to be with your family. You will watch your children be married and, by then, you will be bored and ready for action, I have no doubt."

He did not know me. I would not be bored for I was weary of war. It was not perfect but I would have six months and that would have to do. "Then, with your permission, Your Majesty, I would like to leave on the morrow."

"So soon? But I had planned on a hunt."

"It is winter, majesty and I need to get home. I have missed Christmas and there are two weddings planned in April."

"Very well but I let you go reluctantly. I want you and your knights here for the first week in June. No later!"

That meant that I would have less than six months!

First, I had a feast to endure. It was hard to sit while young Henry took every opportunity to belittle my achievements and those of his brother. There was little love lost between them. At one point Eleanor intervened in the row which threatened to spill into violence. King Henry did nothing because I think he enjoyed the arguments. It kept them divided. The last thing he needed was a trio of sons who might unite and take his lands from him. When Samuel had been their age he had been my son's squire and all that he had wanted to do was become a knight. He was not trying to gain allies and supporters. Richard and Henry were. I was glad when I was able to beg permission to leave. Eleanor retired and that afforded me the opportunity to head for my room.

She was waiting for me outside in the passage. "Do not be offended by my son's comments. Young Henry means nothing. He is in awe of you and this is his way of showing it. Everyone says that you were the architect of my husband's victories. My son thinks that reflects badly on him. He is young but he will mature."

"My lady, he is about to become King of England. If he is not grown then surely he should not be king."

"Perhaps, and there is something else. He misses Thomas Becket. The Archbishop was his tutor before he fled. He has none other to look up to."

"William Marshal?"

The Princes' Revolt

"He is teaching him to be a knight. We both know that William is a great knight but a leader? He needs someone, like you, to make him a King. The Earl is a good teacher of knights. You are a kingmaker."

Despite my afternoon nap, I found it hard to sleep that night for there was too much racing through my mind. Stockton was my sanctuary. Once I was in my valley then I would be able to think again. I would be able to breathe and I would be able to speak what I thought and not use guarded comments.

My men noticed my silence as we headed north through the shortest days of the day. We travelled along snow-covered roads with hoods pulled around our heads. I had a small escort: my squire, my servants and a handful of archers and men at arms. I was not being deliberately silent I was thinking of the situation I had left. Things were not well between the King and the Queen. Worse, they were not well between the King and at least two of his sons. I now saw why he wished me to be in London for the coronation. I was the guarantor of peace. When would my work be done?

Roger de Pont L'Évêque, the Archbishop of York, was a courtly man. He was a handsome man who liked to surround himself with beautiful things and servants and was no friend of Thomas Becket. We were in agreement about that. We also had much more in common. He understood the role the Archbishop had to play. He was happy to ride to war. Archbishop Thurston had done so with me at the Battle of the Standards and, as I enjoyed a comfortable night in his palace in York, he assured me that he would be willing to do so again.

"Your son has had two fine victories and from what I have learned he did so with few knights of Durham." I cocked my head to one side. He smiled and spread his hands, "I have visitors and I receive news from far and wide. Unlike the Bishop of Durham, I am well aware of my duties and responsibilities. King William has become cautious since you defeated him. He sent Balliol and Douglas to probe your defences. He thought that the west, because the Welsh were attacking Chester, would be weaker. He has seen your strengths and my information is that he is now training and building an army which can match yours."

I shook my head, "My days of leading the men of the north to war are gone. My son has assumed that mantle."

"I pray not for your name alone is worth a hundred banners. Your son can lead men but your presence on the battlefield cows our enemies even more and puts heart into our own men. You are the Nemesis of the Scots.

You have had a longevity which is quite remarkable. The more superstitious of the common man believe that you are protected and cannot be killed. We both know that to be a fantasy but when the fyrd goes to war they want to see the Warlord leading them."

I was not certain that, even if that were true, it was possible. My left arm still troubled me. I was not the warrior I had been even five years earlier. However, I took the compliment, "Thank you Archbishop. I have tried to be the servant of God and the King,"

I promised to return at the end of May and, leaving York, headed north through a blizzard. It was as though the land was trying to stop me getting home. We spent a night at Northallerton with Sir John Fitzwaller. He was more of a farmer and less of a knight but his manor was rich and his people happy. His young son Hugh spent the whole of our time asking me about the battles in which I had fought.

His father finally sent him to bed, "I am sorry for my son, Earl. He thinks me a dull father for I never go to war. He does not know yet that the reason for that is your son and his knights of the valley. I fear that if war came then I would be a hindrance rather than a help."

"All it needs, Sir John, is the ability to lead men and be resolute."

He nodded, "Those Durham knights who fled the field at the battle of Gretna have made me realise that I should attend to battle skills. It is just that life here is good."

"Then be prepared to defend it for there is a thin line of knights twixt you and disaster. If the Scots ever cross the bridge at Piercebridge then believe me their wild warriors will pour through your land and it will be devastated."

He looked surprised. "Will they come? King William has tried twice and both times you and your son have defeated him."

"One day he will find a way to slip through our defences. If I led the Scots and wished to invade England then this would be the time of year I would do it. Every English knight is within his walls waiting out the winter." I smiled at the look of fear on Sir John's face. "I do not think that he will do it, not yet anyway but he is building an army and it will be an army such as ours with mailed horsemen. The fight is coming and so you must prepare."

It was quicker to head up the old Roman Road and cross the Tees at Sir Philip's manor where there was a bridge. The blizzard had blocked the road we would normally take. There was less drifting on the Roman Road. We did not stay long at Piercebridge; just long enough for a beaker

The Princes' Revolt

of heated ale and to find out from Sir Philip about the battle. We reached the west gate at Stockton after dark. There were too few of us to send a rider to warn them of our arrival and we had to knock to gain entry.

Ralph of Bowness opened the gate. "Earl Marshal, had we known..."

I smiled, "I am home, Ralph, and that is all that matters." We went directly to the stable. "Simon, when you have seen to the horses then fetch those two small chests from my horse."

"Aye lord."

"When that is done I shall not need you for a while. You have done well. Enjoy some time to yourself. It must be dull with an old man for company all day. I know the roads are bad but if you wished to visit with your parents at Fissebourne?"

He smiled, "No, lord. I will stay here. I will see my parents at the wedding. I will stay with you for I learn much every day."

The welcome I received warmed me more than the fire. Ruth and Rebekah sat me there and Alice brought me buttered, heated ale and fresh oatcakes. Their attention made me smile, "I am not a dotard. I travelled from Northallerton. It is not a long journey."

Rebekah took my hand and rubbed it, "It is in this weather and when you are no longer a young man."

"I forget that you come from a hot country. We are used to this." I waved over Ruth and Samuel. "And I hear that you are to be married."

They both stood and the looks on their faces made them look like children again. They were delighted at my interest. It warmed my heart. I saw that Simon had returned with the two chests. "You cannot begin married life without coin. Here is a little gift from me." I shrugged, "Or the Welsh, it matters not. Use it for whatever you wish."

Simon gave them the small chests. They were filled with coins; gold coins. The two of them hugged me and I saw a grateful smile on Rebekah's face. She knew that beginning married life was always easier with coins. I needed no coins. When would I spend them? My life span could be measured on the fingers of one hand. I put those depressing thoughts from my mind. It was good to be home. William and I were left by the fire when the rest retired. We both spoke of our campaigns. He told me of the men who had fallen. I knew many of them and I was saddened by their loss. I told him what I had learned from the Archbishop about King William's motives.

William nodded, "I did wonder about that, father. It was a good plan and a clever plan but the King was not with them and that made me suspicious. It will take time for the Scots to raise an army. We took much ransom. Balliol has even more cause to hate us for his ransom was high. I think King William will have to gather coin by fighting the men of the islands. He is probing us and he is learning how we defend. He is a clever man."

"And we need to plan what we do about Sir Ralph, Sir Padraig and my grandson. They need manors."

"Gainford is still vacant and Ralph would be close to his father. I always worry about Sir Hugh for he is exposed where he is."

"And Padraig? I gave him Reeth but that was to give him an income. You need knights who are close to you."

"Wulfestun has no lord. It is a small manor but…"

"It is close to here and Padraig could begin with nothing and grow. That is a good idea. And Samuel?"

"I have spoken to my son and he is happy to be as Sir Richard was and Sir John before him, a household knight."

"And you and Rebekah would be happy about that? You will be losing your daughter and you would like your son close to you."

William laughed, "You know me well. However, my son is happy to live here in Stockton."

"That is good for a while but you know yourself that your son needs to be his own man or he will never be the knight to rule the valley when you are gone."

"You are still teaching me even though there are grey hairs in my beard. I will think on your words. He smiled at me. "It is good to have you back even though it will be but a brief time."

The weather kept me inside the castle and the town for eighteen icy days. I did not mind. I was able to spend time with my grandchildren. They might be grown but to me they were still bairns. With Eleanor in Yarm and Ralph at Barnard Castle the company of their grandfather made a welcome distraction. There was ice on the river and that prevented the ferry crossing the river. We were, to all intents and purposes, cut off. I had chosen the only way practical home across the Tees. When the freeze finished and the ferry could cross the river the first visitor was James of Acklam, Wulfric's captain of the guard.

"You had better come quickly my lords; the priest has given the last rites to Sir Wulfric. I fear that my master is dying."

We needed no urging and the three of us crossed the river along with Wilfred. Wilfred had fought as a man at arms alongside Wulfric. As we crossed the chilly and dark river James said, "He began to deteriorate some days ago. We would have sent word then but the weather…"

"I know James." I put my hand on his shoulder for I could see that he was upset. "God has sent this break in the weather so that we can be there. He will not die without his friends around him."

"I would have swum the river if I could."

The faces of the servants and men at arms told their own story. The whole castle was in a state of shock. We were ushered into his chamber. It smelled of death. He had fouled himself. The priest shook his head as we approached. I thought, at first, that he was dead already. He was not and he opened his eyes as we approached. He gave a wan smile when he recognised me, "Warlord, you came! I told this fool that you would. Go priest. You have done your duty. I have been shrived. I can meet my maker, now let me speak with the Warlord!"

I could not believe how gaunt he looked. My son was also shocked. "Peace, old friend, I am here." I took his hand in mine. It was icy. Death was crawling up his body.

He smiled, "And that is the greatest honour in my life. Not my manor, not my knighthood but that the Warlord called me his friend and unlike others, dissemblers and oath breakers, he meant it."

"You have ever been my friend, comrade and staunch shield brother who was always by my side."

"It has been a privilege to serve you and I am only sorry that I leave you early with a worm which eats me from the inside." He closed his eyes and I saw that he was in pain. "It is times like this that I wish I was a pagan and that the afterlife was a Valhalla full of warriors with whom I had fought."

"Aye, that would be something."

"My lord, I do not have long. I can feel neither my legs nor my lower body." I nodded and squeezed his hand. It felt even colder now. "Swear that whoever is your new lord here will look after my people. They are all good folk and have served me well. Give my wealth to them equally. I have no one else. My sword I give to Samuel. I see him there and he is a fine warrior. I know he has a good one but he will have a son and it would please me if he bore this sword. I will be buried with my war axe. James of Acklam knows my wishes."

I knew that he was waiting for my words, "I swear, Wulfric of Thornaby that your wishes will be carried out to the letter. The lord of this manor will treat all of your people well or will forfeit the manor.

More, I say that I swear that once, each year, we will feast and remember all those who have died for this valley, you, Dick, Sir Edward, Roger of Lincoln, Ralph of Nottingham, Erre, all will be toasted. We will drink so much that our servants will need to put us to bed."

"He smiled, "Thank you, lord, I…" there was a soft sigh. His eyes were open but the spirit of Wulfric lay a little above our heads.

None spoke. Wilfred, James of Acklam, Samuel and my son, each of us had our own thoughts and memories. I was still holding Wulfric's hand and I took it and placed it over the other. I took his sword and handed it to Samuel. He said not a word but I saw, man that he was, his eyes filling. Words would have broken the moment. I gestured towards the door and Wilfred, William and Samuel left.

"If you need aught, James then do not hesitate to ask. We have lost a great warrior this day." He nodded. He was unable to speak. If he had he would have unmanned himself. "You will arrange the funeral as he said?"

He nodded and regained his voice, "Despite his words, lord he was fond of Father Nicholas. We will bury him in our church. We have a place prepared. Father Nicholas asked me to ask you when would be a good time for the burial?"

I gave him a wry smile and answered, "Never. But we must get him in the ground. I will send to my knights. They will wish to say farewell. Let us say the day after tomorrow."

The others were waiting for me at the ferry. I did not notice the icy wind flecked with sleet. I felt almost numb already and it was nothing to do with the cold. Wulfric was almost the last of my first warband of warriors and he was gone. I had outlived them all save my first squire, Harold. I was remembering all the battles my former man at arms had fought at my side. He had been a rock. The wound from the Scots had been his undoing.

As we boarded the ferry William asked, "Who do you think should be the lord of the manor?"

"There is but one choice, for the time being; Samuel was given Wulfric's sword. One day he will be Lord of Stockton and we will appoint another when that day comes but for the present let this be Samuel and Eleanor's home. I know that my grandson will look after Wulfric's people and he will guard the sword until his son is born."

The burial of Wulfric was a sobering moment for all of us. Sir Harold was now the last remnant of the first retinue I had led. He had been my squire, Edward and Wulfric had been my men at arms and Dick had led my archers. We had been small in number but great in heart. Now there were just two of us left. When all the rest had left the church Harold and I knelt there. My wife was buried beneath our feet.

"Lord, do you think there is a heaven? I know that the priests tell us there is. I have told my children that if they are good then they will go to heaven but what if there is no heaven? Have we wasted the time we spent being good?" He turned and his face was serious. "I ask you, Warlord for, since Dick died, then you are the closest man I have to a father. Whatever you say I will believe."

I had a great responsibility. Harold had known nothing save Sherwood and the life of an outlaw until I had made him my squire. He deserved honesty and he deserved the truth. I spoke from the heart. "You could not be bad, even if you tried. You and Dick were noble even when you lived outside the law. That is what divides men. It is not titles. You have a title. Dick had one and never used it. It is what is in your heart that decides if you are noble or villain. Would you have your sons as villains?"

"No, and yet I see villains prosper."

I thought about this. The stone slab we had laid over Wulfric was freshly carved, sharp and clean. Like Adela's and my father's, over time it would fade. "Suppose there is no heaven. Will people remember Wulfric?"

He nodded, "I shall." He put his hand on the slab. "We will talk of him so long as we live. I will tell my sons and my grandsons of his deeds and how he fought like a berserker of old."

"Then that is his heaven. He will be remembered. You will keep him in your heart but to answer you truly, I believe there is a heaven. I am not certain what it will be like but if all the good men and women alongside whom I have fought, are there then I will be happy."

He smiled, "You have comforted me greatly." He paused, "I pray you do not tell the others what I have said, lord. I would feel foolish."

I smiled and patted his shoulder, "This is a church. What is said in here remains here. You are a good man. I am proud that you have served with me for all these years. I pray you live a long time my friend."

As we left the church and stepped into the cold air which swept in from the east I felt a chill around my heart. Wulfric's death had shown me that I needed to make the most of my time on this earth.

Chapter 5

The death of Wulfric was yet another reminder of my mortality. My old man at arms had had the presence of mind to make plans for his death. I had not. As April loomed and the women of the castle, not to mention Samuel, were all busy with preparations for the weddings I sat with my son and William the steward. He was a literate man. His son, John, now took on most of the steward's duties and so his father was free to act as a clerk to my son and me. He would take notes during my talk and then write it up so that there would be a record of my wishes.

As he set up his table and wax tablet my son said, "You are not anticipating your death are you, father? We still have need of you here."

"No, there is no death wish but I have been here so infrequently that I believe it is highly likely that I will die far from here. I will die happier knowing that all is in order in Stockton."

"Ready my lord."

I nodded, "And remember, old friend, that all that passes between us in this room is secret and sacrosanct." My steward looked offended. I smiled, "I mean no offence. You would not be here if I did not trust you completely. I leave the bulk of my money, my armour, weapons and horses to you, William. I know that you will use all wisely. There are exceptions. I wish Alice to be given her own home and an income to allow her to live like a lady. The same goes for William here. Aiden, Edgar and Edward will be each given a farm and an income. I would leave a hundred pounds a year to provide the young men of the valley with the opportunity to become men at arms or archers. It will provide for swords and daggers."

I took a drink of wine. It tasted better in this solar of mine and I could not work out why.

"I will be buried in my best armour with the first helmet Alf made for me and my first sword. I would be buried next to my wife, your mother. I hope that you and your wife will be buried close by."

William nodded and added, wryly, "But not for some time eh?"

I smiled back, "Not for a long time!" Other bequests were made and when I was happy William and my son left.

I was left alone and Alice came with a fresh jug of wine. I could see that she had been crying. "What is amiss Alice?"

She shook her head and forced a smile, "It is nothing! I am an old woman but Wulfric, sorry, lord, Sir Wulfric, well, he served with Alan of York, my husband. It just brings it home to me. I am getting old and becoming grey and my husband died when he was younger than your son. Sir Wulfric's death has made me think of all the years I have been without him."

I took her hand and squeezed it, "I am sorry, Alice."

"Do not be silly my lord. If you had not come along then I would still be tending Adamar's pigs, save that he and his family were all killed twenty years ago in a Scottish raid." She crossed herself. "I am a silly old woman. Ignore me lord. We are glad that you are home and all of us pray that you stay."

I spent the ten days before the wedding visiting as many old friends as I could. The King had given me that most valuable of commodities, time. I would use it well. I also spent a long time with my grandson in Thornaby. I helped him to learn to become a lord of the manor. This would not be his forever but it would be a place he could learn. He had watched his father be a lord of the manor but now I was able to give him my help. He was surrounded my Wulfric's men and they were determined to make life as easy for my grandson as they could.

Sir Philip of Piercebridge came to see my son just a week before the weddings. William regarded it as a relief not to be talking weddings and he was grateful for the distraction. "I am sorry to bother you at such a time but I have a boon to beg."

I nodded, "Sir Philip, since your uncle sent you to us all those years ago you have given both my son and me valiant service. Ask away."

He nodded, "Philip, my eldest son, is my squire. He will be a good knight. But I have a second son, Thomas. He is but eleven summers old and yet he would be a squire. He and his brother do not get on. Is there a place for him as a second squire for another knight in the valley? I would keep peace in my home and with these two cockerels it is impossible."

My son nodded, "This is perfect timing. I have need for a second squire. I need someone to help Ralph. He would have to fetch the spare horses and carry the spears in battle."

"He wishes to be a squire. I would be beholden to you, lord."

And so my son had two squires. Gone were the days when I needed two. Simon would do. He was devoted to me and more like a servant than a squire. It was unlikely that I would need to do anything other than point my sword and direct warriors on the battlefield. The last time I had drawn my sword in anger had been four years since when we had fought the Scots in Northumbria.

The weddings went well. I was well satisfied. I had seen my grandchildren married. The knights of my valley and their families also felt a close part of it as it tied us closer together. Wulfric's death had made all of us realise our own mortality. He had not died in battle. God had taken him.

Of course, once the weddings were over then we began our preparations for the coronation. Sir Ralph took Ruth to Gainford and Samuel took Eleanor to Thornaby but they would have just over forty days and then they would have to travel south and swear allegiance to young Henry. We would not be taking men at arms and so our homes would be well protected but, even so, it would be hard for my knights to travel three hundred miles from their home to crown a boy who was just fifteen years old.

As much as I hated to do so I had to leave earlier than the rest. I had to speak with Roger de Pont L'Évêque, the Archbishop of York. I had also visited with the Bishop of Durham. The meeting had not gone well. He was almost belligerent in his manner. I was less than happy about his attitude and his responsibilities as Prince of the Palatinate. The Archbishop understood his role but not so de Puiset. He still regarded himself as being above the rest of us. Rather than being embarrassed at the behaviour of his knights at the battle of Gretna he seemed to blame my son. I intended to speak with the King but I wished to have Roger's advice too.

As I left I bade farewell to Rebekah, "I am sorry that I cannot spend longer here with you. You are a wonderful wife for my son and I know how lucky he was to have found you."

"And you are always welcome. My father and family are dead. You are my father now and we love you dearly."

"You will be missing your son and daughter soon too."

"I can cross the river and see Ruth any time I choose, besides this might be a good opportunity for the two of us to make Thornaby a home. Sir Wulfric was a bachelor and it shows!"

I gave William, my steward, a golden ring with a blue stone. "Thank you for all that you have done for me. Now that your son has taken on your duties you can enjoy your life."

"Lord my life has been bliss since my father sent me to be your clerk."

For Alice, I had a necklace and it, too, had a blue stone. It was made of gold and one of Alf's goldsmiths had fashioned it for me. "Lord, this is too much! I was a swineherd when you found me!"

"No, Alice, you were the widow of an archer who gave his life for me and we both know that you have held this family and castle together. If it were not for you then Gilles and Mary would not be wed and they would not have four beautiful bairns. That is the result of you and your influence." I hugged her and kissed her.

My farewells made I left with Simon, my squire, Roger of Bath and Arne Arneson. My three servants would follow with my son. I crossed the river in a more hopeful and optimistic frame of mind that I had in a long time.

There were just four of us and we rode hard. I was riding Goldie. There would be no war which would necessitate a warhorse. My mail was with my servants. It felt almost like a holy day as we headed south. I was able to look at the land for which I had fought over the years. When we neared the priory of Mount Grace I saw the place we had fought two battles. Further south I saw Osmotherley where Alan son of Alan had joined my men. The whole of the ride was filled with memories. I knew why I was being both maudlin and melancholy; it was Wulfric's death which had prompted this. I decided that each day would now be like the first day of a new life and I wanted to remember everything. When we saw, as the sun began to set, the Roman walls of York, I saw that my world was a circle. When I had been a young Earl then Archbishop Thurston had been my mentor. Now I would be a mentor to Roger de Pont L'Évêque, the Archbishop of York. As Alf, now Sir Morgan of Seamer might have said, '*it was wyrd.*'

This time the four of us were found accommodation. Mine was in the palace itself while the other three shared a room in the guard's hall. The Archbishop and I shared a table when we ate. We were apart from the priests and officials who ate with him. The Archbishop was a careful and precise man. Everything about him was neat, tidy and ordered. "We can speak openly without being overheard." I nodded. "Becket has heard of the King's plan to crown his son."

"That is not a surprise. Knights from across the land will have been summoned to swear allegiance. There will be allies of both the French and the Archbishop amongst their number."

He smiled, "He has threatened to excommunicate me."

"Can he do that? I thought that the Pope was the only one with that power."

Archbishop Roger shrugged, "He can but it does not have the same authority. However, he may have made a mistake for the Pope now wishes this dispute finished. He needs Henry's support against the Holy Roman Emperor." He smiled, "The politics of the church are as complicated as those of court."

I took that information in. "Thomas Becket still expects to return as Archbishop of Canterbury?"

He nodded and cut a tiny morsel of meat which he chewed carefully before wiping his mouth with a napkin. "So it would seem."

"Then that will be a difficult, not to say unworkable, arrangement. There has been much enmity between the two."

"It is in their interests for them to make it work." We ate for a while in silence. "And you, Earl Marshal, when is your work done? You have toiled in this land for as long as I can remember. When I came to this country you were already the most powerful knight in the land."

"I am like Archbishop Thurston. I will serve my King until I am dead. That is my lot."

He made the sign of the cross and then cut another tiny piece of food. I hid my smile as I thought of Wulfric. Wulfric would have hacked a huge hunk of meat and filled his mouth with it.

"And you, Archbishop, do you still desire to be Archbishop of Canterbury?" He flashed me a look of surprise. "Come, you were archdeacon to Archbishop Bec along with Becket. You must have ambition."

He relaxed a little, "I am happy with this see. There is too much politics in Canterbury. This is a backwater in comparison."

"Then this coronation will be your chance for a little glory."

He seemed to wish the matter closed. I did not know why. "Perhaps, now let us enjoy the food."

The Princes' Revolt

The food was excellent. His servants, as in most religious places, were male. The difference here was that they were young. They were eager to please. It had been different in Archbishop Thurston's time. Then the food was functional rather than exotic and the servants had all been priests. It was the same with kings. Each had a different style. I was one of the few who had seen the first Henry. Now the only memory of him would be the events written down in the books written by the priests. According to those books King Henry had died of a surfeit of lampreys. I knew it was poison but I was now the last man alive who knew that. When I died the truth would die with me. The many knights and priests who had committed heinous crimes and were now dead would not be known for their crimes. I wondered if I should get William to write them down for me? It was at that moment that I realised how many secrets I had kept from my son. Perhaps it was the fact that we were so close to the Minster but I felt the need to confess. Wulfric had done so and was unburdened. I would consider it after the coronation and when I was back in my Stockton home.

The next day was spent in making the arrangements for the journey south. My men would be the escort but the Archbishop had his own men he needed to take with him. He had chests which contained his robes and those of the priests who would assist him. My task was a purely practical one. With Simon and my two men at arms we examined the wagons and horses which the Archbishop's men had chosen to take. It was good that we did. The horses were not the best nor was one of the wagons. I used the Archbishop's authority to purchase better horses and a new wagon.

My knights arrived the next day. York had not seen the entry of so many banners for many years. My son and his men made a glorious sight. As they headed through the gate which was close to the Minster, crowds gathered. I had almost sneaked in. My banner was with my son. I did not need the attention. I was pleased that the valley knights were accorded such honour and cheers. They were the ones who had defended the north for them. It was my son and his knights who had kept their land safe.

It took eight days to reach London. As the knights who had escorted the Archbishop, we were housed in the newly built forebuilding attached to the White Tower itself. Intended for defence it saved my son and his knights the problems of finding rooms in an overcrowded and overpriced London. I was given a room in the royal apartments. As a royal guest, I

The Princes' Revolt

was invited to dine with the King, Queen and three Princes. William Marshal and Archbishop Roger de Pont L'Évêque were also there.

I listened more than I spoke and I learned much. Young Henry and Richard argued throughout the meal. Richard's view of Becket appeared to have hardened. Henry was still a supporter of the exiled archbishop. The King seemed happy for them to argue. Geoffrey just sat and took it all in. He was the quietest of the three. It was a sullen silence. John was still too young for such events. I saw Eleanor roll her eyes at the arguments but she did not intervene.

William Marshal was seated close to me. He said, quietly, "I take it, Earl Marshal, that you are like me and long to be away from such talk of politics?"

I smiled, "Perhaps but we chose our places at the high table, William. My son is not here for he did not choose this pathway. He eats with the knights of the valley and I would be with them; if I could. My son's world is simpler than ours. He serves the King and protects the north. We are privy to the King and have to endure the lion's cubs bickering. It is why I keep silent. The barking means little. That is why the King holds his tongue too."

He nodded.

I gestured to the young prince, "You know young Henry better than most."

"He is a fine knight. I know that you were undefeated in the tourney and I am quite successful too. Henry is almost as good as we."

"That will not aid him much when he is King. He will have to command armies not handfuls. How does he think? Does he play chess? Does he read?"

"No, Earl. Why, does he need to?"

"I trained his father and when he was the same age as his son King Henry studied Caesar, Alexander the Great, Charlemagne. He asked me about his grandfather's battles. He studied the past so that he did not make the same mistakes."

"Then I am remiss. I have been making him a knight."

"He has the skills of a knight now. I beg you make him a leader."

"I will try." As events turned out I think the well-meaning Marshal failed.

The next morning, I was woken by one of King Henry's pages. "His majesty wishes to speak with you alone, my lord. He is in the Bell Tower."

The Princes' Revolt

The Bell Tower was in the process of being completed. They were building the embrasures and it was at the western end of the outer wall. Ralph had stirred when I was woken. I sent him back to bed. I wrapped a cloak about me for it was early. I hurried through the gate and across the green. Sentries were on the walls and they waved at me. My surcoat was well known. The tower was empty. There was no one working that day. It took me longer to climb the stairs than once it might have. The King was dressed for hunting. He smiled at me, "Time was, Warlord, you would have reached me quicker!"

"We all grow old, King Henry, and then we die."

His face became serious, "I heard about Wulfric. I am sorry that he died. He was a doughty warrior. I remember, when I was Prince, that, no matter what the odds against us, so long as those two, him and Dick, were there I felt safe."

I nodded.

He pointed to the stones being prepared. "As you can see I intend to make this a fortress. We have many enemies both at home and abroad. This will be the English Chateau Galliard."

"Yet it is not favoured by nature."

"What nature lacks then we will build." He turned. King Henry was ever decisive and liked to come to the point. He had not brought me to the tower just to flatter him for his vision. "When Henry is crowned then one of my sons is secure. Richard shall have Aquitaine. Thanks to my wife that is secure." Suddenly I saw the conversation I had had with Eleanor in a different light. "I need to look to my other two sons, Geoffrey and John."

I looked at him, "Geoffrey is barely twelve and John just four!"

"Geoffrey is going to be Duke of Brittany. The Duchy is not secure. As for John?" He smiled. "You have but one son. I had brothers. Remember how treacherous my brother Geoffrey was? I need balance in the Kingdom. I have four sons. If one has more power then he might get ideas eh?"

"In that case why have Henry crowned?"

"You of all people should know that. Remember the white ship? The heir to England and Normandy was drowned and my mother and you had to fight a war for sixteen years to regain the throne. The French took advantage. Henry is young but he has no power. He has a title and that may help him to grow up and forget his attachment to Becket."

The Princes' Revolt

Henry had changed since he had become King. It had been slow at first but now I saw a different man to the youth I had trained. He had gone beyond me. He had become cunning and calculating. Perhaps that was what power did. His grandfather had been ruthless. Perhaps my work was done and I should retire to my valley. I was about to say that when he spoke again.

"You and your knights exceeded all of my expectations in Scotland and Wales. I need you again." I was bereft of words. Now I saw why he had asked my knights to escort the Archbishop; it was to ensure that we were all here.

"But the Scots! They may cause trouble again!"

"I do not need them all. Your son and grandson must be there. Sir Hugh, Sir John and Sir Gilles of Normanby should be enough to deter the Scots and they can return to the north." He smiled, "I heard the reports. Sir John led the men of Durham well and Sir Hugh held off Balliol and his army. As for Sir Gilles. He was wounded was he not?" I nodded. The King was well informed. Who had spoken to him? "I need your archers and men at arms. They are a weapon the Bretons have yet to meet."

My heart sank. King Henry was entitled to ask for forty days service each year. My son and the knights of the valley had only served for a short time in Scotland. They would be used for more than a month.

"My men at arms and archers are in Stockton."

"Then send for them now! They can follow us. We leave the day after the wedding! We sail for Anjou. I will pay your men. They will be richer for this war." He smiled, "Now do you wish to come hunting with us?"

I shook my head, "No, Your Majesty. I have much to do!"

I sought my two men at arms. "We are needed in Brittany." They nodded. I need you to ride to Stockton. You are to send for Sir Philip's archers, all of my son's and most of the men at arms. Hire ships, John, the Earl's steward will provide the coin. Sail to Anjou. By the time you have your horses saddled then I will have the necessary orders written."

"Aye lord."

As they left I realised that my son and his knights would have wished to send letters of their own. It could not be helped. I sought out the King's scribe. "I need parchment, quill and ink!"

"I can pen it for you, lord."

I shook my head. "I can write and it will be quicker!"

The Princes' Revolt

I sealed the parchment, although there was no need for I trusted Roger of Bath and Arne Arneson. I handed it to them in the inner ward. "If we are not in Anjou when you arrive then have the captain take you to La Flèche."

"Aye lord." They were not worried by my orders. They would cope no matter what the King ordered them to do. It took a great deal to make my men surprised.

Simon must have seen me from within and he came running out. "Is there a problem, Earl Marshal?"

"Aye, Simon. Have my knights gather by the Bell Tower. I have news for them." The Bell Tower had been chosen by the King for our clandestine meeting because it was still under construction and there were no sentries there. They were on the walls. I would be able to speak more openly here. It took some time for them to reach me. I had time to check that there was no one in the upper floors. The ground floor would, eventually, become the guardroom and was large enough to accommodate my knights and their squires. When they arrived, I saw the questions on their faces but they knew me well enough to refrain from asked me anything.

Simon, my squire, was the last to arrive, "That is all of them, Earl."

"Good then see that we are not disturbed." There was no point in trying to sweeten the pill they all had to swallow. "The day after the wedding we will all take ship for Anjou. We go to war with Brittany. The King wishes to quash the rebels. Sir Hugh of Barnard, Sir John of Fissebourne and Sir Gilles of Normanby will return to the valley. They are charged with guarding it from any enemies. I have sent for Sir Philip's archers, the Stockton archers and the Stockton men at arms."

I saw Sir Ralph and my grandson. Their faces fell. They were recently married. Sir James, too, looked unhappy; his wife was with child yet none spoke.

It was my son who broke the silence. "This is the King's command?" I nodded. "And is part of our service to him?"

"It is. You have all served for six days already. He can have thirty-four days and after that he must pay you."

Sir James burst out, "Coin cannot compensate for the time away from my family."

My son said, "That is true for all of us. You at least have your men to guard your family. It is not fair but he is the King."

"Blame yourselves." They looked shocked, "You defeated the Scots so quickly that the King thinks you can do the same to the Bretons."

None looked happy at the prospect but all would do their duty. Brittany was not their land; it was not even their King's land. It was land he wished to appropriate. Sir Harold was now the most senior of my knights, "Well," he said, "at least we will have fine wine, warm weather and enemies who are not half-naked barbarians trying to take our jewels as mementoes."

The knights all laughed for the words could have been spoken by Wulfric. I looked at my former squire and nodded. He had taken on Wulfric's mantle.

The coronation was not my first. For many of my knights, however, it was. They took in all the pageantry and the ceremony. I was watching faces. I looked at the clusters of lords who huddled together. Some, like my knights, were lords who came from the same part of the country. My eye was drawn to those who did not. I also looked for Norman knights. There were few of them. That was ominous. They were not swearing allegiance. I saw that Leicester and Norfolk were together with others who had land in Normandy. I trusted neither of them.

The Archbishop and his two bishops were nervous and it showed but we made it through the ceremony. Unlike a wedding, or even a funeral where there is celebration afterwards, when the coronation was over and we had all sworn our oaths the majority of knights left. The exception were my knights and the others who would be taking ship to Angers. Prince Richard and Young King Henry would not be with us. I thought that to be a mistake. Left together in England they would be exposed to those who wished to undermine the King's authority. I saw that Leicester and Norfolk were amongst the first to congratulate young King Henry. I was glad that William Marshal would watch over Henry, and Richard le Breton and his three friends, Richard. Those five knights I could trust. Geoffrey was coming with us. He was just twelve but already they expected him to behave and to act like a man. John, in contrast was cosseted like a child. The Queen and her young son and daughters, Joan and Eleanor would be travelling with us to Angers. Then they would head to Mirebeau and the Queen's favourite residence.

There was a small feast to celebrate the crowning. It was the royal family, the Archbishop, William Marshal and myself who were invited. As with the other feasts I watched and I listened. The placing of the crown on Henry's head had enlarged the gulf between the two elder brothers. Geoffrey, like me, watched. The difference was that his expression was sullen. Young Henry drank too much as did Richard and as the evening progressed the tensions surfaced. King Henry seemed to encourage the bickering and it was left to Queen Eleanor to stop it. She stood and declared the feast over. She ordered her children to bed. I had to smile as Henry and Richard, one a king and the other a youth who would be a warrior, meekly obeyed. She glared at her husband and said to me, "Warlord, you are the one my husband listens to! I pray that you can make him act more like a father and less like an eastern potentate!"

When we were alone, for William Marshal left with his charge, Henry laughed, "I married a strong woman, did I not, Alfraed?"

"She reminds me of your mother."

"My mother? She was kind and gentle and she never raised her voice to me. My harpy has grown shriller each year."

"You are remembering one Empress Matilda; I saw others. She was strong. She often spoke thus to your father. Good wives do that."

He nodded. I knew that he was thinking of his mother. Her death had deeply affected all of us. "You know that my daughter, Eleanor is to be betrothed to King Alphonso of Castile?"

"I did not but she is just eight years old."

"I know and she will not be wed until she is twelve but it is an alliance which strengthens us in the south. When I give Aquitaine to my son Richard then the French will feel pressure from all sides. That is why we must crush these Breton rebels and crush them quickly. Having a six-year-old as Duchess of Brittany is not the best solution to our problem. I know who the leaders of the unrest are. The Count of Nantes, Matthew is the one who is building alliances. Another is Mathuedoï, Count of Poher. I intend to march from Angers to Nantes by way of Poher. As de facto Duke of Brittany, I will have them swear allegiance to me." He smiled, "Now you see why I wanted your son and his men. We must be swift and decisive. This will not require large numbers of men but men who know how to win and to win quickly."

"They are good men. They should not be wasted. In the north, they can subdue many times their numbers of Scots."

"And, Earl Marshal, I will pay them for their service. I have other knights in Anjou and Normandy I could use but yours are worth the coin." He smiled, "That way I do not have to count the days that I use them." He waved a hand, "Besides it will not cost me anything for I shall take the coin from Nantes and Poher! They will learn the folly of rebellion!"

As I left the cathedral I reflected on the fact that Henry, Richard, Geoffrey and John, not to mention Eleanor and Joan, were all my grandchildren yet Samuel and Ruth meant more to me than the pampered and spoiled princes whom I barely knew.

The Princes' Revolt

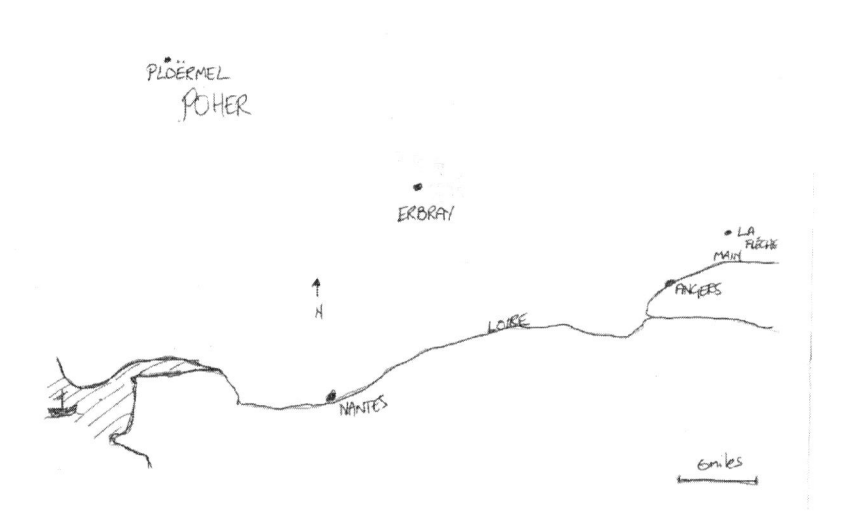

Chapter 6

When King Henry learned of my decision to have my archers and men at arms meet us in Angers he roared with laughter. "You can out-think any man I have ever known Earl Marshal. I should keep you with me at all times! This speeds our journey to Anjou and means that we can reach the rebellious Bretons even quicker."

"You realise, Your Majesty, that we have no warhorses."

"There will be enough for your knights. I will commandeer as many as you need in Angers. Besides, Earl Marshal, you will be watching your knights fight. I will not risk the architect of my success in a battle with Breton rebels."

We sailed in a small fleet of seven ships. I was with King Henry and the future Duke of Brittany. I would rather have been with my son and grandson. I suspect the conversation and the laughter would have been better there. The voyage was, mercifully swift. It took just nine days. I got to know Geoffrey a little better. What I discovered did not impress me. What I had taken for shyness and a reticence to speak before his peers was, in fact the hallmarks of a brooding plotter. He was clever. With the parents he had that was no surprise. For a twelve-year-old he was able to think things through. Brittany was not going to be enough for him. He saw his brothers with England and Aquitaine. He wanted Normandy. Geoffrey was not just sullen, he was dull. All that he could talk of was tourneys and how many he would hold when he was Duke. Even his father tired of him and sent him to the opposite end of the ship. I was glad when we reached Angers. I had had enough of his company.

I saw no English ships at the quay. My men had not arrived. That was no surprise. They had a longer journey than we did. We had passed Nantes at night. That was deliberate. The King did not want Matthew, Count of Nantes, to know that we had come to end his rebellion. My men's ships would probably pass Nantes during the day. Then the Breton rebels would recognise the threat. It could not be helped for the King wanted my men sooner rather than later.

We were housed in the Duke's castle. I sent Sir Harold and my grandson to La Flèche. Despite the King's words, I wanted a warhorse. Sir Leofric would provide the horses for my knights. The King was not relying on my men only. He needed more knights and so he sent orders for the knights of Anjou to muster. Henry was Duke of Anjou and could demand service from the Angevin knights. He would not have to pay them. As he had told me on the ship they had had an easy time since the time of the civil war. They had prospered and become rich. This was his way of enforcing his rule.

We had breathing space and my son and his knights were able to make purchases in Angers. Most were married and presents for their wives would mitigate their absence somewhat. Sir Harold and Samuel returned with Sir Leofric. They had ten good horses and forty men. A day later seven ships arrived from England and forty men at arms, eighty archers and their horses disembarked. My men had arrived. Once the knights of Anjou were mustered we would be ready to go to war. When the bulk of his knights had arrived, we held a council of war. The counts of Tours and Saumur joined myself, the King and Geoffrey in the King's quarters. Geoffrey would just listen but now that I knew more of his real character I watched him in a new light.

The King knew exactly what to say and he made each point with an aggressive finger. He used his hands as weapons. "This will not be a chevauchée. We will not raid and then leave. I intend to ride first to Ploërmel. Mathuedoï, Count of Poher, thinks he is safe there. Now that the Count of Nantes has seen English ships carrying warriors up the river he will expect an attack. He will not expect one at Ploërmel. I will remove the Count and replace him with a lord that I can trust."

"Do you have one in mind, Your Majesty?"

He looked at me, "There are some lords of Anjou who might suit the title. We have a hundred miles and battles to fight first. When Ploërmel is in our hands then we ride to Nantes. With luck we might not even have to fight but whatever the outcome Count Matthew will also be removed from office. My son, Geoffrey will be the new Count of Nantes."

Henry was clever. His son could not be Duke until he married Constance. This way his son controlled the most important port in Brittany. He also protected Angers. It may have been that he sought to appease his sullen son.

Richard, Count of Saumur said, "The land around Ploërmel is not horse country lord."

"I know and that is why we have the Earl of Cleveland's archers. The Bretons use the crossbow and they will soon discover that the English war bow is superior. If you have never seen it being used, Count, then you are in a for a pleasant surprise. The Earl's men helped to win my crown for me and I am grateful to them."

Stephen of Tours asked, "And when do we leave, my lord?"

"Tomorrow. Earl William's men all brought horses. They may not be in the perfect condition after ten days at sea but we have four days to acclimatize them while we ride through Brittany."

The one aspect of this campaign that I was less than happy about was the paucity of local scouts. We had no Bretons with us. King Henry trusted no one from the Duchy. We would have to use Sir Leofric's men. Although they knew the borderlands they were unfamiliar with Poher. They would have to guide us safely to a place where we could launch an attack. If this was England, Scotland or Wales then the local knowledge we had would have helped us to choose a perfect battlefield. King Henry was relying on my mind to make whatever ground we found to our advantage.

It was hotter in Anjou than in England and our men at arms and archers took some time to adjust to the heat. I rode with my son and Samuel. This was my grandson's first visit to Anjou and he looked around in awe at the terraced vineyards, gently flowing rivers and could not help but contrast it with the land of the borders.

"This is land worth fighting for grandfather. The land north of the wall is fit for nothing save trees. Why do men die for it?"

"To protect the land which we farm."

"But the valley of the Tees cannot compare with this."

I smiled, "The valley where I made my home?"

"I am sorry, I meant nothing by the comment. I should have thought first."

My son shook his head, "That is true more times than you know Samuel. It is my home too. I chose to come back home from Aqua Bella. It will be your home too."

Samuel shook his head, "You misunderstand me. I am not saying this land is better than ours. It is just different."

I smiled. I sympathised with Samuel. "Your view, Samuel, is the same view as many of the Norman knights who came over with Duke

William. They did not want the land of the north. I think that is why King Henry chose to give it to my father. My father was coming home and, to him, it was all he ever wanted. I felt like you too. I had been a pampered young lord living in Constantinopolis. I turned my nose up at ale, the cold winds, the harsh winters, the smell of warriors. Wulfstan soon knocked those airs and graces from me. Your father's scout, Masood thinks highly of our land. When we are back home then ask him what he likes about it."

Samuel had decided that he had said too much and remained silent.

Sir Ralph nudged his horse next to mine, "Warlord, how do the Bretons fight?"

"They fight like all Franks but they use more light horsemen than we do. The light horsemen wear no armour but they are fearless. They ride close and hurl javelins. With fast horses they will try to draw you away from the protection of your peers. If they can catch a knight on his own then they will surround him and bring him down. Do not be tempted to chase them. They have knights too and they are armoured much as we are but they have larger horses."

He nodded, "Worth capturing then?"

My son laughed, "First, Ralph, you must defeat them and they are good warriors. They are superior to the Scots. Despite what the King thinks this will not be an easy war."

I listened as my son, Ralph and Samuel debated the merits of various warriors. What I learned was that Ralph had much more experience than Samuel. Part of it came from being so close to the Scots. He was also older and had taken part in campaigns before Samuel was even a squire. Sir Ralph would be good for my grandson. They worked well together and had an easy familiar manner. Now related by marriage they were even closer than they had been.

The first night in enemy territory we stayed at Erbray. Although in Brittany its lord was loyal to King Henry. Robert d'Erbray had fought alongside us when we had fought the French in Normandy. There would be few such havens over the next seventy miles. Some of the knights of Anjou were in for a shock. They were not used to campaigning. They had taken part in the odd chevauchée but they had been able to return to their own castles each night. When we crossed into more hostile territory, the next morning, we were entering a world of ambushes where, potentially, every man could be an enemy. The closer we delved into Poher the more likely it would be that we would have to fight.

The Princes' Revolt

We had Leofric's scouts and his archers out ahead of us. They could sniff out an ambush. We had risen before dawn for King Henry wished to get to Guer by dark and that was forty miles away. We knew, from our scouts, that there was a castle there but it was an old wooden one. If the castellan chose to defend it we would overcome it easily. As events turned out he did not. Robert de Guer swore to King Henry that he was a loyal subject. To ensure that he was King Henry co-opted the knight and his men into our army. If he was an enemy then we would keep him close.

He might well have been a vacillating lord but the presence of so many knights and notable lords swung him to our side. I saw that King Henry had chosen the right course of action. He would be able to pick off the lesser lords and thereby weaken the Count of Nantes. Everything hinged on victory at Ploërmel. With Poher subdued then we could encircle Nantes and starve the Count of his support.

We found our first enemies as we closed with Ploërmel. It was just fifteen miles away. We were approaching Augan and the Broceliande forest loomed large to the north of us. Griff of Gwent led the scouts and he rode back to us. Although he spoke to the King his eyes were on me. He had served with me when Sir Leofric had been an English knight.

"Lord, I like not the forest. There are fresh tracks in the eaves."

King Henry knew my scouts and when the two Counts of Anjou looked to become irritated he silenced them with a wave of his hand. "You suspect an ambush?"

"It is a perfect country for an ambush, my lord. Let me take thirty archers into the forest first."

The Count of Tours said, "I protest! We will be late!"

I laughed, "You have an appointment you need to keep? It matters not when we get to Ploërmel so long as we get there. If we have to camp another night before we reach it then so be it."

King Henry nodded and dismounted, "Go, Griff of Gwent. Choose your men and we will rest here until you return." There was a small stream nearby and the King led his horse there. He smiled at me as I followed him. "Now you see why I use your men. They know their business. These knights of Anjou are brave enough but they have no idea of how to campaign."

"To be fair to them lord they did not hone their skills in a civil war."

"How do you see us attacking this stronghold?" We had spoken with those who had visited the castle recently and we know what to expect.

The Princes' Revolt

"Divide the army into two. If we attack the two gates at the same time we will split their defence. We do not attack on a broad front but a narrow one. Use our superior knights to take the walls. Our archers can keep the walls clear for an attack."

"A good plan." We went through some of the details while our horses were being watered by our squires.

After our horses had been watered we led them back to the road where we could see the forest. Suddenly we heard shouts and screams. Horses neighed. The King shouted, "Mount! Prepare your weapons!" Even as he spoke horsemen burst from the forest. There were more than forty of them. They galloped down the road towards Ploërmel. The King raised his sword, "On!"

The archers had flushed out the ambushers. Their arrows felled a few more and then, as we passed the first of the bodies Griff of Gwent led his mounted archers from the forest. He saluted the King as he headed up the road to continue his scouting duties. "There will be no more surprises, lord."

We could travel towards Ploërmel knowing that there were no enemies hiding in the forest. Samuel asked, "Grandfather, there were only forty men, how could they have hurt us?"

We were passing the body of a Breton slain by one of the archers. I pointed to him. "These are the Breton light horsemen I mentioned. We know not how many Griff and his men killed in the forest but even these forty could have burst from the trees, hurled their javelins and been gone before we could have done anything."

"But what would a few javelins achieve?"

"They could have killed the King, the two counts, your father and me. Without us five then who would lead this battle? In one fell swoop, the rebels would have achieved all. It was a gamble but it did not cost our enemies much. These light horsemen are cheap and expendable. But for Griff and his archers this might have ended the campaign before it even started."

It was yet another lesson for Samuel. I had learned, years ago, that the knights with experience were honour bound to pass on their knowledge. Samuel would be a better knight for it. We saw no more enemies until we reached the town of Ploërmel but our scouts reported that the Bretons knew we were coming and that their ambush had failed. The wooden wall around the town was manned and the gates closed. Sending the archers to the far side of the castle and the town we made camp. The King did not want a siege. As the sun set in the west the five of us walked their walls to identify weaknesses. We saw no signs of stone throwers or catapults. We would just attack the walls rather than the towers or the gatehouses themselves. Back at the camp he explained our plan. "We attack the east and the west sides simultaneously. I will lead, along with my son, the men of Anjou. We will attack the walls by this gate. The Earl Marshal will lead the rest. He will attack the walls by the west gate. It is a wooden wall. Have the men make ladders."

And with that, he left us to it. While Wilfred organised the ladders, I spoke with the younger knights. Few, if any, had assaulted a castle walls. "Attacking walls is tricky. We will use just two ladders. William you will lead half of the nights up one ladder and you, Sir Harold, the other. Aelric you and the archers will keep the walls clear for us. It is why I am using a narrow frontage. My squire, Simon, will use the horn to give you my commands." I smiled, "Unless you would like me to lead one of the attacks?"

My son grinned, "No, lord. We are more than happy for you to be a spectator. Perhaps you can advise us, when we return, how we might improve."

"Just come back alive is all that I ask."

Even though I had said I would not be fighting I had Simon sharpen my sword and polish my helmet. I had one weapon which only I could use: me. The Count of Poher would know I was commanding this attack and he would know my reputation. As he polished my helmet Simon asked, "How will they attack the walls lord? You cannot hold on to a ladder, a sword and a shield all at the same time."

"It is not easy. The best way is to hold your shield horizontally and above you. That way your left hand grips the ladder, protected by your shield, while your right is free to swing the sword. When you move your feet, you keep a grip on the ladder. If our archers do what they have done in every battle up to this one then there will be few men on the walls who can hit our knights." I saw the apprehension on his face. "Squires are not expected to lead an attack and as my squire, it is unlikely that you will even have to wait at the bottom of the ladder with your knight's spare spear."

"Some knights use spears?"

"It gives them extra reach. You will see tomorrow."

There was no point in attacking at dawn. There would be little advantage to be gained and so the men ate well after a good sleep and

The Princes' Revolt

then made their way to the walls. I went with them. It would give them more confidence and I would be in a better position to view the battle. Simon and I rode to the battle lines. We all halted three hundred paces from the walls. My son and I had decided that we would attack to the right of the gate. The gate had two towers. There were no such towers along the walls. My men at arms carried the two ladders. The forty men at arms laid the ladders on the ground and held their shields before them and with two archers sheltering behind them marched in a solid line towards the wall. The crossbow bolts cracked into their shields. My men wore chausses. Some even had greaves. It would take a lucky bolt to hurt them. Even so I knew that the advance would be nerve wracking. When they were two hundred paces from the walls they stopped.

I was not wearing my helmet and my arming hood and ventail lay around my shoulders. I heard the clash of steel from the other wall. King Henry had begun his attack. When the archers were ready I heard Aelric shout, "Draw!" The sound of eighty war bows being pulled back makes an audible sound. It is a mark of the power of the bow. The crossbowmen could not see them and my archers would send their arrows into the air to fall upon the walls. Aelric had told me that he would clear the walls and the gate for forty paces. I believed him. "Release!" Even as the eighty goose feathered messengers of death headed towards the wall another eighty were in the air. My archers could send ten flights so quickly that it would seem like we had five hundred archers.

I saw men plucked from the walls. Shields were pulled into position. A plunging arrow can be stopped but only by a well-made shield. The poor standard of shields could be seen as more men fell.

I turned to my son, "Now, Earl, now is your time!"

Raising his sword, he led the knights towards the archers. The Breton crossbows had appeared on the walls. It was a disastrous mistake. They had no shields and before they could send a bolt all were slain by archers who hated them worse than any other enemy.

The squires picked up the two ladders as soon as they reached them. When they reached the men at arms twenty of them joined the knights. They were replaced by the squires of my knights who stood with their own shields to protect the archers. Sir Harold and Sir Tristan carried one ladder while my son and Sir Morgan of Seamer carried the other. Our knights held their shields above and before them. I heard the clatter of stones as brave slingers risked the wrath of my archers. The boys were slain but they managed a storm of stones before they died. The wall had no ditch for it was a town wall. The two ladders were held against the wall just ten paces apart. It made the archers' task easier and the two bodies of knights could support each other.

I found myself gripping the pommel of my sword as I watched William climb the ladder. His former squire, Alf followed him and that gave me confidence. The son of a Varangian Guard Sir Morgan of Seamer was like a man mountain. A spear was thrust over the top of the wall and the owner tried to keep my son from ascending. I saw Griff of Gwent send an arrow into the hand to pin it to the wooden wall. The spear dropped. My son took advantage of the arrow and leapt up the last few steps. He landed lithely on the fighting platform. Sir Morgan then showed his strength by gripping the top of the palisade and leaping up to join my son. Their swords were out in an instant and I saw a Breton pitch over the side. Sir Harold and Sir Tristan quickly cleared their section of the wall.

I shouted, "Roger of Bath, take the rest of the men at arms to the gate! Aelric!"

"Aye Warlord!" He knew that he had to change targets.

The archers switched their targets to the two small towers over the gate. Now that we had a bridgehead it was safer to try to weaken another section of the defences. The archers also began to move closer. The closer they were the more effective would be their arrows. I saw Tom the Fletcher get to within thirty paces of the gate. His arrow penetrated the mail of the knight who was attempting to rally the men at the gate. As the knight flew backwards so John son of John and Peter Strong Arm began to hack into the gate with their axes. I saw that the two groups of knights and the men at arms had now cleared one section of wall. I could not see my son, nor Sir Morgan and my grandson. I had done this, myself, enough times to know that they would be descending to the gate. When I saw the gate opening then I knew that my son was alive.

"Come, Simon! We will risk the gate." I spurred the warhorse Sir Leofric had brought for me. He was a fine horse and he had a noble name, Ridley. Sie Leofric had named him after my father.

My men at arms and archers were no stranger to assaulting a town. They had burst in and spread out. They would head for the castle. Unlike many armies we were well trained. Our men would not be distracted by plunder. They knew that they would all receive their reward when the fighting was done.

The Princes' Revolt

As we headed through the gate I shouted to Simon, "Draw your sword. Men may still attack us." I wore no helmet and my shield hung over my left leg but my senses were attuned to battle. I felt the Breton rise, like Lazarus where he had been feigning death on the ground near my horse's foreleg. He lunged at me with his pole axe. I flicked the head away and it rasped along my mail and then I brought the blade back to hack into his neck.

Tom the Badger had seen the treacherous blow and he shouted, "Make certain the dead are dead! Unless they yield, kill them!"

Two men rose from the ground where they had been hiding and tried to run away. Tom picked up a spear and hurled it into the back of one. Simon galloped after the other and brought his sword down on the man's unprotected head. By the time we reached the castle the King had also fought his way to the walls. He raised his hand in acknowledgement. I saw that my son and grandson, as well as Sir Ralph, were still alive. The Count we fought was still alive. His banner flew and he stood on the gatehouse of the castle donjon defying us.

Simon asked, "What now? Do we assault the castle too?"

"That can prove a costly exercise. King Henry is not wasteful of men. He will try to persuade them to surrender."

A silence fell and King Henry took off his helmet. I saw a crossbow raised but before I could even speak Aelric's arrow had killed the would-be assassin.

The King's voice was loud and filled with authority and confidence, "Mathuedoï, Count of Poher, you have broken the oath you made. You are sentenced to death. Surrender and your people will be spared."

"You are a fool, Henry Curtmantle! Why should I surrender? If I do then I die!"

"Your walls are made of wood. Your hall is wooden. I have here eighty archers who can send fire into your hall. Would you burn alive? Would you have your family burned to death? It is your choice. We are going nowhere." He turned to me, "Warlord, have your men search the town for food and treasure. We might as well eat before we burn this castle and those within!" He shouted it loudly. The words were intended for those within the castle.

I turned, "Wilfred, make it so!"

My archers stayed where they were. Their arrows were aimed at the walls. My men at arms hurried to obey their orders.

The Princes' Revolt

I said, "Aelric, one flight of arrows, if you please. See if you can clear the gatehouse!"

"With pleasure, Warlord."

Eighty arrows flew high and when they descended men fell. I think thirty of those on the walls were hit. Suddenly there was a commotion, voices were raised and I heard the clash of steel on steel. Suddenly the body of Mathuedoï, Count of Poher, was thrown over the wall. He landed with a thud at King Henry's feet. It did not need a healer to know that he was dead. His head had struck the cobbles and was caved in. A voice from the walls shouted, "We surrender if you will keep your word!"

King Henry's voice was calm and measured as he replied, "You will surrender and that is an end to it!"

We heard voices arguing and then, slowly, the gates swung open. The warriors came out with open hands. They had surrendered and we had won.

King Henry showed how astute he was. He made every knight swear allegiance to him and he made them do it on a Bible while the body of Mathuedoï, Count of Poher, lay close to them. It was a reminder of the risks in fighting Henry. He made them join our army for the march to Nantes. The losses we had taken, mainly among the men of Anjou, were more than made up for by the new men we forced to join us.

We ate in the count's hall. We ate well. The Count of Tours asked, "Can we rely on these men?"

King Henry shrugged, "It matters little. I will send them in first. Let them show me their loyalty by either winning through or dying. Either way we win."

Chapter 7

We spent two days in the town. We ate well and we took all the treasure from the town. King Henry was true to his word and all who were in the battle received rewards. The knights of Anjou found it hard to accept that they received the same as men at arms and archers. None would argue with the King. He had shown a ruthless streak which frightened them.

Samuel and Ralph had both been chastened by the experience. The evening after the capture of the town we had found a place where the four of us could drink quietly away from the exuberant knights of Anjou celebrating the victory.

Sir Ralph turned to me, "It is easier, Warlord, to ride to war on the back of a warhorse. Watching a knight climb a ladder, knowing that if any threw a spear or released a bolt at you then you would have no defence is not something I would like to repeat."

I nodded, "And climbing an assault tower is no easier. Do you remember, William, the castle in Normandy when they fired it?"

He nodded, "Do not remind me. I thought you were dead that day."

Samuel said, "You escaped?"

I laughed, "Unless I am a ghost then yes. Remember this, Samuel and you too Ralph, when you think all is lost then choose any way you can to escape. Life is too precious to lose. As for assaulting a castle walls; we always take archers to war with us. As your father knows they are the equal of a knight in a battle." Just then three drunken knights of Anjou staggered by waving their flagons of wine. "Those three would not believe so but we know different. King Henry's attack cost him five knights. He had crossbows defending the knights. We lost not a knight because we had Aelric and his men. Your father's life was saved when Aelric's arrow struck the hand with the spear."

The Princes' Revolt

My son nodded, "The King knows the value of archers. It is why he brought them and why he shared the coin out evenly."

Ralph said, "Yet he took half."

I shook my head, "Ralph, he is King. He could have had it all! He needed not to share. You owe the King service for the manor you hold. Forty days a year is the price of your fealty. The men on your land at Gainford will serve you for forty days too. Will you pay them?"

"No lord but like you, I would not take them to war unless I had no choice." The two young knights had much to reflect upon. They were learning how to be lords of the manor even here in the county of Poher, many miles from home.

King Henry sent word to the Count of Nantes that we were coming and he expected the Count to bend the knee. There was no point in trying to approach Nantes without alerting the rebels. Our capture of Ploërmel was known. The rebels knew where we were. King Henry sent riders to Rennes and Mayenne. He let them know that he would be visiting them in due course. Neither manor had a lord who was overtly rebellious but many Breton lords were just waiting to see the outcome of this rebellion before choosing sides. King Henry was giving them a good reason to choose his side.

Our approach to Nantes was slower than our march north had been. The men of Ploërmel who were now in our army had no horses and they marched afoot. We had wagons with the treasure we had taken. King Henry wanted other Breton lords to see the folly of revolution. If they did not revolt then they would keep their treasure. If they opposed the King then they would lose all. The new Count of Ploërmel rode behind the King. Phillippe de Rideau had shown great courage in the assault and he had impressed the King. The fact that he was the second son meant he would not inherit the manor on the Loire. When the Duchy was quietened he would have to build up the manor of Ploërmel with little help from the King. I did not envy him his task. It would be like asking Samuel to be lord of Gretna!

Sir Leofric's scouts had proved their worth and King Henry chose them over the new Bretons who had joined us. As we neared Nantes they reported that the Count was marching north to meet us. We were close to Blain when we heard the news. We were eighteen miles from Nantes.

The King turned to me, "What do you think, Warlord?"

"This is as a good place as any. They advance and will be tired when they reach us. We have the opportunity to make this a death trap. I will walk the land and make some suggestions for dispositions."

Henry had learned much from me and he showed his skill as a general and leader. He was decisive. "We will meet them here."

Young Geoffrey who was eager to reach Nantes for he was to become Count protested, "But lord, they will think we fear them!"

"They can think what they like. I would have them march. I wish them to tire out their animals. Question less and listen more!"

We used the small settlement to make an armed camp where the wagons, servants and spare horses could be protected. He had our archers cut stakes and line our flanks. Count Phillippe's dismounted men would be placed between the two sets of stakes.

As the defences were built the King and I walked the battlefield. It was important to know the terrain. I made my suggestions and we returned to the army. The King gathered his captains around him. "We will form three lines and use our knights and mounted men at arms to batter through the Breton lines. If we can break their lines and reach their Count then all well and good but, if they have too many knights and we cannot break them then I will have the horn sounded three times and we withdraw back to Blain."

The Count of Saumur said, "These are Bretons! We defeated them at Ploërmel. We will do so again!"

The King turned and looked coldly at the Count, "And we will do so again!" He pointed to me, "I rode behind the Warlord's banner during the civil war. He taught me that plans do not always succeed and a good general needs to have an alternative. My English knights would not need to be told this. But then," he smiled and it was a cold, chilling smile, "they did not need to be told to celebrate our victory at Ploërmel in a dignified manner, did they?"

The King had been less than happy with the lack of discipline from the knights of Anjou. Women had been assaulted and that would make the new Count's task that much harder. The point was made and the nights of Anjou remained silent.

The stakes were just being sharpened when Sir Leofric's scouts rode in with a prisoner. It was a Breton scout. He was tethered on a rope and had had to run behind their horses. James the Short tugged him so that he fell and prostrated himself before the King and me. "We found six of their scouts. One escaped the others lie dead. We captured this one. The

The Princes' Revolt

Bretons are a mile down the road. We thought you might like to question this one, King Henry!" James had known the King when he had been my squire. I saw the look the Count of Tours gave him. He thought he had been too familiar in his tone. The King did not.

"Well done, James the Short." He took his sword and poked the scout, "Rise rebel! Your lawful master would speak with you."

The Breton had regained his breath. "I am sorry King Henry. I serve the lord of Ancenis. I was ordered to join the rebellion."

The King sheathed his sword, "Then now you can tell me, as a loyal Breton, who else is with the Count of Nantes." He waved his hand and a cleric appeared with a wax tablet. "Speak and you shall live."

The Breton needed no further urging and the cleric struggled to keep a count of the names of the rebel lords. They would be punished by the King after we had won. Their names did not interest me but their numbers did. There would be more than a hundred and ten knights whom we would be facing. We could now muster a hundred. Some of the knights of Anjou had died and others had been wounded or, in the case of two of them, hurt when they drunkenly fought each other over a woman. When the Breton had finished the King said, "Have the horn sounded. We will be ready to fight them if they choose not to camp."

By the time we were arrayed in our battle lines, with our banners fluttering in the late afternoon breeze, we spied the Breton army. They halted a mile from us. The ground sloped down from Blain to the plain and we had a good view of their army. I noted the light horsemen. There looked to be more than two hundred of them. The bulk of their army was made up of the levy. The forty or so crossbowmen would not present a problem for us.

King Henry turned to me, "Do you think he will attack now?"

"If he does then we have won already. His horses have ridden further this day than we have and we have defences prepared. I am guessing that he will be examining our lines and he will camp so that he can devise a way to defeat us."

"Then come with me, Warlord, let us speak with this rebel and plant the seeds of doubt in his mind." He turned to Geoffrey, "You come with us. Bring my standard. You may learn something of negotiation and you Earl William, I would have you at our side."

After Geoffrey had taken the standard we rode towards the enemy. The Bretons had halted and now that they saw us approach four detached themselves from the army and rode towards us. I recognised the banner

The Princes' Revolt

of the Count of Nantes. The other three men were unknown to me. None of us wore helmets and our arming hoods were around our shoulders. We stopped two hundred paces from our men. I knew that Aelric would have archers with arrows nocked in case of treachery.

The Count was the same age as the King but where Henry had the lean and hungry look of a warrior I saw that the Count of Nantes was a little podgier. War was not his business.

"You come to make war on your lawful ruler, Count?"

"You deposed Duke Conan. I do not recognise you as my lord. It is you who have made war on Bretons! You have laid waste to Ploërmel!"

The King laughed, "We took the Count's castle and his people threw him from his walls. Poher has left the rebel alliance. I have no doubt that those in Rennes and Mayenne who may have been swayed by your rebellion will now be reconsidering their position."

"Why have you ridden to speak to me then? What can you gain?"

"Me? Nothing. This is my generous nature. I am giving you the chance to order your men to accept me as their lawful lord and you the opportunity to take a ship into exile. I am being a thoughtful lord."

"Go into exile!"

I leaned forward and said, quietly, "I would take the King's offer, Count, it is better than the alternative."

"And that is?"

I sat up, "Why, death, of course! That is the punishment for treason and you have already committed treason before the four of us. You denied the King's right to rule. It is only the manner of your death which is to be decided."

He jerked his head around, "We will decide this tomorrow on the field of battle."

The King smiled and said, for the benefit of the three men with the Count, "You could save many men's lives by fighting my champion."

The Count looked at my son, "You mean Earl William?"

"No, my lord, I mean the Warlord!"

He had not mentioned this to me but I smiled as though I welcomed the challenge. He should have accepted for I was an old man but he did not for he knew my reputation. I had never been defeated, nor even unhorsed in any tourney. I had fought champions and emerged victorious. He turned and rode away. I saw the looks on his three companion's faces. He had lost their confidence.

As we rode back Geoffrey asked, "Why did the King offer him the challenge, my lord? No offence Earl Marshal but the man is half your age."

My son answered, "The Count is no warrior. He has soft hands and a pudgy face. You have fought in tourneys my lord, you could have defeated him. This was to plant seeds of doubt in his men's mind. I will wager there will be desertions this night. There will be lords hurrying to their homes so that they can claim to have had nothing to do with the rebellion."

As we neared our men I saw my archers unstringing their bows.

The Count of Tours shouted, "We still fight, lord?"

"On the morrow we will decide who rules in this land. It will be me!"

As he cleaned my mail Simon asked, "Will we be fighting tomorrow, Earl?"

"Probably not although we have fewer knights than the Bretons so the King may need me to make up the numbers. If he does then you make sure that you are behind me with my standard. You have not completed enough training to be in the front line." I wondered if the King's offer to the Count had been a way of drawing Breton knights towards me. I would not be surprised if that was a result. The Count would brood and wonder why he did not take up the King's offer. He would have household knights who would be keen to gain a reputation and the death of the Warlord would give them that. "When you have done that then go and check on the horses. Give Ridley an apple. Tomorrow he will earn it."

That night I prayed. Since the death of Wulfric these prayers had had a greater significance. I knew that my time on earth was drawing to a close. My prayers were not for me but my son and his family. I had spent a lifetime saving England for the Plantagenets. Now I had to ensure that my family would be safe when I was no longer around.

I woke before dawn. Old men need to make water more often than young knights. I was surprised to see that my son had roused his knights. My archers had had a fire going all night and there were rabbits cooking. Simon brought me a haunch. It was still warm. Along with a beaker of ale from the archers it was a warrior's breakfast. Simon had been given a leg too and he mused, "Lord, do the other knights have such men as we do?"

"Sadly not, for many lords see their warriors as beneath them. We do not."

The Princes' Revolt

I was mounted before dawn and rode, with Simon and my banner to meet the King. Simon handed me a spear. I would not need a replacement.

The King was eager for the battle. "I prefer this to an assault on walls. This is work worthy of a knight. I will need you with us today, Warlord. Keep yourself safe. I need you for advice." Nodding I saw that Geoffrey held his banner. "And my son can win his spurs this day, God willing."

"Amen to that Your Majesty."

King Henry had his six household knights alongside him and I took my place to the right of them. Samuel appeared on one side of me and Sir Ralph on the other. My son and the rest of our knights filled in the line to my right. I saw my son grinning. "You did not think we would allow others to guard the Warlord, did you?"

I looked behind me and saw Wilfred and the rest of our men at arms. The men of the Tees Valley would go to war together.

The Bretons had their crossbows and their levy moving in two blocks towards our flanks. Perhaps they did not realise the threat our archers posed. They would soon learn. As well as the stakes the archers had fashioned willow pavise behind which they sheltered. The Breton knights were behind their light horsemen. There were a hundred of those. Lightly armed they rode fast horses. They intended to weaken us with javelins. I glanced across to the King. He did not look worried. I wondered if he had a plan to deal with them.

The Breton horns sounded and the levy and the crossbows began to move across the open ground. The horsemen did not move. I think the Count was trying to outwit the King and make him commit our knights. The crossbows and the levy were not a threat. Our archers could deal with those easily. When the crossbows were three hundred paces from us they stopped and the levy began to form ranks. Our two blocks of archers had arrows nocked ready but they were just watching. Another horn sounded and the light horsemen came charging towards us. I realised then the Count had made a major mistake. He did not want to risk exposing his levy to our knights and so he held them while, as he thought, the light horsemen would break us down.

King Henry's voice broke our silence, "Archers, you know what to do!"

Aelric and my archers all shouted, "Aye lord!"

The Princes' Revolt

I heard the command to draw as the horsemen reached the crossbows. Another fifty paces and they would be in range. Aelric waited until they were a little closer and then shouted, "Release!" With no mail and light horses, every arrow found flesh; it was either a horseman or his mount. Both of the results hurt the Bretons. A second and a third flight thinned the ranks so much that I doubted we would suffer a single javelin. I was wrong. Four hardy warriors continued towards us. They hurled their javelins at the King. They were taken on the shields of the King, his son and the household knights. The household knights then spurred their horses and, as the Bretons turned to race back to their own lines were speared for their reckless courage.

The ground over which the Breton knights would advance was littered with horses and men. Another horn sounded and the crossbows and the levy began to move closer. They now knew what awaited them. The lines were a little more ragged. Aelric waited until the crossbows stopped and the men knelt. The next arrows fell amongst the crossbowmen and they died. After three flights there was not a single crossbowman alive. The thirty bolts they had sent were embedded in willow. As the archers switched to the levy the King shouted, "Now is our time, Charge!"

He did not use a horn and we all heard the command. A horn would have ensured a straight line but with so many dead and dying before us a straight line did not matter. I had not intended to join the battle but I knew that men would be watching me. If the Warlord hung back it could hurt our attack. I spurred Ridley. Both Samuel and Ralph were a little eager and their horses began to move ahead of mine. I saw them struggling to rein them in and then we were together. The two groups of warriors who were advancing towards my archers had tightened their lines and were using shields to protect themselves from the arrow storm. It made them move even more slowly and as they had bodies to negotiate our archers had all the time in the world.

Count Matthew decided to cut his losses. He sounded his horns and his knights moved up the slope towards us. We were not galloping yet. Our spears were vertical and our shields hung from our cantles. The Bretons were eager to join with us. They had seen the effect of our arrows and wished to avoid an arrow storm. We were five hundred paces from each other. They were moving faster for Prince Geoffrey had yet to lower his standard to signal an increase in pace. The Bretons, in contrast, were charging and they had a ragged line to show for it.

The Princes' Revolt

When the standard was lowered and then raised we were less than a hundred and fifty paces from the Bretons. I hefted my shield up to my shoulder. I saw my grandson glance at his father to see if he ought to lower his spear. When we were fifty paces from the Bretons and still, largely, boot to boot I lowered my spear. I had seen the man I would be fighting. He was one of the men who had been with Count Matthew. That made him an important man; he was one of the Count's lieutenants. He would not be an easy man to defeat.

The knights from Anjou had not kept the same pace as we had and there was a clatter and a crash as their ragged line met the Breton's equally uneven one. The cracks and crashes seemed to ripple. I did not take my eyes off my foe but he flicked his head to the right when the two lines met. It was a tiny movement but in battles, such movements have a greater effect. I pulled back my arm and then punched towards his side. He had a lance and the glance he had made had broken his concentration. The head of the lance rose. My spear rammed into his side as his cracked off my helmet. I was twisting the spear to remove it as his horse took his mortally wounded body between Ralph and myself. I allowed my arm to be forced back until the spearhead popped out of his bloody side.

I saw that Ralph's spear was also bloody. Then my next Breton was upon me. This one had an open helmet and I saw that he had a surcoat which was similar to the man I had just slain. Perhaps he was a son. I watched him stand in his stirrups. He intended to strike down at me. I jerked Ridley's head to the right. There was now a gap between Sir Ralph and me; I had the room. The tempting target I had made disappeared and the knight had to lift his lance over his horse's head. Even so, he had fast hands. His lance smashed into my shield as I thrust my spear into his thigh. The leather of the saddle stopped any deeper penetration and as the knight fell over the side of his horse my spear was broken. I drew my sword and reined Ridley in for we were in danger of becoming detached from the King who was having a more difficult time than we were. The knights of Anjou and those from Ploërmel had lost men in the charge and the knights from the Breton right were surrounding the King. My son was in danger.

As a lance was thrust at my chest I blocked it with my shield and then chopped the wooden weapon in two. The knight tried to draw his own sword. I punched at his horse with my shield and it reared. As the knight tried to control it I thrust forward with my sword. The blade slid under his right arm and came away bloody.

The Princes' Revolt

The King had lost two of his household knights and Prince Geoffrey was backing away. If the standard fled the field then men would follow and we would have lost. "Samuel, Ralph! With me! We must save the King!"

Without waiting to see if they obeyed me I pulled Ridley to the left and charged towards my beleaguered monarch. A knot of knights saw what the three of us intended. Four of them turned their horses to come for us. We had one thing they did not, speed. Wulfstan had always said that I had the quickest hands he had ever seen. I was older but my hands still moved quickly. As the first Breton raised his sword I pulled the reins to my left so that he struck air and I did not aim my sword at his body but sliced across his arm. It bit through to the bone and his sword fell to the ground. My speed and my change of direction brought me to the right side of the next Breton who was trying to pull his horse around. I watched Samuel as he stood in his stirrups to hack into the shoulder of his enemy as I brought my sword across his back. He arced and fell. Sir Ralph's opponent was distracted. His head flicked to the side and Ralph's sword took him in the throat.

The knights who were trying to get at the King heard the noise of neighing horses and the death cries of knights. The blood from Sir Ralph's victim sprayed in an arc and they turned. King Henry shouted, "England and King Henry! Die, you bastards!" He swung his sword in an arc and it sliced through the coif of a Breton knight. Samuel lunged and his sword went through the back of the knight protecting the Count of Nantes. I could not see his face but when the Count's head turned to see the danger then I knew he was worried. I spurred Ridley and he leapt forward. I brought my sword down over my head as the Count slashed his sword at my chest. His sword hit my mail and pain raced through my body. I was hurt but my sword cleaved his head in two. As Samuel slew the standard bearer the battle ended. We had won.

I normally felt relieved at such times but as I tried to cheer I found that I could not get my breath. I felt as though I was choking yet how could I be? There was no blood on my surcoat. My mail had held. I looked around for enemies but I saw none and I heard cheers. Then all went black.

Chapter 8

When I awoke I was looking into the face of Brother John, the King's healer. He smiled, "You had us worried Warlord."

I touched my chest, "Was I cut?"

He shook his head, "The blow broke your breastbone. At least I think it broke it. I could see no cut. There is bruising and swelling. I have told the King that you cannot leave Nantes for at least two weeks."

"I am in Nantes?"

"The King had a wagon bring you here and I sat with you."

"My son, grandson, squire, they live?"

He shook his head, "My lord but you amaze me. You have been close to death and yet you put others first."

"Did you give me the last rites?"

He hesitated and then realised that he was a priest. He nodded, "Aye lord for you stopped breathing."

"Does my son know this?"

"No, lord. I was alone with you in the wagon." He hesitated, "Forgive me lord but I breathed life into you."

I laughed and it hurt, "You save my life and apologise? Thank you, Brother John. Where are we now?"

"In what would have been the Count's castle. It is now Prince Geoffrey's. "I looked at Brother John. "Aye lord, he ran. His father was less than happy and he has not won his spurs." He stood. "I will fetch your son and grandson. They have watched outside this door for the past two days. He smiled, "I think the bang to your head when you fell did not help."

He went to the door and opened it. My son and grandson entered and both looked relieved.

The King's healer said, "I will tell the King. He was worried." He paused, "Do not stay too long. The Warlord needs rest. I will return with some medicine."

My son took my hand and held it. "Father we thought you were gone. We detected no sign of life when you fell. Brother John came and said that you lived. Why did you take part in the charge?"

I smiled and said, "The King asked me to. You risked your life as did Samuel. Why should I be any different? I have lived long enough. I would rather I died than you or my grandson or even Simon. Why do you worry? I am alive!" They nodded. "Did we lose any men?"

"Harry Lightfoot and John son of John were wounded. They will be with you when we leave."

"You go to Rennes and Mayenne?"

My son nodded, "But we would rather be here with you."

"You serve the King and you make coin. I will still be here when you return and then I will come home to England with you. Perhaps this wound was sent by God so that I may recover in Stockton. I should like that!"

Samuel said, "Prince Geoffrey tried to run away. Had not Wilfred restrained him then we might have lost the battle."

I looked at William. He nodded, "The King was not happy. He is not to be knighted. The Prince goes around like a child chastised for stealing sweetmeats. I will be glad to get back to Stockton. I do not envy the King his sons!"

Samuel said, "And while the King's son vacillated, Simon galloped up and dismounted to protect your body with his own. That was truly heroic and brave. The King was impressed."

I nodded. It was a mistake for my head hurt, "You are lucky. Your children are both perfect. They have chosen good husbands and wives. You will have many grandchildren!"

Samuel blushed, "Grandfather!"

My son laughed, "Your grandfather is well!"

Brother John appeared, "The King is relieved that his Warlord is alive."

My son, William said, "Come we have to tell our men. They have not yet celebrated our victory. Now they can celebrate the victory and the Warlord's recovery!" He put his arm around Samuel and I saw the pride in his face.

The Princes' Revolt

The potion Brother John gave to me helped me to sleep and when I woke I saw Simon sitting in the chair close to me. "Warlord, the King will be here soon. He is taking the army to Rennes but he wished to speak to you first." He smiled, "I am glad you live. When you fell I feared the worst."

"Thank you for standing by me. It must have been hard."

"No lord it was easy. How could I leave the man who saved England? It would be like betraying my own country. I will fetch the King. He said he wished to be notified when you awoke."

There was a jug of water and I poured myself some. My chest hurt. I had a left arm which did not work as well as it might and now my right hand caused me pain when I used it. How could I be a warrior?

The King came in and waved Simon away. The door was closed. "You had me really worried, Earl Marshal. I thought I had lost you." For once his voice was not business like and cold but friendly and filled with warmth. "Once again I am in your debt and owe you my life. I was wrong to ask you to be in the line with me."

"And yet lord had I not been there …"

"I know, I might have died! I thought my son would have more backbone. I fear he is a weakling."

"He is young."

"Yet your squire is the same age and he leapt from his horse and protected your body with his sword. I know what I saw. I will cow the lords of this land and return here by the end of the month. I leave Brother John with you. He is a good healer and I am lucky to have him. I would have you try to make something of Geoffrey. I leave him here. You made a man of me. Let us hope you can do so for my son." The King's voice was filled with disappointment. He had given Geoffrey the chance for glory and greatness and he had spurned the offer. Samuel and Ralph, in contrast, had grasped the opportunity with both hands.

I did not see them leave. Brother John had me confined to bed. My chest was tightly bound in bandages and I was not sure that I would be able to walk. I hated being confined and I decided to take matters into my own hands. I had Simon find four warriors and they brought a board. They lifted me upon the board and I had them take me to the outer ward where I could sit in the sun. Brother John oversaw the transportation. As he walked with my bearers and me to the ward he nodded, "This will probably aid your recovery. I should have thought of this."

The Princes' Revolt

I lay in the fresh air. The river and the sea were close enough to keep a pleasant breeze blowing. I found myself at peace. Simon sat with me each day. The first day he filled in the details of the battle which I had missed. He told me how the archers and dismounted men at arms had driven the levy from the field. When the rebel standard had fallen it had begun the rout. The death of the Breton count had ensured that most of the knights surrendered although a few had fled the field. Simon had told how the King had promised they would be hunted down. My fall from Ridley's back had, apparently, been spectacular. My son and my knights had been cheering me when I fell with no obvious wound save a ripped surcoat and some severed mail. There was neither blood nor wound except for the wound when my head hit the ground. Simon told me that I owed my life to Brother John. If he had not been with us then I might have died on the battlefield.

The second day I had Simon read to me. I had spent my life in war and I had little to do until I was healed, except to lie in the sun. The Count of Nantes had some books in his library. Simon read them to me.

It was as he was reading, just after we had had a lunch of broth and bread, that the new Count of Nantes approached. It was Geoffrey. It was obvious that he wished to speak and yet he did not know how to begin. I smiled, "Congratulations on your new title, Count."

His face looked as though he had just tasted a lemon for the first time. "One brother is King of England and the other will rule Aquitaine. I have this pathetic little Breton backwater! There is nothing for me to celebrate."

I could not lift my head easily and shaking or moving it hurt me still. "Would you take some advice from a man who is old enough to be your grandfather?"

"Will it gain me a throne?"

"When your father was your age he would have leapt at the chance to be Count of anywhere. There were many times where your grandmother and your father and I were hunted the length and breadth of England and Normandy. We did not know if he would regain the throne. Each day we fought not for a crown to place upon his head, but for a victory, no matter how small which would bring that day closer. You will be Duke of Brittany. As soon as Constance is old enough and you marry her then you will be Duke."

"But Brittany is not Normandy, Aquitaine nor England. It is an afterthought from my father."

"And what would you have?"

"Normandy or Anjou!"

It was then that I knew that Geoffrey's silence and his apparent studied contemplation was nothing of the sort. He was brooding. It was no wonder that he had not stayed by his father's side. If his father was killed then he might inherit Normandy or Anjou. I closed my eyes.

I heard Geoffrey ask Simon, "When the Warlord fell you leapt from your horse to protect him. Why?"

I opened my eyes. Simon's face was a picture of shock and disgust in equal measure. "I was carrying the standard and he is my lord. It was my duty to protect him."

"But we all thought him dead. You could have been killed and for what? To protect a dead body?"

Simon's voice showed the depth of feeling, "My lord, I swore an oath to serve and protect the Warlord. That includes his dead body. If that means that I must die then so be it. I will not be foresworn. I would have thought that you owed a duty to your father the King even without an oath. Perhaps I was wrong."

Geoffrey shrugged, "No, you are a fool!" He strode off.

Simon turned to look at me. "We serve a man who does not deserve our loyalty lord."

"We serve the King. Geoffrey is just one of the King's children. Besides, when I am healed we will return to Stockton and the taste in our mouths will not be so bitter."

After seven days Brother John took the bandages from my chest. His hands were gentle as he explored the wound. "It seems to be healing. I will bandage it again but I think you can try to walk a little. If Simon is with you then you should be safe. Your two men at arms are also healed and they can accompany you." He looked at me and wagged a finger at me. "Within the castle and no further!"

It took a day or two for my legs to regain their strength and I was pleased that Harry Lightfoot and Arne Arneson were with Simon. My men at arms were both strong warriors. Harry had lost two fingers on his left hand and Arne had taken a spear to the cheek. Both were philosophical about their wounds. They were alive and they had coin from the battle. We took to walking the walls of the castle. The climb up the stone steps hurt my chest but we were able to rest at the top before we walked around the fighting platform. We never saw Geoffrey. He avoided me after our discussion. I had not done as his father had asked. Perhaps that was a challenge beyond me.

"Well, Warlord, we shall soon be on a ship back to England. This is a fine land but it is not home is it?"

"No Harry. We may not grow wheat in the valley and have to import wine from here but I would not change my valley for this whole Duchy."

Arne picked at the scab on his face. "I know not what Ada and the bairns will think of this when we reach home."

Harry said, "She will be glad you are alive. When your beard grows back she will not notice. I am just glad that I lost the fingers on my left hand. I can still grip a shield with those remaining and wield a sword with my right hand."

The King and my warriors were away for a month. By the time they returned I was able to walk unaided. I was ready to go home. I spoke, not to the King but my son. The King was peaking with Geoffrey. "Was there any more fighting?"

"No, father. We reached Rennes and were welcomed by cheering crowds. The King sent the men of Anjou home and he used just our men. Mayenne was a little less enthusiastic about our arrival and we stayed there seven days while the King made changes. We came back the long way, through Poher to Vannes and then back along the coast. We are weary of Brittany and ready to go home!"

"As am I. Soon it will be autumn. The time for safe sailing will soon be over. I hope the King does not tarry."

We were alone and my son asked, "And Prince Geoffrey?"

"I fear he will not change. The King thought I might influence him but he would have none of it. He spoke to me once and then has kept apart."

"That says more about him than it does you, father. There is none better at moulding young men into warriors. Even if, like me, it takes some time for a fool to see what is in front of his face."

"You were briefly seduced. It happened to me in the east. With Geoffrey, I think it goes deeper."

"The King has promised payment before we return home. I have sent Sir Leofric to arrange for ships to take us thence. You will be coming with us?"

"I hope to be but…"

"The King cannot need you further. We have Brittany. What is there left?"

The Princes' Revolt

"I know not. When the King has time, he will speak with me. If I cannot travel with you then make your own way back. You cannot wait on one man and your knights will be keen to see their families. If you leave soon then you will be home before the harvest."

He gave me a sharp look, "You are thinking of the Scots."

"We have defeated their armies but there are those who would risk much to steal from us. It will be no secret that our knights are abroad on the service of the king. The sooner they are home the safer our land will be."

"And what of you; will you be safe?"

I smiled, "I will. I am almost healed now and a leisurely voyage home will do me good."

He did not look convinced but he left to see if Leofric had secured the ships. I found Simon. "On the off chance that the King allows us to return to Stockton have our bags and chests readied. Make sure that Ridley is returned to Sir Leofric."

"Aye lord."

Despite my words to my son that I was healed, I found it hard to remain standing for long periods. I found a chair in an arbour and sat down. A servant came over, "Can I get you anything, my lord?"

"A goblet of wine would not go amiss."

My son was right. The King would not need me I could go home. Perhaps he was done with me. I know that my brush with death had shaken him. He did not need me any longer. He had made all the decisions in the Breton campaign. I realised that I was his good luck charm. He kept me around for it brought him good fortune. It inspired fear in his enemies. He did not need me. The realisation made me suddenly happy. My work was done. I had turned Henry into a King and a leader. He controlled one of the largest empires in the western world. When the servant came back with the wine he saw my smile, "You are feeling better, lord. Good. This is a new jug I just opened. It is at its best."

"Thank you. I am grateful."

The look on his face told me that he was unused to civility from his betters. He was right it was a fine wine and I had two goblets before the King returned and greeted me. He shouted his servant over, "Wine for the King too!" He took the other chair, "You are lucky with your son and your knights. I sent the knights of Anjou away. They were just a waste of grazing and food! I shall be sorry to see them go but I gave my word."

"Aye, and I will be able to join them for I am healed."

He said nothing. The wine arrived and he sipped it appreciatively. "I would like you to return to London with me. I still need you, for a time at least." I held my tongue and waited for his explanation. "Becket is coming back to England. The Pope has intervened and promised me that Becket will not be so confrontational. He will arrive in Canterbury in December. Stay with me until then. I may need your sage advice." He swallowed the goblet of wine in one and refilled it himself. "Come old friend, can you not give me a couple of months?"

There was little point in telling him that I had wanted Christmas with my family. That would not be a reason good enough for the King. "You wish me to stay and calm the waters with Becket and that is all?"

"He respects you and I just need you there until I can be certain that he has changed his ways."

As I had expected my son and grandson were unhappy especially as they had managed to acquire ships and would be sailing the next day. It would be ten days before we left. The King wished to ensure that Geoffrey was surrounded by reliable advisers.

"William, it is a couple of months. When Becket reaches England, I will visit and speak with him. I believe I am a good judge of men and I will be able to discover the truth and divine his intentions."

He nodded. "Then that will give me the time to add apartments to my hall. I wish you housed comfortably as I intend you to spend the rest of your life there with us. You need not risk your life again. In future I will go in your stead if the King needs you."

I rose early to wave them down the river and I felt very lonely. There was just Simon and myself. The two of us were the only ones at the quayside. We turned and walked back to the castle as the sun rose. Simon had grown in the campaign. It was both physically and mentally. He had become a man. It was the battle of Nantes which had done that. As we headed back he said, "Lord I will become your right hand. While you were recovering I practised with Arne and Harry." He shook his head and laughed, "Even wounded and much older than I they managed to trounce me every time but I learned."

It was my turn to smile, "Much as I did with Wulfstan and my father's hearth-weru. Believe me, Simon, it will make you a better warrior."

"I have used the coin I won at the battle to have a local smith make me a hauberk. I do not think I will grow much. When we returned to

Stockton I will have one of Alf's sons make me a sword. You need not go to war for I will fight in your stead."

"I do not think it will come to war but I am grateful for your oath."

We travelled with the King and we travelled well. I had my own quarters on the ship which Simon shared. We did not have much room but we had privacy. Autumn winds made our journey home slower and we did not reach London until the middle of October. We noticed the cold and the wet but it mattered little for we were home. We were in England.

We went directly to the Tower but discovered that Young King Henry was not there. He had gone to Windsor with William Marshal to hunt. Henry was unhappy for he had warned his son that he was coming home. He smacked the table, when we were alone, "He insults me! He hunts when he should be here so that I can discover what has happened in my realm during my absence."

I said nothing for the King was over fond of hunting. Richard, and his new knights, were in London and when they heard that the King had returned they came to join us. Henry's ire was slightly assuaged. "What has your brother been doing while I have made Brittany secure?"

Richard said, lightly, "He has hunted a great deal. I fear there will be no animals left in the great park at Windsor."

"And what of you? Have you hunted too?"

"I am not King of England, am I? My land is in Aquitaine. I stayed for I did not wish to offend you. Now that you have returned then my men and I can go to warmer climes."

"No, I would have you here. Becket returns."

That elicited the same response from all five of them. Richard le Breton spoke for them all. "That viper has the nerve to return here! After what he has done!"

"Peace, hothead! He returns at my request. We cannot have the office of Archbishop of Canterbury empty. The Pope assures me that Becket will be contrite. The Earl Marshal is here to ensure that it is so."

Prince Richard said, "Then we will stay in England until he has shown that he can behave but if I were King then he would have his head taken from his shoulders."

"And you are not King nor even the next in line! You need to think like a king and not like a warrior."

The Princes' Revolt

Richard was not put out. He smiled, "But I am a warrior. If I were king I would rule as a warrior. I will die as a warrior. What else is there in life?"

He and his knights left us and the King looked exasperated. "What can I do? Perhaps I should have made John the King."

"At least there will be no problem with the succession."

"Always looking on the bright side." I smiled. "And now we wait for Becket. When he comes I would have you go and speak with him. I have asked Roger de Pont L'Évêque, the archbishop of York, along with Gilbert Foliot, the Bishop of London, and Josceline de Bohon, the Bishop of Salisbury to come to London. As they were the ones who crowned my son, they have an interest in Becket!"

Simon and I settled into life at the Tower. It was never a cosy place but without the Queen and filled with the knights of the sons of King Henry it was even bleaker. Simon and I took to wandering the streets of London. I needed my strength building up and walking, rather than riding, seemed to be the best way to do so. I found it a dirty almost shabby place compared with York but then I had been brought up in Constantinopolis and that was a truly beautiful city. What saddened me most, as we walked the streets, were the number of crippled soldiers we saw. None had fought for me else I would have given them coin to go to my valley. There were many Normans and French. When a lord lost a battle, he might be ransomed. A man at arms, a light horseman or an archer had no such option. They could be killed, maimed or simply left to fend for themselves. The ones who were still hale took to banditry. The ones I saw had been hurt in some way and did not have that luxury. I thought that the church might do something for them but they did not. It was sad.

We found an inn by the old palace of Westminster; *'The Lamb'*. It was convenient for we could eat there and rest before we headed back to the Tower. The landlord came to know us. Few lords used inns. I liked them for there you met men you actually wished to speak with and you learned a great deal. I did not wear my surcoat, just a dark blue cloak and I was not recognised. Simon just called me, my lord and others followed that convention. We used the table in the corner. It was both private and yet we could see all who entered. The landlord, if it was not a busy time would chat to us. I know he did so to make coin from us but I found that more honest than many lords who had feigned friendship and then tried to stab me in the back.

The Princes' Revolt

Four men came in one day not long after we had arrived. They did not look like normal customers. For a start they were either men at arms or knights. They had cloaks pulled tightly around them so that their livery was hidden from view. I saw their swords; they were good ones. Secondly, they had the swarthy look of foreigners. That was confirmed when they ordered wine. I could not hear them, they were too far away but they had their heads close together and looked like conspirators.

When John, the landlord came over with our next beakers of ale I asked, "Those four look out of place here. What is their story?"

"I cannot turn away trade lord but they are Frenchmen! What can I do? The law says I have to serve all customers unless they break a law. My son died fighting the French for King Henry. It sticks in my throat that I have to serve them."

"What are four Frenchmen doing here in London and looking so secretive?"

"I am sorry, lord, but Nipper can barely speak English let alone French." Nipper was the man who served ale. John had told me that he had received a wound at the Battle of Winchester and was a little simple. He could fetch and carry ale.

Just then three merchants entered and John hurried to serve them. Merchants spent well. I turned to Simon. "Go outside and make water. See if they have horses or servants."

The four men ordered food. They would be here for a while. When Simon returned he said, "They have horses and they have a servant. I tried to speak to him but he was a surly fellow. I was tempted to strike him with the flat of my sword."

"Finish your ale and we will head back. I will ask John here if he can find more information for us!" I had already finished my beer and while Simon emptied his beaker I stood and slid four silver coins across the bar. "If you can find out where they lodge then there will be a golden dinar for you."

"I will try, lord, but I cannot promise."

"I know. I am just interested in why four Frenchmen are here so close to the old palace of Westminster and the Abbey."

I pulled my hood up over my head as we left. If they were French warriors then I might have fought them. They would be more likely to recognise me than the other way around. I walked deliberately slowly as I passed them. I kept my eyes to the ground. I picked up a few words. One was hunting and a second was Henry. I spied that one of them had

The Princes' Revolt

spurs. There was one knight amongst them. When we passed the surly servant, he glowered at Simon. That too made me suspicious. We had to walk within a few paces of the horses. I saw that they were good palfreys. They were the sort of horse a man at arms used to ride to war. I was even more intrigued now.

"What do you make of it, lord?"

"They could be innocent but my nose tells me that they are not. They were hiding too much for that. They could be assassins. Both King Henry and his son like hunting. When I was a Knight of the Empress in Normandy Frenchmen tried to assassinate the first King Henry while he was hunting."

"Will you tell the King?"

"I will wait until we know a little more. It is possible that they are innocent of any crime and have no intention of causing anyone harm."

Simon smiled, "Yet you do not believe that, lord."

"No Simon, I do not."

When we returned to the inn, the next day, there was no sign of the four men and their surly servant. John brought us our food. "Well, John, did you discover anything?"

He smiled, "I think that they were passing through, lord. They bought food from the baker and the cheesemonger. They headed west."

I gave him the gold coin. "Thank you, John."

"But I did nothing. Heading west tells you nothing."

I did not reply but I smiled. He shook his head, put the coin in his purse and went to serve others who had just entered. "I do not understand, lord, what did the man tell you that made you smile?"

"I know a little more now. We heard hunting and Henry. It is young Henry who hunts to the west of here at Windsor. Tomorrow we will take horses and we will ride to Windsor. I think I would like to speak to Young Henry."

Events conspired against us. Reaching the Tower, we were informed that the King wished to see me. "Becket is back! I would have you go and speak to him. Find out if he is repentant! I will give you an escort of men at arms."

"Aye lord." We would have a two-day ride in December. My heart sank to my boots.

The Princes' Revolt

Chapter 9

The six men assigned to guard us were all known to me. I had fought alongside them in Scotland and in Normandy. The horses the King gave us were sound beasts. We stayed at Rochester castle. It was a royal residence and the constable knew me well. We ate well and had good beds. The next morning, we rode through a storm of sleet, snow and rain. I had a good cloak but by the time we reached Canterbury, I was soaked to the skin. My chest hurt for this was the first time I had ridden since I had been wounded. The cold and wet aggravated the wound. I was not in a good humour as I approached the Archbishop's palace. My mood was not improved by the wait we had to endure. Luckily the cleric who opened the door recognised me from a previous visit when I had tried to persuade the Archbishop to allow the King's brother to marry the lady he loved. I had failed then. Would I fail now?

The cleric's face showed that he remembered me. It had not been a pleasant parting, "Good evening Earl Marshal; what brings you here on such a foul night."

"I am here on the King's business. Admit me." My chest suddenly sent paroxysms of pain through my body. Simon said, "The Earl has not been well. I will draw my sword and force entry if needs be!"

"Pray enter." He looked at the knights with me. "There are stables for your horses and your men." He was pointedly directing them away from the Archbishop's chambers.

I turned, "All will be well. This is just for one night."

Simon put his arm around my back, "This was too much, lord! The King puts upon you. You are not completely healed!"

We were taken to an ante chamber and the cleric hurried off. Simon took off my wet cloak. It was fortunate that I wore no mail for I fear I might have perished whilst on the road.

An old priest arrived with a young one in attendance. "I am Cedric. I understand you are ill, Earl Marshal."

It was finding it hard to breathe and Simon said, "My lord suffered a broken breast bone when serving the King. He has but recently healed."

The healer nodded. "James go and have a bed made up in the hospital."

I shook my head, "I must speak with the Archbishop. I have ridden two days to get here."

"You are ill, Earl Marshal. The Archbishop will come to the hospital. He is in the cathedral and will not be ready to see you for some time." I nodded. "Squire, you are a strong warrior. Help me carry the Earl Marshal."

Fortunately, the hospital was just two corridors away and had a fire burning. While Cedric prepared his potions and drugs Simon and the other priest helped to undress me from my wet clothes and I was given a simple white garment to wear.

"First I will examine you and then I will place a poultice on the chest. Finally, we will make it easier for you to breathe."

I croaked, "No drugs! I must be awake!"

"Aye, lord. There will be no drugs."

The examination was painless. The poultice was warm and soothing. Within moments my chest felt less painful. "Squire, bring your master to the table." Once seated at the table a fur was fetched and draped around my shoulders. A bowl filled with a fragrant and steaming liquid was placed before me and steam rose.

"Put your head over it and breathe." As I did so a cloth was placed over my head enclosing me. I smelled camphor, rosemary and thyme. There were other smells I could not identify. As soon as I inhaled the steam it felt as though a weight had been taken from my chest. I heard voices as the healer spoke with Simon but it was as though I was in a different world. I know not how long I sat there but the bowl cooled and Cedric lifted the cloth. "Good. Now food. I will have some broth sent to you."

I felt that I could now talk. "Thank you, Brother Cedric, but I must speak with the Archbishop."

"He will come, lord, as soon as the service is ended."

Simon poured a mug of ale for each of us and went to the fire to fetch the poker. He plunged it into my ale where is hissed. He put the poker back in the fire. "Drink, lord. Brother Cedric said that it would help the healing. He says that you must stay here for two days, at the very least."

"I thought I was healed."

"You might have been but the ride and the inclement weather has done something within you to the wound. This is a different ailment but it is caused by the wound." As he plunged the poker into his own ale he shrugged, "I am sorry, lord. I did not understand all that he said. But I did understand the fear in his face. If you try to travel back tomorrow then you will die."

I nodded. I still felt weak. "Then whatever news we have must be taken back by you and the men at arms."

"I cannot leave you alone."

"I am in a house of God. What should I fear?"

The broth was well made and served with freshly baked bread. I felt better. It was much later when Cedric returned with the Archbishop. I saw that he was wearing a hair shirt. That was a sure sign of penance. He had aged during his time in France.

"Earl Marshal, it grieves me to see you in this condition. This is not the time of year for a man of your age to travel especially not one with such a wound as you bear." He shook his head, "That King Henry would allow a man of your age to fight in battle astounds and amazes me."

"I come on the King's business. It was important to him." My eyes bored into the Archbishop's and he looked away first.

"Leave us. I would speak alone with the Earl Marshal."

Simon stood, "I will check on the horses and the men at arms and I will return forthwith."

When he had gone, Thomas Becket smiled and shook his head, "You still inspire great loyalty amongst your men."

"The loyalty is mutual much as the loyalty between a subject and his king."

"Yet I am not the subject of the King. I serve God."

"You are the King's Archbishop and he appointed you. Does that not deserve loyalty?"

"Not blind loyalty. I am the church's ultimate authority in this land. I decide and arbitrate on all religious matters. When I was tutor, briefly, to young Henry, I saw in him a future king who would understand the division between church and state."

My heart sank. He had not changed. "Then you will still oppose the King's choice of bishops and priests?"

The Princes' Revolt

He nodded, "I will go further. I have this day sent letters of excommunication to Roger de Pont L'Évêque, the archbishop of York, along with Gilbert Foliot, the Bishop of London, and Josceline de Bohon, the Bishop of Salisbury who were the three men who had crowned young Henry. They exceeded their authority when they crowned young Henry."

I could not believe my ears. "I thought you would have been happy about the coronation! You want young Henry to be King."

He smiled, "And I will be the one to crown him when he will be sole King of England." Simon returned, "And now I will leave you. Brother Cedric tells me that you cannot travel for a few days. You and your squire are more than welcome to stay here. I believe that you are a good man and that contrasts with our King. You are misguided in your blind devotion to a corrupt King but I admire your loyalty."

He left us. When we were alone I said, "Fetch me parchment, quill and ink. I have a letter to write."

Thomas Becket was, effectively declaring war on King Henry. The three priests who were to be excommunicated were the most senior clerics after the Archbishop of Canterbury. It would mean the King would have no say at all in the life of the church. The Archbishop and the Pope would make all the appointments and the church, wealthy as it was, would become an enemy within. What I could not see was the reason for this. Why had Becket returned now?

When Simon returned I wrote. I told him the gist of the Archbishop's words. My written words would tell the bare bones: the excommunication. I gave Simon my innermost thoughts which were for the King's ears only.

When I had finished Simon said, "Lord when I went to the stables I spoke with the stable master. He told me that ten days since a French knight, three men at arms and a servant arrived. They stayed for two days and the knight spent most of that in conference with the Archbishop. I would have said nothing but now…"

"You are right Simon. That sounds like the men we met in '*The Lamb*'. What treacherous game is Becket playing?" I sealed the letter and handed it to Simon along with a purse. "Leave before dawn. When you reach Rochester ask for a change of horses and ride directly to the King. This letter must reach him sooner rather than later. Those five men are up to something. I fear assassination may be in their minds."

I drank more of the ale and studied the fire. What was going on? Then it came to me; the Vexin. This was a way to keep Henry in England dealing with religious matters while King Louis attacked the Vexin. Becket was in the employ of the French King. It still did not tell me why he had five assassins in the land. Then I remembered the Archbishop's words; *'When I was tutor, briefly, to young Henry, I saw in him a future king who would understand the division between church and state.'* The killers were here to kill King Henry so that his young son would be the sole ruler and he would be guided by King Louis' spy. I cursed my wound. I was trapped here and could do nothing. I now saw why the four Frenchmen had headed to Windsor. It was not to kill Young King Henry, it was to pass a message to him.

Simon tried to leave quietly but my ailment and the thoughts which had kept me awake for most of the night meant I was awake.

"I am sorry, lord. I meant not to disturb you."

"Be safe Simon. The message must get through but beware. There is a plot here which is greater than any I have witnessed."

"I will not let you down."

And then I was left alone. For the rest of the day, I just saw Brother Cedric, his priests and the servants who brought my food. I was left by myself for most of what passed for daylight in this dismal time of year. The hospital was like a prison. I was alone with my dark and brooding thoughts. I realised that the King did not have sons on whom he could rely. Geoffrey was weak. Richard just wished power so that he could make war and Henry wanted to be sole king. I had thought, when his mother and I had helped to put him on the throne that Henry's worries were over. I was wrong. They had just begun.

The steaming herbs and spices seemed to have a beneficial effect. The poultice was changed regularly and Brother Cedric appeared happy with my progress. I found that I could walk. On the second morning, when I assumed King Henry would have heard my news, Brother Cedric suggested a visit to the cathedral to thank God for my recovery.

He smiled and spread his hands, "I merely carry out God's will."

I did not go to the church until late in the afternoon, towards evening. I sat, instead, before the fire. Brother Cedric had placed a bowl with the pleasant-smelling herbs and spices. I found that it made breathing much easier. I had conspiracies and plots racing around my head and I needed to make sense of them. Why had Becket come back now? I did not believe that the Pope had forced him back. Becket feared for his life. If he came back then he needed to be in England. He had excommunicated three men. He had to do that while in England. He was isolating the

The Princes' Revolt

King. That was where I ran out of solutions. What could he gain by antagonising the King? He had fled for he had feared imprisonment or worse. He had been safe in France. The only conclusion I could reach was that he had been ordered back. The King of France needed him in England. I could reach no other conclusion than the one I had a day earlier. The knights were here to kill the King so that Young Henry, under the sway of Becket, could be crowned. I had thwarted that by warning the King. He was too clever to be caught by assassins. He could avoid hunting. Even though I felt I had done all there was a nagging doubt. The killers went towards Windsor. That was where his son hunted.

Servants brought my evening broth and fresh bread. There was even wine. After I had eaten and with darkness all around me I decided to do as Brother Cedric had suggested. I would visit the cathedral. Perhaps prayers to God might bring enlightenment. As I donned my cloak I heard hooves clattering on the cobbles before the cathedral. For a moment I wondered if Simon had returned. Brother Cedric was in his cell and when he heard me open the door of the hospital he came out.

"You are going to the cathedral?"

"Aye, you are right and I need to give thanks."

"Then I will come with you. Take my arm."

I did not like to but I knew that I was still weak. I saw four horses outside the mighty minster. They were not tied and they were lathered. Steam and sweat rose in the air like a mist. They had been ridden hard. Even the healer noticed. "Who has come so quickly that they abandon their horses?"

Then we heard the clash of steel on steel. I drew my sword. Brother Cedric said, "We should stay here, lord."

"I am Earl Marshal. It is my duty to investigate this commotion."

We found Gervase of Canterbury at the door with a wounded knight, Edward Grim. He was one of Becket's men. Cedric knelt to tend to the wounded man and Gervase said to me, "Thank God you are here, Earl Marshal. Four knights have come and demanded that the Archbishop accompany them to Winchester. He refused. They retrieved their weapons and I fear they mean him harm."

I ran down the aisle but I could see that I would be too late. By the light of the candles I saw Reginald FitzUrse, Hugh de Morville, William de Tracy and Richard le Breton. They had bloody weapons drawn. Even as I watched I saw that Becket was already wounded but Richard le

The Princes' Revolt

Breton raised his sword and took the top of the Archbishop's head. As he did he said, "Take that, for the love of my lord William, the king's brother!"

Hugh de Morville said, "Let us away, knights; this fellow will arise no more."

They ran down the aisle. They had not seen me until then. I raised my arm, "Stop! I am Earl Marshal of England."

They had weapons drawn. Richard le Breton and the others sheathed their swords when they recognised me. They pushed by me. I was too weak to stop them. "We have done our duty. The treacherous cleric is dead. You are still wounded, Earl, and we hold you in great esteem. We will not hurt you and, as we have sheathed our weapons you will not harm us."

I tried to raise my sword but it was too much and I could not. They rushed down the aisle and out of the cathedral. I sheathed my sword. I was an old cripple and I had let down my king. I walked to the altar. Whatever plans and motives Becket had had he did not deserve to be butchered like this. He had no weapon upon him. The four knights had behaved in the most appalling manner; they had no honour.

Brother Cedric joined me. He shook his head, "A most piteous sight."

I looked towards the door, "The knight, he will live?"

"He will. You had best get back to your bed, lord. The exertions you have made and the night chills will have done you no good."

He was right and I walked slowly down the aisles. Priests and the Archbishop's knights raced through the church to witness for themselves the bloody deed. When I reached the cobbles, I saw that the four knights had gone. I was about to enter the hospital when I heard the sound of galloping hooves. Had they returned. I looked up and saw that it was Simon. He took one look at my face and, as he dismounted said, "I am too late then?"

"If you were here to warn me then aye you were but I could not have saved him. I am finished as a warrior, Simon. I could not even raise my arm."

"But I could!" He shook his head, "Get inside, lord. I will stable my horse and then join you. I have much to tell you."

Once inside I took off my cloak and poured myself another goblet of wine. I raised it in the direction of the cathedral, "Farewell Archbishop. I fear your plotting has been your undoing but you did not deserve such a death."

Simon came in and took off his cloak. "I rode as fast as I could, lord."

"Have some wine and sit. There is no rush. We cannot save Becket and the four knights are long gone."

He did as I had asked. His skin looked almost blue from the cold. "I delivered the letter and spoke with the King. It was a full court, lord. The Prince and young King Henry were there with their knights. After he had read the letter I spoke quietly to him and told him of your suspicions. He was quiet for a moment and a rage took him. He stood and shouted, '*What miserable drones and traitors have I nourished and promoted in my household, who let their lord be treated with such shameful contempt by a low-born clerk!*' There followed a most fearful commotion. Prince Richard and Young King Henry began to argue. I think they and their men would have drawn swords had not the King ordered his guards to separate them. Prince Richard's men left the hall. I was heading out to the stable see to my weary horse when I saw them mounting their own. I heard one cry, '*We will show the King that we are loyal men. We will avenge our lord, William, Viscount of Dieppe. We will take the snake and throw this rebellious priest into a cell!*' They galloped off. I told the King but he seemed distracted. It took me some time to find a fresh horse and I followed as soon as I could. I am sorry I was late."

"If the King knew of the knights' intentions, then he is to blame, not you." I warmed my hands. I had not been out long but the cold seemed to seep into my bones. "This argument between Young King Henry and Richard, what was it about?"

"It was hard to follow, lord for they were both yelling at each other but I think the young King was supporting the Archbishop and Richard was saying that he should be publicly flogged."

I sank back into my chair. The King had thought that by crowning Young Henry it was the solution to all of his problems. It had merely exacerbated them.

Outside we could hear the furore as the news of the murder spread. When all quietened down, Brother Cedric came in to the room. "I think, my lord, that it might be as well for you to leave early in the morning. Your association with the King has made some of those in the Cathedral suspicious."

I flashed a look at the healer. Then I realised that he was trying to be kind. "Brother Cedric, thank you for your warning but I am Earl Marshal of England. I will not sneak away like a thief in the night. I had nothing to do with the murder."

"I know lord but…"

"If you think that I am worried by a few knights who guard a church then you do not know me."

"Lord, in the cathedral, you could not raise your sword."

I smiled, "When I leave I shall be on horseback. I will not need to raise my sword."

After he had gone Simon asked, "You could not raise your sword?"

"When we reach home, Simon, that will be the next part of my recuperation. We cannot have an Earl Marshal of England who cannot lift a sword eh?" The priest's words had brought me from my depression. I would not be cowed. When I left I would ride with head held high.

Brother Cedric came before dawn with food. I think he thought that if we ate we might leave. I waited until the sun, or what passed for the sun on the cloud filled morning, was up. The walk to the stables was without any trouble for they were in the cathedral precincts. It was when we left the church and headed through the town that we might have trouble.

I leaned down to clasp Brother Cedric's arm. "Thank you for what you did. I am in your debt."

He smiled, "Lord we are all in your debt for you have saved England more times than enough. Go with God."

We managed just four hundred paces before a surly looking fellow shouted, "There is one of the killers! He is one of King Henry's murderers."

I could have turned away but that was not my way. I spurred my horse towards the man. He had also thought that I would run. I reined in. "I am Alfraed, Earl of Cleveland and Earl Marshal of England. I have never murdered anyone in my life. You will apologise."

"Or what?"

"Or I will get off my horse and I will punish you with my fists."

A voice from the side said, "You needn't bother my lord, we will deal with this troublemaker!" Three men stepped out of the inn. By their dress they were warriors, men at arms. I did not recognise them but it was likely that they had fought alongside me. "The Earl is a true knight. Let him pass or you will have us to deal with!"

When I turned I saw that the loud mouth had disappeared. I waved my thanks to the three men and we rode through the gates of the town. A mile or so from the gates Simon asked, "Would you have dismounted and fought him, lord?"

"He was a blowhard. If he had been dangerous there would have been a weapon close to hand. He was trying to make a name for himself."

"Nonetheless, lord, I will be happier when we are back in London."

The two-day ride back was without incident. When we stayed at Rochester I told the constable exactly what had happened. There would be rumours and there would be exaggeration. He needed to know the truth. "The knights were wrong to do what they did but their initial plan was to arrest him and take him to Winchester. He refused because they were low born. They were fools. Had they come for me then he might have acceded to their demands. He fought them when they tried to drag him hence and they killed him."

"A bad day for the King, lord. Already we have those in the town calling for the Archbishop to be made a saint."

I shook my head, "He was anything but a saint! I am sorry that he was murdered but I am happy that he is dead for he was an evil man."

"Yet the world will say he was a martyr."

"I cannot help what the world thinks. They will believe what they are told."

I had half expected to meet with the King heading for Canterbury but he was still in London. I sought him out as soon as I reached the Tower. "Your Majesty I came as soon as I could."

He shook his head, "I did not give them any orders! They acted on their own! I cannot be blamed!"

"Yet you will be. Are there men looking for the killers?"

He shook his head. "Why? The deed is done. We can do nothing about it now! I have more pressing matters to deal with. My sons bicker and fight like dogs over a bone! What am I to do with them Earl Marshal?"

I suddenly felt weary. "They are your sons, my lord."

"But you have always advised me well."

On the way back from Canterbury I had had much time to think of my future. I was no longer able to be useful. I was used by the King when he needed me. I did not particularly like his sons and Henry had changed. "My lord, the journey to Canterbury almost killed me. I beg permission to go to Stockton to recover."

He appeared to see me for the first time, "Leave London? But I need you now more than ever."

"No, King Henry, I am the Warlord. This is not a war you fight. This is a squabble between petulant princes. When there is war then send for me and I will be your right hand once more. Until then I have a family and people whom I would like to see. I will travel home to Stockton."

"Then go! Be another ingrate! I will deal with this myself!" It was not the best of partings!

Simon and I left the next day. We took spares horses which I purchased and we engaged four old soldiers as servants. Even though the air was filled with rain and sleet I felt happier than I had for many months. Simon ensured that we travelled at a pace which suited me and that I ate well. He had some of the medicine from Brother Cedric and I was cosseted all the way home. It took almost sixteen days to do a journey which I once accomplished in five days. Then I had been a young man and now I was a wounded old warrior.

**Part Three
William Earl of Cleveland**

Chapter 10

My father had been back in his home for a year. He was a shattered man when he reached us. The ride to Canterbury on the King's orders had almost done for him. We gave thanks to the priest and God who had saved him. I was just grateful that it had been a quiet year. There were events further afield but we were safe in our cocoon that was our valley. The Scots remained cowed and bowed after our swift victory. My knights' ladies had babies and the land prospered.

The King had disappointed both my father and me. He had done nothing to apprehend the killers who hid out at Knaresborough castle. They had, just a few months ago, sought the King's advice and he had not given them any. When Captain William arrived from the Loir he told us that they had gone to Rome to seek forgiveness for the murder. Their excommunication was to be lifted after fourteen years' service in the Holy Land. It was a death sentence but at least they were punished.

My father had recovered in the year since he had returned. Simon had been a rock. He had helped my father by riding out with him and sparring with him. It was not that my father would go to war again, we all knew that was impossible, but he needed to exercise and to have the knowledge that he could, if he had to, fight. Simon had told us of the incident in Canterbury. My father had even been hunting with us. My son and Sir Ralph had taken him to the forest to the south and west of my castle, where it edged towards Hartburn. We had hunted deer. My father had been more of a spectator but he still knew his way around the woods and the joy on his face when we returned made the whole castle and town a different place. The Christmas celebrations had been both long and loud. My father had seen almost seventy summers. As he told me, while we sipped strong wine in my solar, each day was now like the first day of his life.

As the days began to slowly lengthen he began to grow restless. He wished to know what was happening in the outside world. Henry had been to Ireland to build castles. It was a statement of his power but my father noted that he and his queen had not been together for almost two years. Sir Leofric kept us informed. He told us that Richard had spent a great deal of time in Aquitaine. Geoffrey and Young King Henry now lived in Normandy. That was something my father did not like. It was as though King Henry had given up on his sons.

Then rumours reached us that Young Henry had visited Paris. When my father heard that he became angry. I was the one who had given him the letter from Archbishop Roger. He had kept in touch with my father. He read the letter and flung it to the table.

"Your father is a blind old fool, William."

I poured him some more wine, "How so, father?"

"Those Frenchmen we saw in London when Simon and I waited there for King Henry. They were assassins. They were emissaries. They were sent by Louis to suborn Young Henry and they have succeeded. The French plots have borne fruit."

"That is just Henry. He is still young. He must know how treacherous the French are."

"Geoffrey is with him and we both know what a weak fool he is. Conan died but he is not yet married. He has not attained the Duchy. He is not patient." He then picked up the letter and waved it. "And now I read that Prince Richard and Prince Philip of France are close friends. That is all that the King needs. I should be at his side!"

"He is in Ireland and he has created this problem for himself. From what Leofric tells us the Queen is stirring up her sons."

My father sank back in his seat. "Is my life's work to have been for nothing?"

"Look around, father. This is a monument to you. So long as Stockton Castle stands it is a measure of your success."

He nodded and then said, out of nowhere. "I would have great grandchildren."

I laughed, "I have done all that I can do. I have given you two grandchildren and they are both wed. All else is in God's hands."

"They do not visit as often as I would like."

"They have manors to run. You are in a melancholic mood. Soon it will be spring and when the news grass comes and the sun shines then you will feel happier."

He smiled at me, "Each spring takes me closer to my death."

I tried all that I could to bring him from his dark place but could not. It was Aiden who managed to bring him from the depths of despair. Aiden had been a slave and, apart from Sir Harold, had served my father the longest. He came one day, "Earl Marshal. I have a mind to ride along the river path. Why do you and your squire not come with me?"

I thought he was going to say no but instead, he asked, "Is there a reason?"

"Aye, it may be cold but the new flowers are out. New growth after winter is always a sign of hope. Even though the land is cold and frozen there is life waiting to come out. Some of the animals who live by the river have had young. Let us go and see them. We will not hunt but, as two old men we will watch them. If we fall from our horses then Simon is strong enough to pick us up."

They left the next day. They had no sooner left than a rider came from the north. It was a messenger wearing the livery of Durham. He threw himself from his horse. "My lord, the Bishop of Durham sends word that his constable at Norham reports movement across the Tweed."

It was still just the first week of March. I thought it early for the Scots to be considering raiding but it had been two years and I had asked the Bishop to have his men watch for the Scots. I had to react. "Tell him I will bring a conroi of men to his castle on the morrow."

When he had gone I sent for my son, Sir Morgan, Sir Richard and Sir Padraig. Norham and the Tweed was a good five days' ride from us. Wilfred, who had been the captain of my men at arms, was like my father, he was getting old. John of Chester, Henry son of Will, Günther, Harry Lightfoot, Arne, all were getting old. They had chosen Roger of Bath as their captain. He had not yet seen thirty-five summers. I summoned him to join us too.

I would take forty men at arms and forty archers. That would be enough. When my knights arrived, they were happy to be given a challenge. The last battle had been the battle of Barnard. They had young sons and squires they wished to blood. The exception was Samuel. He wondered if they were blighted and would not have children. I think the only thing which kept Samuel and Eleanor sane was the knowledge that Ralph and Ruth had not conceived either.

"We ride to the Tweed. First, we visit Durham for I would have some of the Bishop's knights too. Whatever trouble the constable has discovered cannot be a major attack. It may be just a local mormaer flexing his muscles but I dare not ignore the threat. If we do then they will take it as a sign of weakness. The King is having trouble with his sons. It could well be that they are testing the waters. We will not take warhorses. Each man needs two mounts. Aiden is away with my father and so we will use Edgar and Edward as scouts. Say your goodbyes. We leave at dawn. We will meet at Wulfestun."

My two squires, Thomas of Piercebridge and Ralph of Sadberge were waiting for me as I came from the hall. "Prepare horses and war gear. We may be away for a month. We take no warhorses. I will have Hawk and Goldie."

"Will we need tents, lord?"

Ralph of Sadberge had campaigned before. "Just one. The three of us can share."

"Aye lord."

I then sought Edward and Edgar before telling Rebekah what we would be doing

When my father returned with Simon and Aiden he actually looked younger. He and Aiden were laughing. As he dismounted he said, "I had forgotten just how beautiful the river can be. It is a place of peace. We have done well, my son, to keep the beast away from it."

I nodded, "Thank you Aiden I hope that while we are away you can find other places to help remind him what he has done for this land."

My father's face became serious, "Away?"

"The constable at Norham has reported that there are warriors gathering north of the Tweed. I take a small conroi to investigate. Fear not we will take more Durham knights with us and I do not think this will be a serious threat."

As we entered my hall he shook his head, "I often think that the Romans had the right idea with their wall. They just failed to build it high enough." I saw in his face and heard in his voice that he would not be going to war again. The blow to his chest had been the best thing to happen to him. It had made him slow down and realise that he had done his duty and more.

The Princes' Revolt

We reached Durham well before noon. The horses were fresh and we made good time. The Bishop was not there. He had been summoned by the King to London. His dean told us that the King was trying to build bridges with the Pope to get the interdict removed. I met with his constable Sir Guy d'Auxerre.

"His grace sent word for the knights who have manors along the Wear to meet you at Norham lord. He sent the message when the rider returned from your castle. They will reach Norham before you."

"And is there any more information for me?"

"Sir Richard Bulmer is the constable. He is a doughty if unimaginative warrior. If he says there is danger then the Scots may well be pouring over the river even as we speak. The message he sent was that knights were gathering at Berwick and this was the wrong time of year for such gatherings."

"Then we had best hurry."

I had men who knew how to ride and did so without fuss. The knights I had were all young. They were of an age with Samuel. My older men at arms helped the younger, newer ones fit in well and learn from them. My archers were, quite simply, the best. They were all used to the outdoors and they ranged ahead and alongside us watching for danger. We moved so quickly that we caught up with Robert of Howden and his neighbours close by Hexham. There were ten knights and twenty-four men at arms. They soon found that we moved at a faster pace than they did!

The weather north of the wall was worse than the south and I wondered, again, why the Scots would think of risking our ire. We had just left Alnwick castle when a rider from Norham found us. We had been travelling on the main coast road. We were exposed to vicious winds from the east. All of us were well wrapped in cloaks. "Lord, I am glad I have found you. The Scots have crossed the Tweed. They were heading for Bamburgh."

"Did you pass any other Durham knights?"

He nodded, "Sir James Fitzwilliam and twenty knights took shelter in Bamburgh. There were Scots nearby. I took the inland road and then cut across. I spent the night in the woods for there were Scottish scouts. I do not think they were searching for me but I was taking no chances."

"And Norham?"

"Is surrounded. I was sent out as soon as we saw the banners. I watched the Scots surround the castle before heading for Bamburgh."

Sir Richard might be dull-witted but he had chosen a quick-witted messenger. "What is the size of this army that has managed to trap Sir Richard inside Norham?"

"There are a hundred knights." He hesitated, "Lord, I was with the Bishop when he went to Rome. I recognised some of the banners. They were French. The bulk of the army is made up of men from the far north. I saw the banner of the Lord Comyn's son, William."

"You had better stay with us. What is your name?"

"James de Puiset." He saw my look. "The Bishop is my uncle."

I nodded and turned in my saddle, "Thomas of Piercebridge, ride back to Alnwick. Tell Sir Henry that the Scots are over the border. He is to prepare for a siege! Join us at Bamburgh."

James said, "The Scots might be there already, lord."

I waved Thomas of Piercebridge away. "Then I hope they tried to besiege it. It will be a waste of time. I think they are looking for softer targets. If Sir James and his men are in Bamburgh then we need to combine with them. We are mounted and we can use our speed."

Thomas of Piercebridge had just rejoined us when my two scouts, Edward and Edgar, came to our rescue as we headed up the coast road and passed Seahouses. We would see the rock of Bamburgh up ahead but my two scouts had spotted Scots. The folds in the land prevented us from seeing anything. An encounter battle needs a leader who can think quickly but, even more importantly, it needs men who can react like lightning.

"Lord there are a hundred Scots ahead. I think they are heading for Seahouses." If Edgar said they were heading for Seahouses then that is where they were heading. He had great skills.

I had dismounted my men and they are in wait in the sand dunes. I turned, "Squires stay with the horses. Knights and men at arms with me." Ralph of Sadberge brought me a spear and my helmet. I spurred Goldie and we leapt up the road. I turned and saw that my household knights and James de Puiset were with me as well as my men at arms but the other knights of Durham were still organising their men.

The road, which had been made by the old people of this land was not straight and followed the contours of the earth. Sand had blown over its surface and deadened the sound of hooves. Neither side would hear the other. We dipped into a hollow with steep dunes to our right and scrubby moorland to our left. We were not in a line but I was flanked by Sir Morgan and my son. The other three were just behind us followed by

The Princes' Revolt

Roger of Bath, John of Chester, Henry son of Will and my household knights. As we crested the rise I saw the Scots just ahead. We were less than fifty paces from each other. I recognised a banner. It was the Mormaer of Dunbar. We had no banners and we were cloaked. They would not know who we were.

I lowered my spear and spurred Goldie. My son and former squire emulated me and three spears headed like and arrow for the lord of Dunbar. Even though they outnumbered us the Scots made the classic mistake; they hesitated. They slowed. We hit them when we were galloping. I pulled back my arm and thrust it at the knight who was still drawing his sword. I hit him in the shoulder and he tumbled. To my left Samuel swung his sword and it hit the Lord of Dunbar on his shield but it was so hard that he reeled. Samuel's spurs must have raked the flank of the lord's horse as he passed for it suddenly took off towards the moor land.

My spear was still intact and I thrust it at the man at arms on the small horse. His shield came up but the angle at which I struck him and the speed of my horse meant that he too was hit. The band of Scots were all mounted but they were on the hill ponies the Scots favoured. Hardy beasts, they were capable of carrying a man long distances but they were useless for war. When Aelric's archers' arrows began to descend and hit men and horses they turned and fled. Their ponies might have been hardy but they were not fast. Our horses were powerful. Even though they were palfreys we had brought the best and we soon overtook the Scots. I pulled my arm back and rammed it into the leather mailed back of a Scot. As he fell his body tore the spear from my hand. I drew my sword and leaned out to sweep it into the skull of another.

Sir Morgan of Seamer, my former squire, Alf, was putting his long arms and long sword to good effect. Even when Scots tried to evade him they could not. Samuel still had his spear and he was using it with a precision which impressed me. He had such skill that he was choosing the spot to strike which would ensure that his enemy fell. As we neared the rock upon which Bamburgh stood I saw that the Scots began to flee away from the coast and across the scrub land to the west. We could not risk damaging a horse riding across such unpredictable terrain. We had broken the Scots. The ones who fled were without mail. I held up my hand and yelled, "Stop!"

I reined Goldie in and took off my helmet. Turning in my saddle I saw that the tardy knights of Durham were finishing off knots of Scots who had escaped us. Aelric and his archers were moving amongst them. My household knights were all unscathed. When they removed their helmets, I saw the joy of victory on their faces.

"We were lucky! Had Aelric not warned us then things might have been different."

James de Puiset shook his head, "No lord there was little luck involved." He pointed to the knights of Durham. "Your men and knights reacted as one. The Scots stood no chance."

Roger of Bath pointed west, "Four of their knights escaped yonder lord. You want us to go after them?"

"No, Roger. Gather the horses, mail and weapons. We will seek counsel in Bamburgh first."

Bamburgh was a royal residence. The only knight was the constable, Richard of Bayeux. It did not have a large garrison; there were but forty men at arms and ten archers who lived within the mighty fortress. It needed no more men for it rose from the land and seemed to be part of the rock upon which it was built. One gate was only accessible at low tide and the other road twisted and turned as it climbed to the south gate. An attacker would have to endure a missile storm. The castle was cunningly crafted. A ram would not be able to build up speed and could be attacked from the gatehouse and the walls which abutted it. We would have plenty of room for our men and horses and we could use it as a base from which to scour the land of Scots.

The knights from Durham were ebullient as we rode the last mile or so to the castle. We had no prisoners. My men valued their own lives above any ransom which they might have taken and the Durham knights had been too slow to react. We had horses, ponies and weapons. My archers had taken the coins from the bodies. They would share the bounty with my men at arms.

Sir James Fitzwilliam and Richard of Bayeux greeted me as I entered. The Constable was older than I was while Fitzwilliam and I had been squires together with my father. "Magnificent Earl! We watched from the walls."

I dismounted and nodded, "Thank you, Sir James. What do we know about the rest of the Scottish raiders?"

As we walked to the keep Sir James said, "We were north of this castle when James de Puiset found us. I sent him to find you straight away. I hope I did right to take shelter here."

"If there were a hundred knights then aye for you would have been slaughtered. You confirmed the numbers?"

Sir Richard said, "They approached the castle but stopped on the other side of the harbour. There were one hundred and three banners. It was hard to make out the numbers of their foot and light horse. They are camped to the north of us. We saw the men whom you slew ride out this morning. I think they had a chevauchée planned."

I turned to Sir James. "You said Norham was surrounded." He nodded. "Were there more knights there?"

"I saw some banners as they made their camp but it seemed to be men on foot who surrounded it. You know the castle, lord, there is but one way in and out. It does not have a large garrison but my uncle has made it hard to take." He hesitated and then went on, "I think they just mean to keep Sir Richard and his men within Norham so that they can raid the land." He shrugged. "I may be wrong lord."

I liked Sir James, "No, Sir James, I think you are right. That means we need to do something about this Scottish army which squats like a toad on yonder headland."

Richard of Bayeux said, "We do not have enough knights for a single battle."

"Then we whittle them down and we use the land to defeat them. What is their camp like?"

"There is water there. A small stream pours into the sea. There is grazing and the dunes give shelter. They must know the area to have chosen it. We cannot easily get to them because of the harbour. They can raid north, head through the woods and reach the west and the south."

"As you say, well planned out."

I was summoned to the north gate towards dusk. The sentry pointed to the west, "Lord, we have seen men returning from the south west for the last hour or so."

I peered and saw that they were the survivors of our attack. They must have feared pursuit and headed as far west as they could get. "How many others have returned?"

"I saw ten or so and there are another fifteen there, lord. Four were knights."

"Thank you."

I peered towards the distance camp. It was protected on one side by the sea and on another by the steep slope which led from the harbour. There was a way to attack them. It would involve a night time manoeuvre. We would have to leave the castle after dark and head west before turning north. We would be attacking from the woods to the west and the north. It was clear that I could not use the knights of Durham. They were unreliable. Samuel came to join me.

"You are planning an attack, father?"

"I am. I would weaken them before they begin to raid. When we rode north I saw that most of the farmers had their animals close to home. That is why they have chosen now. They are able to collect a large number of animals and slaves without travelling too far. If we can thin their numbers in a swift attack then we can use our horses to prevent them raiding. They will grow hungry and return home. Then we can relieve Norham."

"And you have a plan?"

"We use the night to aid us. Tomorrow we will ride forth with our knights. It may be that they try to challenge us and we can fight them. If they do not then when it is dark we take our archers, men at arms and the knights from the valley. We ride west to those woods you can see. We will leave the horses with horse holders and then close with their camp. We use the knights and men at arms to form a human shield and the archers send arrows blindly into the camp. Then we withdraw."

"That sounds like a hazardous plan."

"If we were using the knights of Durham it would be but I plan on just using our men. The knights of Durham will be satisfactory when it comes to riding down their raiders but night work and knife work require skills which I know my men have." I saw doubt on his face. "If you think you do not have the skills then there is no shame in saying so."

He coloured, "No, I am ready. I think I have the skills but I have never had to use them yet."

"We do not wear helmets nor do we carry shields. We wear no surcoats and we oil our leather and mail so that it makes no sound. The archers and our two scouts will be ahead and they can move like ghosts. All that we need to do is to follow."

I told my knights what I intended knowing that they would tell the men at arms and archers. I gathered the knights and the constable in the Great Hall and told them there. "Remember to listen for my squire and the horns. If it sounds three times then we ride back to the castle. There is nothing to be gained from throwing lives away. We are outnumbered. We deal with the Scots in the best way that we can."

"And in the night? What then? You said that you had plans. What are they?"

I smiled, "The men who are involved know the plans. That is enough."

"You do not trust us?"

"Sir Walther, of course, I do but what I do not trust is that if one of you is captured tomorrow when we go to antagonise the Scots then they may inadvertently give something away."

When the knights had gone to speak with their men I sat with Richard of Bayeux. He smiled as he poured me some wine, "You are right, Earl. The fewer who know your plans the better. You could send to the lords further south for more men and knights, lord."

"I know but this is not the real attack. We will know when that comes for King William will lead it. I will use cunning and not numbers to defeat this Scottish raider."

I sounded more confident than I was. The truth was that I now knew that my father would no longer lead the knights of the north. It looked like it would be my lot to do so. I needed to get to know my knights better and that would be easier with a smaller number of knights. Robert of Howden seemed solid enough. I also found that I liked James de Puiset. He came to see me as I headed for my chamber, "Lord, I beg you to take me with you tomorrow night."

"You know not what I plan."

"No, but I have sat at Norham for two years and seen no action. I volunteered to bring you the message for I want to serve with you." He paused and took a breath. "Do not judge me by my uncle. My father was a good knight and died bravely. The Bishop took me in but I have been kept cooling my heels in Norham and other castles of the Palatinate. What is the use of being a knight if I cannot use the skills I have learned."

"Do you have a squire?"

He shook his head, "The Constable of Norham has a number of young men who serve him."

"Then get yourself a squire and I will consider taking you on. As for tomorrow…I will put you with my son. You will obey every instruction he gives you."

"And what do we do tomorrow?"

"You will see. Now get some rest for tomorrow you will need all your wits about you."

The Princes' Revolt

Samuel and Alf were in the chamber next to mine. "Tomorrow night we take James de Puiset with us. I put him in your charge, Samuel."

"Do you trust him, father?"

"I think so but I rely upon you to discover the truth." It was time for my son to develop new skills too.

There was no point in riding before dawn. My men and I would be losing sleep the next night anyway. We ate heartily and then mounted. I kept the archers on the walls and half of the men at arms. We had just forty knights and forty men at arms. I hoped that we would give the Scots the impression that we had few men. Dunbar would have reported large numbers and dissension in the Scottish camp could only aid our cause. We took spears and headed out of the south gate and then travelled along the road to the Scottish camp. We heard their horns when their sentries spied us. We had travelled two hundred paces before they did so and that told me much about their discipline. The road followed the harbour. There was neither quay nor jetty. The boats were either drawn up on the beach or moored. The ground rose steeply. We passed through a small stand of trees and I led the column west, off the road. The road passed within a hundred paces of the camp and the last thing I wanted was for them to gain an advantage by using their bows and their slings. We halted three hundred paces from their camp and we faced them in four lines. My knights and the ones I had chosen especially were in the front rank. Our squires had our banners. Some, like Morgan's, Samuel's, Padraig's and Richard's were small but they told the Scots that they were knights. I saw James de Puiset looking uncomfortable. He had neither banner nor squire.

Our arrival had certainly discomfited the Scots. Many of the ordinary warriors, the men from the north and the east stood shouting belligerently at us. The knights and their mounted men quickly mounted their horses and were hurriedly heading towards the mob who chanted and cursed us. Some turned around and lowered their breeks. It was their way of insulting us. I saw the knights of Durham look towards me for a signal. None was forthcoming. My men at arms had seen and heard this sort of behaviour before. It was sound and fury. It meant nothing. I saw Scottish leaders, that was a guess for I only recognised Dunbar's livery, gather around the main standard and hold a mounted discussion. They must have decided to attack us for horns sounded. I had not donned my helmet. I turned and shouted, "Front rank only will charge with me!

Second rank you will receive the Scots charge and let us pass through when we return."

I did not wait for an answer as the Scots were moving. I donned my helmet and shouted, "Charge."

It must have looked like madness for there were just twenty of us and a hundred Scottish knights but it was a cold and calculated move. I intended to hit and then run. The press of men on foot forced the Scottish horses into an even narrow frontage; there were just fourteen knights and the ones behind were not in ordered lines. They were just joining the mob of horses which galloped towards this impudent island of English men. Their archers and slingers could not get close for the bigger, burlier men on foot had been at the fore. Timing would be everything.

I held my spear behind me. Many of the Scots charged with just a sword or an axe. Our spears would strike them first. When we collided, the sound was like thunder and hailstones mixed as spears shattered and splintered and swords cracked on shields. My spear went into the chest of a knight. His falling body dragged his horse down and crashed into the horses following.

I drew my sword and shouted, "Fall back!" as Samuel and Sir Morgan despatched their foes. My men wheeled their horses. The Scots we had struck lay dead and dying. I saw Robert of Potto fall from his horse but he was the only casualty. Our second rank had opened up to allow us through as had the men at arms behind. The Scots had to negotiate dead knights and horses. Their men on foot also got in the way. As they hit our second line more of their men were unhorsed. Now was the time to withdraw. We had done that which I had wanted. We had hurt their knights.

I shouted, "Fall back!" As the knights withdrew to join us Roger of Bath led the men at arms to smash into the disordered knights, men at arms and foot.

"Ralph sound the horn three times!"

My men at arms were well trained and they wheeled and followed us as we galloped back towards the castle. We rode down the road through the stand of trees. The slope was with us this time. The trees afforded us cover but the Scots were angry at their losses and they hurtled after us. We rode, in good order, along the castle walls to the south gate. The Scots discovered my archers. Aelric waited until the majority of the Scots were within range of his bows and then unleashed a most terrible arrow storm. Men and horses fell. A Scottish horn soon sounded and they headed back to their camp. They left behind at least fifteen dead and wounded warriors. There were dead and dying horses too. We would eat well that night.

I reined in. "Roger search the dead and despatch the wounded. Robert of Howden, have your men butcher the horses. We might as well eat fresh meat!"

Chapter 11

We were all in good humour as we rode through the gates. Our losses had been light and the enemy had lost more than thirty men. The majority of the men we had killed and wounded had been knights. Ralph took my horse to the stables and I waited for Roger of Bath to return. Edward and Edgar were already in the stables. It was where they had slept. Like Aiden they were comfortable around animals and preferred the stables to a strange warrior hall. I waved them over. "I want the two of you to leave at dusk. You will scout out the woods to the west of the road. We will join you when it is dark."

"Yes lord."

Roger of Bath was checking the hooves on one of the horses, "Roger, I want us to be as dark as an African at midnight."

He grinned, "Aye lord. We will oil the mail and the leather. The men will leave their shields and helmets behind. When we have eaten we will get our heads down."

I went to the walls where Aelric and his archers still watched. "Have your men rest. Tonight, we will leave as soon as it is dark. I want us in those woods. Edgar and Edward will scout them out so that we are not surprised. When it is clear we slip across the road and you will send as many arrows into their camp as you can."

He nodded and pointed to their camp, "Although we hit them, hard lord, I have been watching their camp and they still have many men. We have not begun to hurt them yet. Twenty of them rode west while you were crossing the inner ward."

"They are raiding." He nodded. "Then we hurt them tonight and tomorrow we make certain that they cannot raid more."

The Constable was also in a good humour until I told him about the twenty men who had gone raiding. "That is not good, lord. The people hereabouts are hardy and hardworking but they have few animals. The sheep and the cows give them milk for cheese and their fowl eggs. If the Scots take what little they have then they may starve."

"Then it is up to me to ensure that they do not suffer. Tonight, I will take my men out. Tomorrow we will rest and we will see what the men of Durham can do."

Thomas of Piercebridge and Ralph of Sadberge met me in my chamber and I took off my mail and arming hood. "You know what you must do?"

"Aye lord."

"And then you will rest. That is a command. Tonight will be hard."

By the time I reached the Great Hall the majority of the Durham knights were there and eating the fresh bread and hot meat. It was a rowdy atmosphere. Their nerves had been calmed by our apparently easy victory. They did not know that it had only seemed easy because we had caught the Scots unawares. I waved over Fitzwilliam and Howden. They had emerged as two leaders.

"Robert, I need your ten best men at arms to go out with us tonight and act as horse holders. I will go out with my men."

"Should we come with you, lord?"

I shook my head. "Tomorrow my men will need rest. You two will need to lead your men and stop the Scots from raiding. Twenty men left this morning. Tomorrow you will be where you can be seen to deter the Scots from leaving their camp. Your knights and men at arms must prevent any of the people hereabouts from suffering."

"You will not be with us, lord?"

I laughed, "Am I your mother teaching you how to tie your breeks? You are knights. You will learn how to do this."

I did not heed my own advice. I did not rest. I ate, at noon, with the Constable and then he and I walked the walls. This was a royal residence and the Constable had improved the defences year on year. It was an ancient fortress. It had been a hill fort in the time before the Romans. The ones who had fought the Saxons had called it Din Guardi and they had held off those raiders for many years. The Kings of Northumbria had made it their refuge but it was William and his Norman knights who had made it impregnable.

Richard of Bayeux pointed to the southern gate. "We have plans to make that gate even stronger, lord. We are going to make a wall which abuts the gate so that men can sally forth and attack men who bring a ram."

"Do you not have another sally port? I saw none when we rode around the walls."

He smiled, "We have a hidden one." I was intrigued. "There is a well in the castle. If you climb down it then there is a tunnel which leads under the rocks and emerges at the beach. At high tide it is flooded but it is a useful way to get messages in and out."

I stored that information although I did not see why we would need to get to the beach. "I hope to drive the Scots hence. It will be within the next ten days. The speed of their departure will depend upon how much we can hurt them. A harder task will be to relieve the siege of Norham. I will write a letter for the Sheriff. Have a rider take it to him. I do not have enough men here to relieve the siege."

"Norham is a Palatinate castle lord."

I nodded, "And I am Earl of the North. He will obey my command."

I went to the Great Hall and wrote the letter. I made it quite clear what I wanted and when. After sealing it I gave it to Ralph to hand to the Constable. Samuel came to me. He had just risen, "Father, it is time you rested. You have often told me that a tired man makes mistakes. We cannot afford to have our leader make a mistake, can we?"

I laughed, "The cub chastises the wolf!"

He laughed, "As I believe you did with your father. It must be something to do with the blood. It is not just me who wishes this, your knights, men at arms and archers are also concerned."

He was right. "Very well but I want to be wakened before dusk."

"I will send Thomas of Piercebridge to wake you."

I was weary and I slept well. My head seemed to have barely touched the bed when Thomas of Piercebridge shook me awake. "Lord, Edgar and Edward are about to leave."

I washed, mainly to refresh myself, and Thomas helped me to don my oiled mail. With a sharpened sword and dagger in my baldric, I went to the hall where my knights awaited. Ralph had food ready for me. I was hungry. The horsemeat had been freshly cooked and the Constable ensured that I had a good wine to drink. The knights of Durham looked at us curiously. There was no bravado amongst my young knights. They chatted easily with each other and their squires. My knights' squires were the only ones in the hall who were eating with their knights. The rest were just acting as servants.

Richard of Bayeux leaned over, "They are confused, lord. They wonder why your squires are accorded such honour."

The Princes' Revolt

I laughed, "It is simple. All of my knights were squires for me or my father. They are merely doing what we did. I cannot understand knights treating squires like servants. Will it make them better warriors? I do not think so. When we go amongst the Scots this night then my men will know that the squires will behave and perform as well as any."

"You go amongst them then?"

"We do. My plan is to cause as many casualties as we can without losing too many men. When the knights of Durham harry them tomorrow they may grow tired of this and return home."

"You do not desire one great battle?"

"That rarely happens, Constable. I would take one but with barely a handful of knights on whom I can rely and not enough archers then I will take the Scots running home with their tails between their legs. When we have marched to Norham and relieved that siege then I will return to my valley."

Richard of Bayeux lowered his voice, "We are remote here, lord. Little news reaches us but I have had visitors who have asked me if I think King Henry should abdicate in favour of his son."

"That is treason!"

"Perhaps but if I was asked that, up here in the wilds of the north of England then what questions are being asked further south? You are close to the king or rather, your father is. He needs to speak with the King and alert him to the danger."

"My father is not a well man. He has done more than enough for this land and King Henry's lands in France! There are others who need to bear that mantle!" I was aware that I had raised my voice and men were looking at me. I cared not. I pushed the platter of food away. "I have lost my appetite. Knights of the valley let us arm. We, at least, know our duty!"

I glared at Richard of Bayeux. He shrugged, "I am an old man with a worm-eating out his insides. It matters little to me lord who rules this land. I will do my duty too. It will not do me any good but I will die knowing that I was a true knight."

I felt slightly guilty about my words. I realised now that the Constable had meant well and was asking me to help the King. I could not allow my father to do that. I would have to speak with the King. It might mean leaving my home but the King needed my family and it would be my responsibility.

Samuel hurried after me, "What is amiss, father?"

The Princes' Revolt

I shook my head, "Politics! A knight should never get involved in politics. His duty is to defend his lands and his people. Remember that!"

"Aye father."

I rode Goldie. I needed a clever horse and she was lucky. A knight needed luck. We left the gate and headed west. Darkness had fallen. My two scouts were already in place and my archers were two hundred paces ahead of us. We needed no words and so we rode in silence. We turned when the woods appeared to the north of us and headed along the trail. Robin Hawkeye awaited us. He said nothing but he waved and we followed him. We reached a clearing. I had lost track of where we were but I trusted my scouts and my archers. The archers' horses were already there and were being watched by three men. As we dismounted the three disappeared east and the men at arms from Robert of Howden took over. I tied the reins of Goldie to an oak tree. I waited until my knights and men at arms were with me and then I followed the archers.

We moved in silence through the trees. We had seen the forest from the road but the darkness had a way of distorting time making the obvious seem strange. Suddenly Aelric appeared in front of me with Edgar. He put his head to my ear, "Lord, the Scots are in the woods. I think they meant to launch an attack on us."

I had to think quickly, "You cannot use your bows. Tonight, you become assassins. Have your men hide behind trees and await the Scots." He nodded and disappeared. I waved Roger of Bath forward. "The Scots are coming. We will ambush them. Spread the word."

My knights and squires were close to me, "What is it, father?"

"The Scots are here in the woods. We ambush them!" I waved James de Puiset over. "You do not know my men. Stay with me." He nodded, "Thomas, Ralph, behind us!"

I drew my sword and dagger. I waited. The Scots had tried something I had not expected. What could they have hoped to achieve? Then I remembered the tunnel which Richard of Bayeux had mentioned. Perhaps they knew of it too. To get to it they would have to go all the way around the castle and approach the tunnel from the south. If there were French knights with them then it was possible. Speculation would have to wait.

My eyes were now accustomed to the dark. Since we had ceased walking my ears could now listen to the woods. My men would all be still so when I heard the crunch of a foot on a leaf or a dried twig then I knew there were Scots close by. I heard the first Scot die, just up ahead.

The Princes' Revolt

There was a soft sigh and the sound of someone being lowered to the ground. One of my archers had made his first kill. Unless you were listening for it then you would not have heard it. The Scots would be making noise as they walked. There would be a knight, at the very least, leading them. They were not as stealthy as my men. That was why we had walked with our knights and men at arms at the rear.

There may have been other silent deaths. I heard nothing but suddenly the silence of the night was ripped apart. As soon as a noisy Scot died screaming, I heard a Scottish voice shout, "Ambush!"

James made to move and to pass me. I put my hand on his middle and shook my head. Stillness was still our best weapon. My patience was rewarded when two Scots came towards us. They had not seen us for the tree behind which we sheltered hid us and I peered between the forks of two large branches. I tapped James on the shoulder as I stepped out, swung my sword and hacked through the middle of the first Scot. James, stepping to the other side of the tree, brought his sword from on high and cut across the neck of his foe. Having stepped from behind the tree I now saw the battle raging in the forest. It was hand to hand and no quarter was given. It was the kind of work in which my men excelled. My men at arms were protected by mail and my archers knew how to use the forest.

I noticed that there were no more Scots heading our way. I raised my sword and waved it forward. To my right I saw Samuel copy my action and to my left Alf did the same. We moved towards the Scottish camp. Roger of Bath signalled the men at arms to spread out like a line of beaters. We would drive the survivors of the aborted attack on the castle into a killing field. We passed the bodies of dead Scots. I heard a horn sound from the Scottish camp. Then I heard a voice shout, "Form a line! We must hold them until help can be brought from the camp!"

That order was a warning that we might be the ones who would be trapped. I began to hurry. I heard the thrum of an arrow. My archers could not use their bows as well as they might like but if the Scots formed a shield wall then they would be easy targets for my bow men. I reached Aelric. I had to step over the body of Ralph of Ely. My archer had been hacked almost in two by an axe. Aelric had formed his men into a line. If the Scots rushed them then there was a danger they might be hurt.

"A wall for the archers!"

I stepped before Aelric. James and Samuel took their places next to me and then the archers started to work. The Scots were ten paces from us. Although it was night they could still be seen at that range. If my archers could see them then they would die. Some of the Scots had shields and they stood behind them. It mattered not for my archers were close enough to choose which eye they sent their arrow through. The arrows did not just thin their lines, they reaped them like wheat. As I had hoped that was too much for some of the Scots. They left their line to rush us. In the dark they might have thought that we, too were archers. I fended off the axe with my sword and ripped my dagger across the throat of the first Scot. Dark blood spurted; showering me. Samuel excelled in this sort of work. He had an efficiency which I admired. There was no wasted effort. He used his height and long arms well as did Alf. The few who ran at us were soon despatched. James' lack of experience showed. He tried to block a sword with his dagger and did not have enough room to swing his sword. Had not Ralph, my squire, been close at hand then this might have been James' last battle. As it was the Scot fell. When Robin Hawk Eye sent an arrow into the Scottish knight's mouth the survivors fled.

James made to move towards the Scottish as I went to examine the Scottish knight's body. Samuel said, "Hold Sir James. We have done what we intended. Roger of Bath, collect our dead and wounded. Aelric, take what we need from the bodies."

I saw that the knight next to the Scot was a Frenchman. I said, "Samuel, search this warrior. He is French."

James asked, "How do you know?"

Samuel said, "Look at his sword and his dagger, they are French made. His surcoat has a fleur de lys upon it. This is a French warrior. He may be a man at arms. His lord will either be fleeing back to the Scottish camp or lie dead in the woods. That is why our men search."

"I thought you were just grave robbers."

Samuel shook his head as he stood with the items he had recovered from the body. "You have much to learn James de Puiset."

I had found a seal as well as a purse of coins. I recognised the surcoat as that of the lord of Falkirk. The knight I had killed was too young to be the lord and had to be one of his sons. Edward and Edgar ran towards me, "Lord the Scots come. We have made a few traps but they will be upon us soon."

"Back to the horses!"

We hurried back through the trees. We passed the dead. Any wounded had been given a warrior's death. Even a Scot did not deserve to have his face eaten by a rat or a fox. I heard cries from behind as the Scots discovered the traps set by my woodsmen. We reached the horses. The wounded were mounted first and then the dead draped across the backs of their horses. Four men would not return to Stockton. We headed back to Bamburgh.

Richard of Bayeux must have been watching for us. The gates swung open to admit us. He looked puzzled, "Did you not attack their camp, Earl? We watched from the north wall but we heard nothing from the camp until the horn sounded."

"They were planning an attack. I think, Constable, that others know of this tunnel. It is low tide now, is it not?" He nodded. "Then we were lucky. Had I not taken my men on this foray we could have woken to enemies within."

"I will have a pair of men set to watch the well. Then your raid was not a success?"

"Just the opposite. Had we attacked their camp with arrows we might have killed men but we could not have been certain to kill knights. Ten knights fell in our attack as well as men at arms. A French knight and two men at arms were slain. Make sure that the knights of Durham are roused early so that they can prevent the Scots from raiding."

Our squires saw to our horses and took our mail to be cleaned. I sat with my knights in the Great Hall. It was too soon to go to bed for our minds would be racing. We sat and drank. "What is the French connection, lord?"

"I think Padraig, that it is the normal French mischief. They like to use a little gold to encourage our neighbours to raid. There is an uneasy peace with France. This way Louis can have those knights eager for war, fight over here under Scottish colours."

Samuel snorted, "Then they are fools for they fought under French colours. If they wished to stay hidden they should have either discarded surcoats or ridden under false colours."

"Is that honourable?"

Alf, Sir Morgan, looked at James and shook his head, "You think there is any honour in what they did or what we planned? The Earl is right to make war this way. The Scots wish to make England their land. We do all that we can to stop it! Would that every lord of the north did the same."

Alf's tone could be a little blunt. I saw James colour as he took in Alf's words. "You mean my uncle?"

My knights all looked to me. I would not lie to this young knight. He had shown courage. "That is what Sir Morgan means. Your uncle has sent less than forty knights to retake his own castle. He is not committed. He is Prince Bishop and should act accordingly." I stood. "You all did well this night. Get some sleep for we ride again this afternoon." I had a plan which would, hopefully, drive the Scots home.

My father had told me that when you led you did not get much sleep. I was learning that now. Until I had returned from the crusades I had had a life which was free from such worries. I made my own decisions and did not worry about others. Now I worried. Robert of Howden was a competent leader of knights but he lacked imagination. I had told them to ensure that the Scots did not raid. My knights would have known what that entailed. I was unsure about the Durham knights. I rose just before noon and I went directly to the north gate. Richard of Bayeux was there.

"Well, constable?"

"I have heard the sounds of fighting but it came from the north of their camp."

I nodded. That did not worry me. The Scots would raid that side first. What did worry me was that we had had no report back from the knights and men at arms we had sent. "Tomorrow I will rid this land of the Scots." I saw the question on the constable's face. "It is not arrogance but we have weakened them. No matter what Robert of Howden does this day he will have weakened the enemy."

"He may have weakened the men you have at your disposal."

"Perhaps but I intend to use my archers behind a wall of knights and men at arms. And I hope that High Sheriff William de Vesci will bring his men north in the next day or so. The longer the Scots are here the more parlous becomes the position of the Constable of Norham. They are perched on the edge of this land and surrounded by enemies." I turned, "I will go and eat. If you hear anything then send for me.

I had eaten and my knights had just awoken when I heard a shout from the walls. I went up the stairs to the top of the keep. There I saw a sorry sight. The men of Durham had been badly handled by the Scots. There were horses with men draped over them. I saw that there were just twenty knights returning and less then ten men at arms.

Samuel joined me, "They must have fought a battle, father."

"And I told them just to stop the Scots from raiding. I did not want a battle from them. Come we will go and hear the bad news for ourselves."

When we reached the outer ward, the knights had begun to enter. Robert of Howden had been wounded. I said nothing but looked at him. He dismounted and handed his reins to his squire. "The Scots came to challenge us. We fought them."

I nodded, "And you lost."

"We slew many of their men."

"Knights?" His silence was eloquent. "You should have ridden away. I sent you there not to fight but to contain the Scots. They will now be raiding north of Bamburgh. The people there will suffer." I shook my head. He did not understand my plan. Perhaps that had been my fault. "Tomorrow I will lead the knights who are fit and we will end this incursion."

"You will fight them then? When I do it then it is wrong and when you do it then it is acceptable?"

"Aye, it is but come tomorrow and you shall see how I do it." I saw that my words had been like a slap to his face. I turned and, with Samuel, headed for my archers and men at arms.

"He wanted glory such as you enjoy, father."

"I do not have glory."

"That was the wrong word; success is what I meant."

"I have had success, that is true but I have had my setbacks too. Perhaps I was hard on him."

Samuel shook his head. He was becoming wiser, "No, father for the men who died paid the price for his misjudgement."

After telling my men at arms and archers what I intended I went to the chapel which they were using as a hospital. That was one advantage we had over the Scots. We had healers and beds inside solid walls. They had nothing save an open and exposed camp. Even if they had healers it was unlikely that they could do much. The victory that morning might have raised Scottish spirits a little but as we had had more success I guessed that the mood was one of depression. I hoped so.

The next morning, we ate early, before dawn and I led my men and the fifteen knights who were fit from the Durham contingent. Even though he was wounded Robert of Howden insisted upon accompanying us. He went up in my estimation. Edgar and Edward rode ahead and we took the same route we had done during our night attack. We rode further west and used the cover of the trees.

Robert of Howden said, "We rode up the road, Earl."

"And they spied you. This way we will arrive unseen."

Just then Edgar and Edward galloped in. Their speed made my men at arms and knights pull their shields up and my archers to string their bows.

"Lord, there are Scots heading this way. There are thirty of them and they are all mounted. I think they raid."

"Aelric take your men and cut off their escape. We will give them a surprise."

"Aye lord, come men. Robin Hawkeye you take half south and I will head north."

I took the spear Ralph offered me and donned my helmet. I spurred Goldie. The early warning from my scouts had given us an edge. We outnumbered them anyway but they would be so surprised when we fell upon them that their judgement would be impaired. Robert of Howden's failed attack would have given them confidence. With Samuel at my side we rode along the narrow trail. We held our spears vertically. It was easier that way. Suddenly I saw a flash of white and blue and I lowered my spear while spurring Goldie.

There were two Scottish knights leading a column of men. They had no spears. This was a chevauchée. They were going for animals, food and slaves. They did not expect to encounter knights. The knight who led was quick thinking. Seeing our spears, he recognised that he was outmatched. He shouted, "Back to the camp!"

They had to turn their horses and on the narrow trail that was difficult. The two knights and their squires had better horses and they managed to turn and gallop down the trail. The men they led were not so blessed. Two of them could not control their horses. Samuel and I stabbed them in their sides with our spears. Their bodies fell and their mounts fled. Three tried to evade us by taking off through the woods. Behind me I heard John of Chester shout, "We will get these men, lord!"

Two more of the Scots were tardy and died. Then I saw, just ahead, lighter ground. We were emerging from the woods. Then arrows flew from my right and left. Men fell. As we cleared the woods I reined in for four hundred paces from us was the Scottish camp. Just two knights and a squire had escaped us.

"Form two lines. Aelric, have your archers ready behind us. Squires, take post behind the archers!"

James de Puiset nudged his horse between mine and Sir Morgan's. He smiled, "I think I will be safer here, lord, than in the second rank. Sir Morgan is built like Bamburgh itself." James was learning. He wished to

The Princes' Revolt

survive the battle and the safest place to do that was within my men's ranks.

The Scots had learned from our previous forays. There were now stakes at the edge of their camp and a ditch. I had no doubt that the ditch would be full of traps. We waited three hundred paces from the ditches. The Scots formed up. Their men on foot now had long spears to hold us off. They had fewer horses now. I saw the knights' squires lead their horses forward and the knights mounted in the gap between the stakes.

"Samuel, you have younger eyes. Can you see fleur de lys?"

He nodded. "One knight has a single fleur de lys. He has red chevrons quartered on blue and there are four men at arms with the same livery."

"Then the French are still here."

The Scots stayed where they were, as did we. Robert of Howden rode along to me. He had been sent to the rear with his squires for he was wounded. "Why do we wait, Earl?"

"This is what I wished you to do yesterday."

"Wait? That is all?"

"Can they raid?" He shook his head. "Then we have won. When the men of the New Castle come then we can be more aggressive. For now, this suits us. Our horses are grazing. It is a pleasant day for it is not raining. We wait. Let us see who becomes bored first." I was confident that it would be the Scots. My banner intimidated them. When they had sent this army south the King of Scotland, and I had no doubt that he was behind it, would have assumed that he would be fighting the men of Northumbria and not the son of the bane of the Scots, the Warlord!

They were close enough for us to see a heated debate. The hot heads won. As the sun reached its zenith they formed battle lines. Their handful of archers and slingers moved closer to the stakes. They had hunting bows and not war bows. They would have to endure the arrows from my archers before they could send a missile in reply. Aelric and his archers were hidden behind my two ranks of horsemen and could not see their target. It did not matter for they knew the range. "They advance, Aelric."

"Just give the word, lord and they will die."

The men on foot, the highland and island warriors had their shields ready. In the main, they wore leather caps but a few had helmets. The horsemen, the knights, men at arms and hobelars were wary of attacking us. We were a mailed wall. A horn sounded and the men on foot, the highland and island warriors, along with the bowmen and slingers advanced. I let them cover fifty paces and, as the Scottish bowmen nocked an arrow I shouted, "Now Aelric!"

"Draw!"

"Shields!" My knights and men at arms swung their shields around.

Aelric's archers were in two blocks. Their arrows soared and even when the first flight reached their apex then the second flight followed. The lines stopped. The highland and island warriors held shields up or sheltered beneath a neighbour's shield. Arrows cracked and thudded into willow. The Scottish slingers and bowmen had no protection. Two arrows and a stone thudded into my shield. I heard a stone ping off Samuel's helmet but none was hurt.

Samuel said, "They should have aimed at the horses. They would have had more success."

Five further flights followed and then I heard a Scottish horn and they pulled back out of range of our archers.

"They fall back!" I saw that there was a line of dying and dead. Wounded men crawled or were helped back to the stakes. The knights had not come forward. They had lost enough already to us and were saving what remained.

"Aye, lord! Change bowstrings."

James asked, "And now we wait?"

"It is neither exciting nor glorious but they cannot raid. Had your uncle sent more knights and men at arms then this might have been easier. We could have charged them and ended this. I dare not risk the handful of men we have. Robert of Howden hurt us yesterday."

I decided to have the men dismount. The archers were our guarantee that they could not catch us unawares. Our squires brought us food and water for our horses. The stream the Scots were using was not large. I spied it as it left the woods. We could have fouled it but that would be unnecessary. It was not large enough to keep them supplied for long. I now knew why they had been so keen to raid. They needed ale as well as food. I spied, on the headland, twenty cattle they had taken and a dozen sheep. They would feed upon the sheep. I also saw a huddle of women and children; slaves.

Leaving my horse with Thomas of Piercebridge I walked to Aelric. "Let us see if we can spur them to a fight and hurt them a little more. When we mount, advance your archers and send ten flights into their ranks. We will open lines and allow you through. If they do not attack then we will wait until dark and then return to the castle."

The Princes' Revolt

"Aye lord."

He went to his archers and I walked down my knights and men at arms giving them the same message. "When Aelric and his men fall back then open our lines."

We mounted and Aelric and his men walked fifty paces in front of us. The Scots who had shields raised them. My archers could, with a following wind and fresh strings, send an arrow more than three hundred paces. The wind was not that strong but I watched as they pulled back and each archer sent ten arrows so quickly that the Scots must have thought they were bewitched. The arrows reached further into the camp. There men walked around thinking they were safe from attack. They wore neither helmet not arming cap. I watched as one knight, racing to get his shield was struck in the neck with an arrow. Horses were hit. Two became so maddened that they galloped through the camp tearing tents from the ground. Even as the horns in the camp sounded my archers were racing back. Their faces reflected their joy. We moved our horses apart and the archers scurried through. We closed ranks as the Scots, enraged and angered, ran at us.

I pulled up my spear and lowered my spear, "Charge!"

Aelric and his archers were already sending arrows overhead. They were no danger to us but they caused confusion amongst those trying to get to grips with us. I spied a French man at arms. He and his comrades were protecting the knight who charged at James de Puiset. The French man at arms was good but I was better. I flicked his shield away and rammed my spear into his thigh. I tore the head out sideways and so much blood spewed that I knew it was a mortal wound. A Scottish knight suddenly found himself face to face with me and he rammed his spear at my head. A head inside a helmet is the smallest of targets. As I punched with my shield I ducked my head and the spearhead scraped and rasped off my helmet. My spear, thrust almost blindly, took him in the chest. His dying hands clasped the spear and his body took it from my hands. Drawing my sword, I hacked at the back of a man at arms who was fleeing the battle. I saw that it was a Frenchman and that he was following his knight. The arrows continued to rain upon the Scots. I knew that we could not continue this for too long. I was about to sound withdraw when the Scottish horn sounded three times and they fell back.

"Pull back."

As we walked our horses backwards, keeping our shields towards our foes I saw that there were empty saddles. We had lost men. One of the horses belonged to James de Puiset. When we reached the place where we had first fought I saw one of the healers kneeling next to him.

"How is he?"

"Lucky, Earl. The axe which hit him struck his helmet first and then his shoulder. He will recover but it will be some days until he can ride and fight again."

I turned Goldie and looked at the Scottish camp. They were pulling back to the headland. They now respected the skill of my archers. The wounded and dead were taken back to the castle. Our numbers were depleted. Jean of Angers would never see his home in Anjou again. We waited and, as the sun dropped lower in the sky I decided that we could return to Bamburgh. With our archers before us we headed home.

Robert of Howden came to me, as we ate in the Great Hall. "Now I see what you meant, Earl. I misunderstood your commands."

"Then the next time ask for clarification."

As we were discussing our plans for the next day a dusty messenger burst in. "Earl William, I come from the Sheriff. He will be with you in the mid-morning tomorrow."

I banged the table in delight. "Then we have them. We will rise early and, when the Sheriff arrives we will end this and then relieve Norham.

When I was woken, by Ralph, before dawn it was with the news that the Scots had decamped. They were heading north. They would escape us!

"The sentries heard movement, lord, but when it did not draw close to the walls then they thought it was just preparations for the day."

I gave him a wry smile, "Our sentries would have woken us." He nodded. "Are our preparations made? Is the war gear packed?"

"Aye lord, but we are down to one spear for each of us."

"Then I will have to use it well!"

Chapter 12

De Vesci was most apologetic when he arrived. "We came as quickly as we could but the coast road is not made for such traffic."

"I fear that the delay may have helped our enemies. I will take my men and the men of Durham. I would keep our swords in their backs."

The Sheriff did not look happy. "We will follow but we have men on foot."

"Just so long as you are behind us then we will try to discomfit the Scots as much as possible." I turned, "Edward and Edgar, ride directly to Norham. Let me know what awaits us."

"Aye lord."

"Can I come with you, lord?"

"No, James. You are wounded and would slow us up." The Bishop's nephew looked unhappy to be left behind.

Once again, my men, more experienced than the men of Durham, were ready to move first. We had spears already and each of us rode our best horses. I did not wait. The knights of the Palatinate could catch us up. I had the squires and our servants bring the horses and the baggage at the rear. I left our three wounded men at arms and two of Aelric's archers as guards. The rest of us rode hard. The Scots had a start. They would be slowed by the men on foot but the Scottish men of the highlands and the islands could move almost as quickly as horses. The difference would be that when we caught them they would be tired and we would not.

We found the first Scots just ten miles up the road at West Kyloe. They had been carrying wounds and could not continue. One was dead and the other two would not last long. Their fellows had not given them a warrior's death and neither would we. Having caught up with the rear I was anxious to make them aware that they were being followed. We hurried north knowing that Norham was less than fourteen miles away. There was flatter ground towards Duddo and we saw the tail end of their

The Princes' Revolt

army. As I had expected it was their men on foot. The knights and horsemen could be seen further north. We would not catch them before Norham but we would catch those on foot.

Duddo was a small settlement with, perhaps six houses and farms. It was uninhabited. The Scots had seen to that. The rear guard must have realised that we would catch them and they began to deploy in the huts. If they could hold us off until nightfall then there was a chance that they could escape in the darkness. They had more chance of that than being caught in the open by horsemen. Even as we approached them I saw them building barricades between the houses. We could have delayed but that would only have enabled them to make their defences even stronger.

"Samuel, take Padraig, Richard and half of the men at arms ride to the west of the huts and attack there. Aelric close to within bowshot. The rest of you with me." I knew it meant I only had one knight for support, Sir Morgan, but I had John of Chester, Henry son of Will and my best men at arms. Even as we headed east I saw the knights of Durham labouring down the road. They had almost caught up with my squires and their horses.

We cantered to the east. We had to cross fields which had already been cleared of crops. The ridge and furrow made for an unpleasant motion. I headed for the trees I had spied from the road. They would, briefly, mask our intentions. As we passed the trees and turned to face west I saw that we were riding across common grazing land between two stands of trees. Even as we turned to form line I saw faces in the woods. The villagers of Duddo were taking shelter there until the Scots had gone.

The Scottish warriors had managed to build barriers facing south but they were improving them to the east and west. I led my line of twenty men across the grazing land. Our hooves thundered. Once we cleared the woods to our left I saw Aelric and his archers begin to send arrows into the cluster of huts. There was no point in riding boot to boot. Alf was to my right and John of Chester to my left. Next to him was my wild man, Henry son of Will. When we were forty paces from the huts I lowered my spear. Those on the far right of our line would be able to attack behind the defences. The Scots had kept the northern exit clear. I saw that one of the barriers they had constructed was made of three wicker baskets. Four men with swords sheltered behind them. Goldie was a better jumper than any other horse I had ever owned. I spurred her and we leapt in the air. As I soared above the men who were trying to avoid

Goldie's hooves I stabbed down with my spear and hit one of the Scots in the back. Goldie's trailing leg clattered into a Scot and smashed his head to a pulp. As we landed I pulled back my spear and rode at a Scot sheltering behind a shield which was too small to be effective. He punched it at my spear. He deflected the spearhead into his shoulder. He fell clutching the spear which had caused the mortal wound.

Ahead of me, I saw Samuel and my other men. They had not jumped the barrier. They were spearing the men sheltering behind. I saw that Sir Morgan had also failed to jump the barrier but he was spearing men like fish in a barrel. Roger of Bath had led men from the north and, as I turned I saw Henry son of Will. "Henry, with me!"

"Aye lord." He rammed his spear through a Scot who was trying to hamstring his horse. Drawing his sword my wild man gave a feral scream and we rode at the Scots holding off my son. Hearing our hooves some men turned. Samuel and his horsemen were beyond the barrier but we were within. Some tried to run. Four tried to face Henry and me. I rode Goldie at one and leaned to strike at the one to his left. I felt a blow on my shield and then my sword first bent and then broke a Scottish sword. When the blade broke my sword bit into his neck. I wheeled Goldie around as wild Henry swung his sword and took first one Scottish head and then a second. He did not even seem to notice that he had been wounded in the leg. The last of the four was caught out by my manoeuvre and my sword bit into the back of his skull and took off the top of his head.

It was the last act for my archers and my men at arms had slain so many that the few survivors who fled across the fields would not be a threat. I reined in. "Henry, you are wounded. Get it seen to!"

"It is nothing lord!"

"Get it seen to! The healers are with the squires!"

Robert of Howden rode in with the knights of Durham. "We seem fated to be late." I said nothing for he was right. "Do we carry on the pursuit while you see to your men?"

I shook my head. "The horsemen will be at Norham now. We have done what I intended. There were two hundred men here. That is two hundred less for us to fight. The ones we did not kill or wound will flee across the Tweed and head home. They will have no heart left for a fight. We await William de Vesci. Our horses have done well. They need to rest."

The Princes' Revolt

We had our wounded tended to by the healers. We had lost another man at arms. Red John would be a hard man to replace. His horse had done for him when he had tried to jump the barrier. A Scot had hewn the horse's legs. Red John had broken his neck but his dying horse had broken through the barricade and the rest of my men had avenged him.

By the time the Sheriff and his forty knights had arrived we had food and we had shelter and Edgar and Edward returned from Norham. "We are less than four miles from Norham lord. There were another two hundred warriors on foot who escaped you. They have joined those besieging the castle." Edgar was good with numbers. "Some of the knights did not stay at the siege lines. They rode to Berwick. We did not follow."

"You have done well. What are the siege works?"

"They have dug a ditch around the castle. It looks to us as though they have attempted to divert the river."

"It failed?"

He nodded, "It is a damp ditch. Before you ask lord, there are no defences facing south."

That was all I needed to know. "Then go and eat. I have plans to make."

I had worked with William de Vesci before. He was a good knight and knew his business. As the King's representative in the north east of the land he had a large area to control. I saw that he had brought another twenty archers. They were not mounted but would be a welcome addition. Even better were the five thousand arrows he had brought on wagons. He had fifty men at arms. I saw that he had brought half of his garrison from the New Castle. He was taking the threat seriously.

"I would have come sooner had you asked, Earl."

"Until I reached Bamburgh then I did not know the size of the threat. I sent as soon as I did."

He seemed happy with my explanation, "And so our plan; what is it?"

"Simple; we have thinned their ranks of knights and men at arms. Some have gone to Berwick. I have no doubt that they will bring reinforcements but they do not know about you and your men. We strike in the morning before their reinforcements can reach Norham. My scouts report no defences to the south."

He nodded, "You did not bring many knights when you came north, Earl William."

The Princes' Revolt

"No, for I did not wish to leave the valley unguarded. We have, in times past ridden north and my people have suffered." I lowered my voice, "We are doing the Bishop a favour and I know not why. He sends less than sixty knights north yet it is his castle we save!"

He laughed, "Aye I noticed that and yet his nephew is here."

"His nephew is nothing like him and I suspect that he has been dumped at Norham to keep him out of the Bishop's way!" We sat and looked at the campfire for a while. "There is something else, Sheriff. The French are involved. We have found evidence of French knights. That is more sinister than a chevauchée across the Tweed."

"Then how about this as a strategy, Earl. The next time you suspect there is a raid you send a rider to me. It is but thirty-five miles to my castle. With a change of horses, a rider would be there in less than half a day. Like you I am not worried about the Scots but the French are something else." We spent some time working out how we might work together. When we were agreed her said, "Yet, Earl, it still comes down to Hugh de Puiset and his lack of backbone."

"I think I have the solution to that problem. He has set a precedent, albeit without his knowledge for he is in London; he has allowed me to lead his knights. They are like rough clay and need work but the ones I have here might be moulded into an army which could aid your knights and mine. If he chooses to delegate then I will use that delegation to our advantage."

We rose at dawn and, leaving the servants in Duddo, we rode towards Norham. I counted on the fact that the Scots would assume I just had my men and the men of Durham. They might reinforce from Berwick and so I sent all of our archers west to cross the Tweed and wait in ambush for any reinforcements who might ford the river at Norham. It meant we were attacking with just horsemen. The men the Sheriff had brought who had no horses would be held as a reserve. They had marched a long way. We rode beneath the Sheriff's banner, my banner and the banner of the Bishop of Durham. The Scots would know, as soon as they saw them, that we had been reinforced. We were seen from a mile away and immediately we caused a stir. They began forming their men into three blocks. The men who fought on foot were in the centre beneath the banner of Dunbar. The two other blocks were made up of a mixture of knights and hobelars. My father had often used complicated battle plans. I remembered the battle of Herbault where he had totally outwitted the French and the rebels by switching knights from one flank to another. I

The Princes' Revolt

could not divine a clever approach to this battle. The Scots were arrayed with the woods anchoring their right flank and the ditch around the castle their left. Without a large number of experienced men who could work their way through the woods then we had no choice but to charge in three lines.

I talked through my plan with the Sheriff. Samuel was next to me, "Recall the archers and send them through the woods, father."

"If I had more then I would but the archers are the only ones who can stop the Scots from being reinforced. We know not when the men of Berwick will reach us. Sheriff, you and your men form the left flank, Robert of Howden, you and your men will be the right flank and I will have my men at arms and household knights in the centre. God be with us!"

We formed our lines and the Scots waited. The ones who had been at Bamburgh would be looking for our archers and the dismounted men at arms. There would be doubt in their minds. Ralph of Sadberge had the horn and Thomas of Piercebridge the banner. They rode just behind me and in front of the men at arms from Durham and the New Castle.

"Ralph, sound the horn, for God and King Henry!"

The men chorused, "For God and King Henry!"

We walked our horses. I was riding Goldie. I might have preferred a warhorse but I had made the decision not to bring them. Our spears all had pennants on them and they fluttered in the breeze. I heard the Scottish horns and they stood to. The men in the centre, those on foot would be filled with fear. In such a battle as this their horsemen would desert them and they would charge our flanks. The men on foot would be facing me, the son of the bane of the Scots. Those who had been at Bamburgh would have told them of the way we had slaughtered them when we had fought at their camp. I raised my spear. Ralph sounded the horn and we began to canter. The ground was shaking. Our hooves sounded like thunder. The Scots had a decision to make. When did they attack us? If they waited to take our charge stationary then they would die. I saw helmets turn as they looked to Lord Dunbar. I could see him now. He was flanked by French knights, two of them. One pointed towards me. I began to hope that the French, in their desperation to get at the Earl of Cleveland would make their knights attack me! When their horns sounded and they moved forward I saw that they had done just that. They were converging on me. It was a disastrous mistake. They would take the men on foot out of the battle and they would expose

The Princes' Revolt

themselves to an attack in the flank from my knights. Lord Dunbar and his advisers remained where they were. We were one hundred and fifty paces from them. I took a chance and I gambled. If we increased speed then they would match ours but we were already travelling faster. If we galloped, with luck, we could strike their men on foot before their horsemen could get up to speed and hit ours.

"Ralph, sound the charge!" In every battle, my father and I had ordered the charge we had been within a hundred paces, often closer. I could see that it affected the Scots. The horn sounded and they went from the walk to the charge. They were not ready and they had an uneven line. I would be reliant on Robert of Howden and William de Vesci but I was confident that they would be resolute. I saw the Scots trying to get at me. It would be a close-run thing but, as I spurred Goldie again and she leapt forward I was confident that we would hit the men on foot and, more importantly, they would not see us coming.

The knights struck my men at arms first. My household knights and I hit the surprised Scottish foot warriors. My spear struck one in the cheek and he reeled. He was a big man and as he fell he created a gap. Using my knees and Goldie's natural intelligence I guided Goldie into the gap, spearing a surprised Scot in the chest as I did so. As I was striking down the man I killed pulled the spearhead from his own body and I was able to pull back and stab once more. The front rank had had spears and shields. Some even had helmets. Now we were fighting men with either a spear or a sword and no shield. I broke through, having slain two Scots in rapid succession.

Reining in I turned. As I did so I saw that the knights from Berwick had arrived but were prevented from crossing the river by my archers who used the cover of the trees to pick them off. We had little time for eventually they would force a crossing and then we would be outnumbered.

"Samuel, Alf, Richard, Padraig, with me!"

I turned Goldie and rode back into the fray. I was no longer using my horse's speed I was selecting enemies who posed a threat to the rest of our horsemen. I saw one Scot wearing a short mail hauberk with a helmet on his head. He was swinging a war hammer. Even as I watched the war hammer connected with a man at arms' horse. The horse fell, killed instantly. As the Scot raised his war hammer to impale the man at arms with the spike I rammed my spear between his shoulder blades. The grateful man at arms leapt to his feet and grabbing the warrior hammer

The Princes' Revolt

from the dying man's hands he swung it around his head. Two Scots fell immediately. Samuel and my knights were also reaping the rewards of breaking through the enemy lines. Attacked on two sides many of the Scots failed to protect against either attack.

I wheeled Goldie around. Lord Dunbar and the two French knights were with the banners. "Cleveland! With me! Ralph sound the charge! Thomas keep my banner close."

With three knights close by me and our squires in close attendance, we rode towards Lord Dunbar. We had already cleared the field of living warriors and our horses picked their way through the dead and the dying. We could not gallop; our horses were too tired and so we rode together. Miraculously my last spear was still intact. The knights were too busy watching the battle unfold and we made it to within thirty paces before we were noticed. Lord Dunbar tried to flee with his standard bearer. If the standard fell then they would have lost. The two French knights rode at me but Samuel and Alf spurred their horses extracting the last burst of speed. Two spears crashed into two French shields and Thomas and I, along with Ralph, were through. Lord Dunbar was slow to turn his horse and I was gaining on him. I did not want him dead, I wanted his surrender. As I neared the Scottish lord I rammed my spear into the hamstring of his left leg. His scream sounded like that of a vixen. While he fell from his horse Ralph's sword was at the standard bearer's throat. He lowered the standard and Thomas threw it to the ground.

"Ralph sound the horn! We have won!"

Turning I saw that the two French knights lay dead. They had not surrendered. My son and Sir Morgan had shown their skill. The French squires were nowhere to be seen. It as a pity for I would have liked to question them. I pointed my spear at the prostrate form on the ground. "Your standard has fallen, Lord Dunbar. Do you surrender?"

His standard-bearer leapt to the ground and began to bind his leg. The Scot nodded. "I surrender but I curse your family!"

I laughed and handed my spear to Thomas. "Insults merely add to the ransom demands. Watch him, Thomas and Ralph. Samuel, Alf, come with me. Bring the Scottish standard. There was still fighting. Men who had their backs to us had not seen the fall of Lord Dunbar. When we neared the fighting, I took off my helmet and, standing in my stirrups shouted, "Hold! Lord Dunbar has surrendered! See I have the standard."

Men's heads turned and when they saw me, flanked by my knights, holding the standard, they lowered their weapons. One knight saw me

The Princes' Revolt

and turned back to continue fighting with William de Vesci. The Sheriff was angered at the flagrant disregard for the rules of war. He blocked the blow from the sword with his shield and brought his war axe to split the knight's head and helmet in two. Men began to cheer.

Long after the battle people said that the victory was due to the heroic charge of the knights of the valley. That was not true. There were too few of us. The victory came because three conroi of knights joined together and fought as one and my archers had done something few other men on foot had done. They had defeated a column of mounted knights.

Samuel, Alf and I turned our horses and with William de Vesci we headed for the castle. The gates opened and Sir Richard Bulmer, bareheaded, rode from the castle to greet us. As he neared us he patted his horse's head. "It has been many days since she has had the opportunity to ride. We thank you gentlemen for allowing us to do that!"

I found myself smiling. I suppose you needed a wry sense of humour to be here at the furthest point from the King of any. "You are welcome Sir Richard. We will not impose upon your hospitality. We will camp here this night and then return to Bamburgh until reparations are made and ransoms are paid. Do you need anything?"

He nodded, "Fresh meat and, if you have it, ale."

"That will be part of the reparations. Samuel, go and fetch Lord Dunbar and his standard-bearer. Do you have a healer?"

"Aye and a good one too."

"Then if he stitches up the Scot we can take him back to Bamburgh."

I dismounted as did all but Sir Richard. Our horses had been the heroes of the day and they deserved a rest. When Lord Dunbar arrived, he was pale but his leg was no longer bleeding. His standard-bearer was no youth. He was a man grown.

"Standard-bearer."

He raised his head up proudly, "I am James, lord of Galloway and Lord Dunbar's son."

I nodded, "You surrendered and as such you and your father belong to me. Here are my ransom demands for the two of you. I want ten head of cattle and six barrels of ale delivering by nightfall. In addition, I will have a thousand crowns for the two of you. There will be demands for the other knights we have captured."

Lord Dunbar raised his head, "You do not wish a treaty?"

I laughed, "Why? You never keep them. Your word is like the wind, it blows one day and disappears the next. Let us just say that if you come south again then we will deal with you as harshly but we will increase the reparations each time until Scotland is bled dry. It is your choice. You might advise your King to choose his alliances more prudently. He has been used by the French."

The two of them looked at each other and then at me. Lord Dunbar said, "This has nothing to do with King William. We did this of our own volition."

I laughed, "Of course you did and the French knights my son and knight slew just happened to be in Scotland admiring the scenery. I am not a fool, Dunbar, and you would be advised to remember that." I turned to Lord Galloway. "Is that acceptable? Do I have your word that you will return to Bamburgh with the ransom?"

"You do and the cattle and ale will be here by nightfall. I would not have my father go hungry." I nodded and he rode away.

Sir Richard rose up to me. "If Lord Dunbar gets any food it will be the tripes and the offal! Damned Scotsmen! Robbers and bandits every one."

The Bishop had chosen a good constable for this outpost of the Palatinate.

The battlefield took some time to clear. We had captured many Scots who were not worth ransom. They were disarmed and set to clearing the battlefield. The English dead were buried in the churchyard of the small settlement which had grown by Norham Castle. The Scots were burned. The survivors of the battle were then sent on their way. They marched disconsolately across the ford of the Tweed. They were not happy and their burning eyes told me that they had not finished fighting the English.

The next day we set off south with our captured knights and wagons filled with weapons, standards and treasure. Twenty warhorses had been captured. I took six and the other fourteen were divided between the Sheriff and Robert of Howden. As we headed back down the road to Bamburgh I detected a change in Robert of Howden. He had learned from the experience. As he said, when we neared Bamburgh, "I will not wait to be ordered to follow you north next time, lord. I will volunteer. We have lost knights but that was because they were not good enough. We need to practise our art. Most of us gained our spurs and then thought that was all there was to being a knight. This has been a valuable lesson for us."

William de Vesci said, "It is unlikely that the Scots will raise their heads for some time, Howden."

The Princes' Revolt

I shook my head, "Do not be too sure, Sheriff. This was King William's chevauchée. He was not present but he was behind it. He was testing our defences. Those men we released hate the English. They will follow again. They are fools but they are brave fools. They think they can win. If you wish some advice from one who fought in the crusades then this is it. Do not relax your vigilance. The Seljuk Turks have been defeated by Christians many times but they come back for more. The Scots are the same. The moment we relax our vigilance then they will pour through this land."

Robert of Howden said, "Then how can we stop them?"

"The Sheriff and his lords need to make their castles stronger. Bamburgh, as we have seen is strong but what of the others? Is the New Castle strong enough? What of Alnwick and Prudhoe? I task you with that Sheriff. This was a probe. He has seen that this is too strong a place to attack. He will find another route to England." I turned to Robert of Howden. "To answer you lord, I will advise the Bishop to have a bigger garrison at Norham. I will write to the King and ask him to increase the men Richard of Bayeux has at his disposal. The harbour is under used. We can send men by sea from the New Castle and Hartness. That would be a way to reinforce the garrison in times of war."

William de Vesci reined in as we passed through the gates of Bamburgh. "I can see that you are like your father, Earl. You think beyond your last battle and anticipate the next war."

He did not know it but that was the greatest compliment he could have paid me.

James de Puiset had recovered. He sought me out before we left when all the ransoms had been paid. I was anxious to return home for we had spent two months in the north. "Earl William I would serve you as a knight."

"And I would have you, gladly but you are a knight of the Palatinate. Your uncle may have something to say about that. if he gives you permission then you can be a household knight but there will be neither manor nor income."

"I care not. I have much to learn and you are the man to teach me."

I liked James and I wondered if the Bishop would agree or not.

Chapter 13

We managed a peaceful year, at least in the north. King Henry continued to allow my father to remain at home in Stockton. He recovered from his wound completely although Brother Peter was insistent that the Warlord never returned to war. I think my father was happy about that, albeit secretly. He was old but until the Empress had died he had not looked it. Since her death and his wounds, he now looked his age. What he craved were grandchildren but neither Ruth nor Eleanor showed any signs of bearing children. My wife was philosophical about the whole thing. "Jehovah will send them children, in his own time. You men want your women to be with child giving you young warriors! Let Ruth and Eleanor enjoy their husbands and their homes. Both are young and there is time enough for them to bear children."

Life in Stockton and my valley returned to the peaceful ways we had enjoyed in the years after the civil war. We had time to train our squires. Simon and Thomas of Piercebridge needed the skills which only Ralph of Bowness could give them. They could ride but the former Varangian Guard could teach them how to kill with a sword. It seemed unlikely that we would need to go to war again any time soon. A year, almost to the day after our victory at Norham, a messenger arrived by ship. It was Sir Richard Fortescue, who was one of King Henry's household knights. I had a sinking feeling in the pit of my stomach. A messenger from King Henry was rarely a good thing. He carried with him a small chest.

Sir Richard was a good knight. He was not a courtier. He was a warrior who had gained his spurs in Ireland with King Henry. That alone made my father and I listen to him. "The King would like your lordships to come back with me to London. He has need of your counsel."

I saw my father's shoulders sag. I asked, "Just my father and me? He does not need my knights?" If he did not need my knights then we would not be needed for war.

The Princes' Revolt

Smiling Sir Richard said, "There is no war looming if that is what you mean, Earl William, he needs your advice." He lowered his voice but there were just the two of us in the room with him. "To speak candidly, the King is having problems with his sons. I can say no more. It is just advice he seeks and then you can return here to the north." He opened the chest and took out a seal. It was similar to the one worn by my father. "As a reward for your service last year against the Scots, Earl William, King Henry makes you Earl Marshal. With it comes the power to command all the knights and lords who live north of the Tees and south of the Tweed. You are now lord of the north. With it comes the income from all of the lands which border the Tees."

That was an incentive. The lands to the south of the Tees paid their income to York. I guessed that the Archbishop was still grateful to both myself and the King. It was a bribe to ensure that I headed south with Sir Richard. My father looked pleased but it did little to increase that which I already had. My father seemed to read my thoughts. "At least this way you do not have to ask the Bishop for his men. You can order them."

The Bishop of Durham had agreed that James could serve me. I think he was pleased to have the encumbrance taken from him. He gave his nephew a warhorse and mail. James had brought with him a squire, Henry of Auckland. Even so the Bishop and I still had an uneasy relationship. Perhaps the seal would be a good thing.

I nodded, "We cannot leave until the morning tide. I will have a room prepared for you and I will tell my wife." I left Sir Richard to speak with my father. They knew each other.

Although Rebekah would understand she would not be happy. I found her speaking with Alice and John, my steward. "My father and I have been summoned to London."

As there were others close by she controlled her feelings and her face. "Will you be away long, husband?"

"I know not but I hope it will be brief. The King wishes advice."

"And he has no one closer than two knights three hundred miles away?" Her words were laden with sarcasm.

I was going to mention the new title but realised that would be the wrong thing to say. Money and power meant nothing to Rebekah. "Is there anything you wish from London?"

She gave me a wry smile, "Aye, my husband and his father safely returned."

Alice crossed herself and said, "Amen to that my lady."

The Princes' Revolt

I could not win. I sought out Thomas. He was in the outer ward practising with James de Puiset and his squire, Stephen. Simon, my father's squire, was watching and giving advice. I waited until they had finished their routine and said, "Thomas, Simon, you need to pack chests for my father and myself. We sail on the morning tide for London. The King wishes to speak with us."

Thomas asked, "Will we need horses, lord?"

"I have been promised that there will be no war. Leave the helmets and shields here too."

The two hurried off. James came over. He sheathed his sword, "Lord, I would deem it an honour if my squire and I could accompany you. I have learned much already and a visit to London could only add to that."

Since he had joined us James and Henry of Auckland had worked diligently to become part of my household. He deserved the opportunity. "It will be dull. Court is not what you think. It is full of backstabbing politicians who are only out for themselves."

James smiled, "Then I ought to see how the Earl of Cleveland deals with such people. I beg you to let us come. Your son and your other knights are married. I am the only bachelor knight. You will take servants, let us be your bodyguards."

"We should not need them but if you are willing to suffer the ennui then come."

I was actually happy to have the company. Samuel would have come but my son and his wife were still trying to have a child. It would be unfair to drag him away from her.

The year and a half my father had spent away from Henry and the politics of England and Normandy had done him good. He looked healthier and he was back to his old self. He knew, as we all did, that his days as a warrior were gone. Although his chest had healed he had had a poor winter when the damp made him cough and he was confined to a bed for ten days.

As we headed south James probed Sir Richard about the court. My father and I watched our landslip by as we tacked and turned our way around huge bends in the river. My father pointed to the bend we had just come around. It was close to the manor of Norton. The gap between the two sides of the river was less than three hundred paces. "You know, William, I have often thought that if we made a cut between the two sections of the river we could save hours on this journey to the sea." I nodded. "Since I have been home I have looked at my land with new eyes. I have spent less than a third of my life here and yet it is my home. There is so much I could have done had time and the needs of the realm allowed."

"Perhaps, when we return, we could devise a way to do this. We have the labour. Our ranks are full and idle hands make for mischief."

"I should like that. It would be good to work together to make our valley stronger. You will have more coin soon. The lands to the south of the river are rich fiefs. The Archbishop must think highly of you to gift them to you."

"It might have been a bribe from the King. Perhaps they are also intended for you. We keep the Archbishop's lands safe."

"No, my son, take nothing away from yourself. This is a reward for a task completed which few other men could have achieved. That you make it look easy is a compliment to you."

I noticed that the motion of the ship was changing as we entered the tidal waters. Soon the air would be cooler. I waved over Harold One Eye, my servant. "Have Wilfred fetch a cloak for the Warlord. We will soon be at sea."

My father stared north, towards the sands where the seals basked. "I wonder if the King thinks that the problem of Scotland is gone. I hope that he does not wish you to go with him abroad again."

"Neither do I. The problem of Scotland is still there. We now have a plan in place to deal with William should he decide to attack but that is dependent upon me being in the valley. If the Scots attack while I am serving the King then it could prove disastrous for us."

"If this is a problem with his sons then I would not worry overmuch. They are all young and we know that young men are sometimes reckless but they change."

I looked around and saw that he was studying me, "You are talking about me."

He smiled, "You were seduced at the court of Geoffrey of Anjou and your head was turned. We were lucky that King Henry did not have the same experience. His sons are without Eleanor. The Empress Matilda was always there at her son's side or if not then it was me or his uncle, Gloucester. They will emerge from this dark place and be better men for it. You were. You returned from the crusades a different man."

"But I was of your blood," I remembered the dark days in Normandy when I hunted, caroused, wenched and neglected my family. Worse I had disparaged my father and ignored his sage advice. I had been punished and done my penance. Perhaps he was right. The blood of Henry ran through the veins of young Henry, Richard and Geoffrey. John was still too young to be a rebel!

The ship was a basic one with little in the way of accommodation. The servants and squires were worse off than we four. We had a small cabin which we shared but they were in the hold. We learned much from Sir Richard despite his reluctance to tell us anything. We learned that Richard was spending more time with his mother in Aquitaine and that King Henry did not like it. Geoffrey was still unhappy about his lack of land. He was still just Count of Nantes and he wanted more. Young King Henry appeared to be the most rebellious of the sons. He wanted to be able to spend money and King Henry was, in my view, wisely withholding the treasury from him. He had the title but neither power nor influence. My father had told me that he thought making Young Henry joint king was a mistake and he was being proven to be right.

Sir Richard was more forthcoming about events away from the palace. "Ireland is now firmly under the King's control. De Clare and King Rory O'Connor, the High King, appear to have the island under their control."

"The castles helped then?" My father had been the one to suggest strategic sites for the castles.

"The Irish cannot fight against them. The Welsh are contained but the King thinks he needs castles there too." It begged the question of why he did not build them but I suppose he was preoccupied.

My father knew the right questions to ask, "And France? The Vexin?"

"They are still problematic, Warlord. King Louis fosters rebellion and resentment from across the border. He has tried to have important lords married off to the daughter of his leaders. There are rumours that he has employed hired killers to eliminate the leaders who are loyal to King Henry."

I asked, "Have any died?"

"Not yet and it is just a rumour."

My father nodded, "The rumour itself will be as successful as a killing. It is the fear of what might happen which will distract the loyal lords. The rebels will then be abler to gain power subtly."

This was depressing. "Then the King's lands in France are in a state of uncertainty?"

"Aquitaine and Anjou are not. For the moment Brittany is quiet. The rebels there have been dispersed but they need a Duke."

"And Constance is still too young to be wed."

The King had made what he had thought were good plans but they were unravelling a little.

By the time we entered the Thames estuary we had a better idea of the situation into which we were walking. James de Puiset had said little but when we were alone he confided in me that he found the whole experience fascinating. "My uncle sees himself as a man with power. Listening to Sir Richard I can see that, in reality, as Bishop of Durham he has little. You and the Warlord have more importance. Why else would he summon you to London?"

"There may come a time, James, when you have to choose between your uncle and me. That will be a test of your loyalties."

He laughed, "It will not. I know that you and your father work for England. My uncle works for himself. There will be no divided loyalties."

The river was a crowded and busy waterway. My river saw barely a ship every four or five days. Here the captain had to wait for the ships before us to move. The river also reeked of human and animal excrement. Waste was hurled into the river. There were no fishing ships on the Thames or if there were then no one bought the fish they caught. Each year the city sprawled further east and south. I was glad I lived in the north. There we would breathe the air and fish the river. It was no wonder that the King spent more time at Windsor than in London.

"The King is at the Tower, is he not?"

"Aye lord. He prefers Windsor but he needs to be close to his treasury and his counsellors. We are a rich kingdom now and it takes many officials to make it work."

I could not help smiling. At home we had just John and he might be aided by his father if it was a busy time.

Simon came along to me. "Will we be long in London lord?"

I looked at Sir Richard who shrugged, "I know not, why?"

Simon pointed at the river. "Brother Peter told me that the Warlord's chest and his breathing will become worse if he is close to pestilential water. This looks like a river which would make a healthy man ill. I would have him housed as far away from the river as we can manage, lord."

The Princes' Revolt

Sir Richard shook his head, "That might be difficult for the Tower is on this river."

Windsor was a healthier place and I said so, "Then I will ask the King if we can be housed at Windsor. The air there is cleaner."

Sir Richard looked at me as though I had spoken blasphemy. He did not know the relationship my father had with the King nor the one I had enjoyed. I had been a close friend of his father, Geoffrey of Anjou. Added to that was the fact that I did not care if I offended the King. He needed my father and me more than we needed him.

The King was not in the Tower. He was meeting with his '*curia regis*' at Westminster Hall. As we were heading for our chambers Thomas asked me, "Lord what is the curia regis?"

"It is just a royal counsel. The great officers and churchmen meet and advise the King. If we lived close then both the Warlord and myself would be there. Believe me I am glad that we live in the north for they are dull beyond words. I think the King finds them dull too but it is a way to govern and keep the great lords on his side. If there is trouble in his family then he needs as many lords on his side as he can get."

Sir Richard had managed to get my father a chamber as high up as he could. Simon made certain that the Warlord was as comfortable as possible. James de Puiset took everything in. This was his first time in London. He had not been there to swear an oath to the Young King Henry. I wondered about that. He was full of questions. My father knew more about the Tower than any. He had first visited it in the civil war when Princess Nesta was a guest of the first King Henry. My father was more patient than I would have been. He answered them all. I suppose it was his age although he managed to ascend the stairs easily.

The King arrived back in the late afternoon. I was showing James de Puiset the new buildings which had been erected by the King. King Henry frowned when he saw James, "Who is this lord?"

It was curt but the King had had a day of interminable talk with his counsel. It was to be expected. "This is James de Puiset. He is one of my household knights."

"De Puiset? The Bishop of Durham?"

"He is my uncle, Your Majesty."

A frown appeared on the King's face. "Sir James served with great distinction at the Battle of Bamburgh."

The King nodded, "Leave us." James flushed and left us. The King led me away from the sentries. "Forgive my brusque manner, Earl, but I am beset with enemies. Until I know him then I do not want him near me."

"I confess that I am uncertain why my father and I were summoned here. We are best used in the north."

"You are best used where I determine and right now that is London."

I stopped walking and faced the King. "You know me, King Henry, I served your father and I serve you. I speak my mind. That is my father's way and it is mine."

"Be careful, Earl. I have had a difficult morning."

"We have come as soon as you sent for us but my father is not a well man. The river here is bad for his health. He would be better served if our meetings were held in Windsor."

"You have a high opinion of yourself, Earl William if you think I would move my court to suit an old man."

"An old man who won your kingdom for you." He glared at me. "Then let my father stay there. Surely you cannot need his advice all of the time."

His face softened. "I sometimes forget that there are warriors who have stood shoulder to shoulder with me and fought off my enemies. They deserve the chance to be honest with me. The trouble is, William, that I cannot trust even my own family."

"My father and I are more than family, lord."

"You are right." He smiled and rubbed his beard. "This suits my purposes. We will leave for Windsor on the morrow. If the council wishes to speak with me then they can come there to find me. You are certain of this Sir James?"

I suddenly realised that I was not. "It will not be a problem to keep him from discussions. He came here as a bodyguard."

"And that is wise. Rumour has it that the King of France has killers at large."

"Templars?"

"Not this time. We interrogate every Templar who arrives in London. They may be in disguise but you can smell a Templar." He laughed, "Why am I telling you this? You were a crusader."

"We heard that you are to take crusade too."

He frowned and then changed it to a smile. He spoke conspiratorially, "Saying that you will take a crusade and travelling halfway around the world are two different matters. When my lands are

The Princes' Revolt

settled then I will take the cross." The King was a pragmatic man. He would go on crusade when he would reap the benefit.

We returned to the Great Hall. He waved a servant over, "Tell Sir Walter D'Amphraville that we will be moving the court to Windsor on the morrow."

The courtier must have been waiting in the anteroom for the King had barely poured a goblet of wine when he hurried in. "You wish to go to Windsor, Your majesty?"

"Aye, I do. Send a servant to let them know."

"But King Henry, why?"

It was the wrong thing to say and the King turned and glowered at him, "Because I command it!" The man hurried off. "I took him on as a favour to my son. He is the second son of a knight in Normandy with no prospects of a manor. I can see why. I give him until the end of the month and then he returns to Normandy."

We feasted and King Henry, now aware of my father's condition, was most solicitous. For his part, my father was in good humour. As much as he enjoyed being with his family he always enjoyed being close to the King. I saw something in his eyes I only saw when he looked at Samuel or Ruth and, occasionally, me. Perhaps it was because he had almost raised him. I knew, from personal experience, that Geoffrey of Anjou was not a good father. Once his sons were born then he ignored them until they could lift a sword.

Simon stayed close to my father anticipating his every need. I wondered at his training to be a knight. He seemed, to me to be more of a servant than a squire. Thomas and Ralph both had more skills and more experience in battle. When we returned north I would ask Simon if he was happy with his position. He had skills to be a knight; he had just neglected them of late.

It was not a long journey to Windsor and the King did not wait for baggage. We rode swiftly along well-maintained roads and he swept into the castle. This was Henry's royal hunting lodge as well as his castle and he was a frequent visitor. However even my father surprised when he was greeted, as we entered the hall, by a stunning beauty. No more than seventeen summers old, Ida de Tosny threw her arms around the King and kissed him. I thought he might have been embarrassed but he was not. He smacked her on the buttocks and said, "Go warm my bed! I have business with these lords."

The Princes' Revolt

I saw disappointment on my father's face. He remembered Geoffrey of Anjou. He, too, had had mistresses but he had been a little more discreet than King Henry.

The King turned to Sir James, "You and the squires see to the horses. I would speak with the two Earls privately!" Sir Walter D'Amphraville smirked and he stood patiently with Sir Richard Fortescue. "And you two can make yourselves scarce. Wait without. I need privacy."

Once alone my father asked, "What is amiss, Your Majesty. This is not like you."

He nodded, "I have missed your wisdom Warlord. I decided to give John three castles. He has nothing. I thought it inconsequential. First Geoffrey objected saying that he had had to work and to fight for his poor little fief of Nantes."

"But he will be Duke of Brittany one day. Has he no patience?"

"Apparently not, Earl William. And Henry has taken himself off to one of his castles in the north. He is unhappy too."

"But why?"

"Because Warlord, the three castles were in Normandy and belonged to him."

I said nothing but I thought that he had missed more than my father's wisdom. He had missed basic common sense.

"And you wish advice?"

"I have not yet finished. My wife and Richard plot to usurp me."

"Surely not, the Queen?"

"Aye Warlord, the Queen. I need more than advice. I need you to go to Aquitaine and to stop her."

I was shocked. I could see that my father was too. Neither of us knew what to say at first.

The King said, "My son is due to meet me in two days' time at Westminster. I need advice on how to deal with him and then I would have you two board ship and sail to Aquitaine to speak to the Queen."

"Speak to her?" My father's voice was laden with other unspoken questions. He and Henry had an understanding which was not enjoyed by many. The King seemed to be able to read between the lines of my father's words.

"I would have you bring her to me. I will be in Normandy. I know that Louis is behind all of this."

"You would have us kidnap the Queen?"

175

The Princes' Revolt

He looked at me. "She is my wife and the Queen but she is in danger of behaving in a treasonous manner. I am her husband and I would have her close to me."

"If Richard is with her then he might object."

The King sighed, "I have chosen you, Warlord, because of your unique position. You were the one who saved the Queen when she fled Louis. You were, albeit briefly, Richard's mentor. They will listen to you."

"And me?"

He turned to me and I saw the coldness in his eyes, "Your father is old; he needs someone to care for him. In addition, if it comes to war then you are the man who can defeat any of my enemies. Richard is just a boy!"

"And what forces are at my command? Surely you do not think that three knights and four squires with four servants can do what you ask?"

"Be careful Earl William. I have been patient with you but I am the king."

My father said, "Then behave like one! You ask us to risk our lives and to do the impossible. My son has every right to speak the way he does. Had we been warned we could have brought our men from the north. I am too old to be worried by your threats, Henry FitzEmpress. Whom do we use to perform this impossible task?"

I thought that Henry might strike my father. Had he done so then I would have started the great revolt there and then. As it was his fingers clenched and unclenched and then he smiled, "God but I have missed you Alfraed! You are the one man who I would allow to stand up to me." He drank some wine and I saw that his hand was shaking. The drink was to let his temper go. "I sent a message when I sent the ship for you. I used your William of Kingston. He has sailed to La Flèche. I have given Sir Leofric the authority to raise an army of loyal Angevins. He has archers and you know him. Is that good enough for you?"

"It will have to be."

"Good. Do not tell your squires or your knight what you are about until you are on the ship. There are many spies and traitors in my realm. You two I trust and there are few others in that position. Now I must leave you. I have a wench warming my bed."

Now I knew why he had agreed to come to Windsor. It was not for my father's health. It was to satisfy an itch in his breeks. He was a colder and more calculating man than he had been. The whole loss of temper had been an act. I did not like it.

When he had gone I poured my father some wine. It was as though the last couple of years had disappeared. He looked old once more. He drank some of the wine and said, sadly, "I am sorry about this William. This is my fault. I thought I had been a better teacher to him. I was wrong."

I shook my head, "It is not you. It is the blood he has from his father. He was the same."

He gave me a strange look and then sipped his wine. He seemed lost in his own thoughts. "Leofric is a good man. That, at least, is in our favour."

"We will have to send a message home. My wife will need to know." I stood. "I will tell the squires that we are to visit Sir Leofric."

My father smiled, "They are clever and will know that something is amiss."

"And they are loyal and will not ask too many questions. Sir James, on the other hand..."

"You do not trust him?"

"I thought I did but the King has planted seeds of doubt in my mind."

"William, you are as true a knight as any. Do not change now. You trusted him enough to allow him to come. Trust those feelings. Besides we need to keep him close. I agree with you, I do not believe that he is an enemy." He poured himself another goblet of wine and looked like a man who had lost everything. I knew not why.

The squires were not surprised when I said we were going to Anjou. Sir James was and that made me suspicious once more. "But why lord? I thought that when the King had done with us we would return home."

I decided to make light of it, "Regard this as part of your education. La Flèche is part of my father's fiefdom. You will enjoy the experience."

We returned to London two days' later. Young King Henry was already there. The King decided to show who was the real ruler by keeping him waiting. It was a mistake. It irritated and angered the Young King Henry. The King insisted that we accompany him. I knew not why for young Henry did not like either of us. We entered the Great Hall and I saw that the young King had surrounded himself with allies. Prominent amongst them were Robert de Beaumont, Earl of Leicester and Hugh Bigod, Earl of Norfolk. Both were powerful barons. I noticed that

The Princes' Revolt

William Marshal was not there. The knight was either showing great sense or he was keeping himself safe from the King's wrath.

The King sat on his throne. Young Henry sat on the throne next to his father's. Symbolically King Henry's was bigger. "Now, my son, have you reconsidered your position? Do you regret the harsh words which were spoken?"

"Harsh words? Is that what you call the truth now? Harsh words! You cannot give my castles away! I wish them back."

"But I can give them away. I made you King of England and not Normandy. They are Norman castles. As Duke of Normandy they are mine to give or take as it pleases me. Your brother, John has no lands. Would you have me give him English castles?"

"So long as they are yours then I care not." He pointed a finger at me, "Give him Stockton! The Earl of Cleveland could do with some of the air knocking out of his pompous body."

I said nothing but I could see that even High Bigod and Robert de Beaumont were uneasy with their young King's words. You did not upset the son of the Warlord of the North.

The King turned to me, "I apologise for my son, Earl. It is the people he associated with who have made him thus. You should be grateful to the earl, my son. He has just saved the north for us."

"I care not a fig about the north! The Scots can have it. It is a land without wheat nor vines. Do I get my castles back or not?"

The King turned and said, very slowly, "No, you do not. They are the property of your brother, John!"

Young Henry said nothing but he stood and walked from the hall. His allies followed him. I saw then that there were more than Leicester and Norfolk. The King sat for a while and said nothing. Then he stood. "That has given me an appetite! I hope that the Constable has laid on a fine fare for us."

Sir James had been a witness to the row and, as we headed to the outer ward to get some fresh air he said, "Did you expect that, Earl?"

My father smiled, "When it comes to kings and princes then any man who expects normal behaviour is a fool. A word of advice James. Keep your ears open and be discreet. There are dissemblers who will feign friendship to trap you. We are loyal to the King. Say nothing and do nothing which would put you or us in jeopardy!"

"You can trust me, Warlord."

The Princes' Revolt

My father laughed, "All that you have seen of me, James de Puiset, is an old man cosseted by an overprotective squire. When I was Warlord then I was a force to be reckoned with."

I smiled. "You still are, father!"

The feast was a good one and we were enjoying fine food when the door burst open and Sir Walter D'Amphraville rushed in. He knelt by the King. "My lord, your son has fled England. He has taken ship to the court of King Louis in France."

The King wiped his mouth and then emptied his goblet. He smiled, "Then you had better get hence and follow him, spy! If I find you in my court when I rise from this table then you will be executed." It said much that Sir Walter D'Amphraville did not object but rose and ran. The King said, "So it begins. Warlord, you and your son can leave on the morrow. Your ship awaits at Tilbury."

Chapter 14

After sending a rider north with the letter I had penned we travelled by horse to Tilbury. It was a faster journey than by the river and meant we did not have to wait for the tide. It was not the same ship we had travelled south in. It was a larger one and there were men at arms on board as well as archers. King Henry had sent the thirty of them as our bodyguards. It showed that the King was worried. He had told us that he would be following his son to Normandy. He must have feared this situation would arise for he had ordered the levy to be called up. This would be war. As he had told us, just before we left, "This is King Louis's opportunity. He has the King of England with him. My plan has failed. Worse it might have lost me my kingdom. I rely on you and, I suppose, on the skills you taught me. If I defeat my son then that will be a testament to your teachings, Warlord."

Once on board, we told the squires and Sir James what we had been commanded to do. For once the Bishop's nephew had nothing to say on the matter. I think he was impressed with the confidence the King had in us. The King had come to Tilbury with us and have given us more information. We now knew that the Queen was at Poitiers. We would have to travel through lands loyal to Eleanor of Aquitaine. I now saw why the King had chosen my father. He had a reputation as an honest warrior and the one who had fought for the Empress, her son and also Eleanor of Aquitaine. I was there to be the one who led men into battle; if it came to that.

The men at arms and the archers were unknown to me. I would need to be as close to them as to my own men. I had a short voyage to get to know them. After my father and I had spoken briefly with them to discover where they had fought we allowed them the rest of the voyage to prepare themselves for our journey south. I made certain that I spoke to each of them during the days we were at sea. The men we would rely

The Princes' Revolt

on the most were the ones whom Sir Leofric had gathered. They would the cutting edge to our sword.

"So, father, you know this land better than I do. What is our best course of action?"

"I only know it slightly better. However, I do know that if Anjou is loyal then Tours and Saumur, not to mention Chinon, will be safe places to cross the Loire. The Gascons are loyal to Eleanor." I nodded and looked east to the coast of Flanders. "Did you know that I met her when she was just twelve?" I remembered the story and I nodded. "She was a clever little thing, even then. I cannot believe that she would turn against her husband. She chose him over Louis! She brought more land to the marriage than he did. For him to publicly humiliate her by flaunting his mistresses at court would be something which was quite unacceptable. However, she is a clever woman. She is more intelligent than most of the men alongside whom I fought. She will listen to reason, I hope."

"And if not?" He remained silent. Neither of us relished the thought of taking a Queen by force. It was not in our nature but we both knew that it might come to that.

"Let us be optimistic. We persuade the Queen to come with us; then we head for La Flèche first and then Rouen?"

"That is where the King will be. Let us hope that there is no war already for that would make the journey across Maine even more fraught with danger. Young Henry is no leader... yet but Leicester and Norfolk are seasoned campaigners. Both had fiefs in Normandy and Maine. They could make life hard for the King."

This was not like my father. The King's behaviour had seriously upset him. I could not fathom the reason. We both knew that kings were, literally, a law unto themselves. The King's grandfather had done many things which had both surprised and disappointed my father and me. This disappointment seemed personal. Perhaps it was the years my father had invested in the King and his mother.

I turned to the squires and Sir James. "All of you are now considered to be our household knights. Along with Sir Leofric, you are the only ones on whom we can truly rely." I looked at Sir James as I spoke. "This will be a test for each of you." I saw Ralph and Simon straighten their backs. Within a year or so both could be knights. Thomas was the youngest of the squires but I saw a steely determination on his face. "You will sleep with a dagger close to hand. As you saw at court there are spies and traitors littered throughout the realm. I have no doubt that there will be more in the Duchy. Until we know more we trust no man and we let none close to the Warlord."

My father bridled, "I am not in my grave yet! I can defend myself!"

"I know father but you are not a pawn on this chessboard. You are a major piece. The King has put you in grave danger by sending you to do this. I know that you are the one man who might persuade the Queen but there are many of your enemies who would love to get their hands on you or, failing that, put steel in your back. Until we are safe in Stockton we get little sleep and we will be vigilant."

It took eight days to reach Angers. We would not have stopped there save that we saw Captain William with my father's ship. He was heading downstream. We hove to and hailed him. "I would have you go to Stockton, Captain William."

"Aye lord. I thought you might. You need men?"

I shook my head, "By the time they reached us it would be too late. Have Sir Harold increase the patrols to the north and tell my wife that we will return as soon as we can."

"Aye lord." He waved, "You take care, lord."

We were a family.

As we continued our slow journey upstream Sir James asked, "Earl William, why do you speak to the captain as though he is one of your men at arms or knights?"

I laughed and saw my father smile, "His family live in Stockton. His ship is the one which uses our river the most. He helps us and we help him. Your uncle's port of Hartness is easier to reach but Captain William is loyal to Stockton. Such loyalty should be rewarded."

My father said, "Another lesson for you James de Puiset. Look after all of your people and they will look after you."

When we reached it, La Flèche was like an armed camp. I recognised many of the banners. It took time to negotiate the other ships and I had time to count the banners. There were forty knights. I hoped that would be enough. Our delay in docking meant that Sir Leofric was able to join us. He and his son, Alfraed, were so similar that one could have taken them for brothers. Their faces however were not the smiling ones I had expected.

My father left the ship first. Leofric had been his squire and they embraced. "It is good to see you both but your faces are dark. What is amiss?"

The Princes' Revolt

"Geoffrey has fled Nantes and headed to Paris along with his brother Richard. They are gathering rebel lords close to the Vexin. The Counts of Flanders and Boulogne have invaded Normandy from the north. I am sorry to be the bearer of such dire tidings, Warlord."

My father turned to me, "It seems we have our work cut out for us, son."

I nodded, "We can do nothing about the north for we have a task to perform. The sooner we do it then the sooner we can go to the aid of the King. He will need us 'ere long. How many archers have you gathered?"

"We have fifty and they are all mounted. I told the knights I summoned that I only wanted mounted men. I do not think there is a spare horse in the whole of Anjou! I have horses for you." He looked behind me at Sir James.

"This is Sir James de Puiset. He is of my household." Sir Leofric said not a word but I saw questions in his eyes. "He can be trusted." He nodded. "We are in your hands now, Sir Leofric. Have you scouts ready to find the Queen?"

"We believe that she is still in Poitiers but the rumour is that she wishes to join her sons. She could have moved already to Mirebeau."

I looked at my father, "Then the King might be right, the Queen might be behind this."

I saw him frown, "We delay! We should go now." He looked at me. With the King here in France then this is the time when the Scots will rear their snake like heads!"

He was right. We had followed a King who had caused his own problems. Those problems would now hurt us!

It took time to disembark and to have our gear loaded on to horses. Our four servants were all ex-soldiers. They knew their business. With Sir Leofric's scouts ahead of us we took the road to Saumur. Our journey to Poitiers was less than a hundred miles. Even with mounted men that would take us two days. The good news was that Sir Leofric's scouts, Griff of Gwent and James the Short had spare horses and they would reach Poitiers in a long, hard day. The rest of Sir Leofric's archers formed the vanguard. We would not be surprised.

While we rode my father and I spoke with Sir Leofric and his son, Alfraed. "How is Brittany?"

Sir Leofric looked over his shoulder to make certain that none could overhear him save his own men at arms. "All the worse for Prince Geoffrey. He antagonises the other lords and barons. He tries to impose his will over them and yet he has no authority for he does nothing. He wants power but does not know what to do with it."

My father was astute. He read between the lines, "Then what you fear is rebellion."

"Aye Warlord. With King Henry assailed then those barons who bowed the knee when we fought in Poher, Rennes and Nantes will seize the opportunity to wrest the Duchy from the King. Duke Conan died. King Louis has demanded that as Brittany is a vassal of France the children should be in his care. Once he gets them then there will be no marriage for Geoffrey and the King will lose Brittany." He shook his head. "All those men we lost in that war would have died in vain."

My father regarded Leofric as another son. He patted his arm, "We are true knights. We are true to our word and our deeds are noble. We ignore those who are not. We will find the Queen and take her to the King. You and your son will return to La Flèche and you will guard your home. So long as your manor is safe then all will be well."

That set me thinking about Stockton. We had left it exposed. My son and my knights would have to do that which I could not. Was Samuel ready?

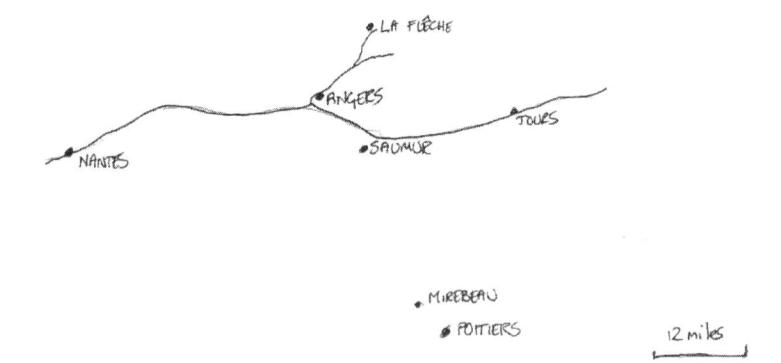

We passed Saumur and crossed the Loire. There was a manor at Angliers. My father knew the lord of the manor there. Although loyal to Eleanor of Aquitaine he was also loyal to my father and Duke Henry of Anjou, our King. Our men camped there and we stayed in his small castle.

The Princes' Revolt

Sir Jocelyn was of an age with my father. He was perhaps ten years younger but he looked the same age. They had fought in the wars against Blois. A landless knight, Angliers had been his reward from Eleanor and her husband. "Duchess Eleanor has called the muster. She has excused me the call as she knows my obligations to her husband. Warlord, this is a Gordian knot is it not?"

"It is, old friend. With luck, we can avoid bloodshed. It would sit heavily on my heart if I had to spill the blood of Gascons for they were ever loyal to us in our wars."

We left the manor with heavy hearts. Sir Leofric sent archers ahead to meet with Griff of Gwent. They had not been gone long when both our scouts and archers returned.

Griff of Gwent dropped from his horse, "Warlord, we have let you down. We headed for Poitiers and skirted Mirebeau. When we reached Poitiers, we discovered that the Queen had left for Mirebeau two days since. We found that she has since left Mirebeau too. She has taken the road to Chinon."

My father smiled, "Clever. That is one of her favourite castles. The Constable there is a friend of the Queen's. She can cross the Loire there with ease. How many men has she with her?"

"Fifty banners."

I turned to Sir Leofric. "Is there any way we can cut her off?"

"If we head north and east and ride with no regard to our horses then we should be able to find her. We take the road to Loudon. I know that she is a hardy lady but she will have women with her and will move slower than we."

My father counselled, "We want no bloodshed. Send your archers ahead to block the road south of Chinon. She knows the efficacy of your archers and she will not risk her knights."

As we cantered north and east I feared for my father. His chest might have been healed but he had seen almost seventy summers. This was not the journey for an old warhorse. We ate up the miles. With no archers ahead of us we followed Garth of Sheffield and Walter of Derby. Both were good men at arms and knew their business. It was the middle of the afternoon when we caught up with the baggage of the Queen. Whoever led the knights for Eleanor had made a grave misjudgement. There was no rear guard. The baggage was protected by servants.

The Princes' Revolt

As we galloped up the road they panicked and most abandoned the baggage. Sir Leofric shouted, "Alfraed, have some of the knights of Anjou take charge of the baggage."

"Aye, lord!"

I drew my sword, "Simon, watch the Warlord. James, guard the Warlord!" I spurred the warhorse which Sir Leofric had provided. There were knights ahead and I did not want to risk my father in a skirmish. This was not worth his death. Sir Leofric kept pace with me. We rode under Sir Leofric's banner. I had no helmet on my head and my surcoat was well known.

Ahead the knights of the Queen realised that something was amiss and they turned. Garth and Walter had swords drawn. Sir Leofric shouted, "Charge through them!"

I was aware of his men at arms galloping alongside us to protect our flanks. Garth and Walter knocked the three knights who tried to stop us from their horses. Our men at arms might not know how to win in a tourney but they knew how to fight. They rode to the side to allow Sir Leofric and I to power through on the backs of our horses.

I yelled, "Yield or we will kill you. I am the son of the Warlord."

My reputation won the day for us. That and the overwhelming numbers we had. The knights around the Queen could not defend her and they knew it. Eleanor had chosen a small escort to help her travel quickly. I saw her banner and her carriage. I also noticed that the knights ahead of her had stopped. As we neared I saw why. Our archers were spread across the road. The column was going nowhere. I reined in next to the carriage.

Eleanor's face was a mask of fury. "How dare you stop me in my own realm."

I heard hooves behind. I saw my father approaching. "My lady, it grieves me to do so but I am under orders from your husband, my lawful liege, to fetch you to him for your own safety."

My father reined in and dismounted. He held his arm up and the Queen dismounted from the carriage. She spread an arm around us, "Who is a danger to me save you?"

My father shook his head, sadly, "Yourself my lady." He pointed to the archers, "Tell your knights to stand down else they will be slaughtered to a man. You know their skill."

She nodded, "Alain, have the knights return to Mirebeau. It seems I will no longer need their services." As her Captain left to give the

The Princes' Revolt

command she looked sadly at my father, "Warlord, that it has come to this. Where did it go wrong?"

He shrugged, "I am sorry to say, my lady, where it always goes wrong, in a man's breeks but your sons are wrong to rebel against their father. You know that. All that he did was to give land to your youngest son. Is that a bad thing?"

She had no answer to that. I said, "Thomas of Piercebridge, take over from the driver. You can command the carriage."

Eleanor smiled and patted my father's hand, "If you had been my husband there would be no revolt."

"And you would not be Queen." He leaned in and said, quietly, "Even as a young girl you wanted to be Queen. Sometimes we wish for things which turn out not to be as attractive as we first thought. You and the Empress Maud both wished for power and were granted it. Were either of you happy?"

We headed north and took the road back to Angliers. We stayed overnight and then journeyed to Saumur. We stayed just one night at La Flèche before, with barely a handful of Angevin knights and the escort sent from England we headed to Rouen.

The Queen decided that she had enough of travelling at the speed of a carriage and, much to the chagrin of her ladies, insisted upon riding. I rode on one side of her and my father rode on the other. We talked. Rather she spoke with my father and I listened. I heard the hopes and dreams the Queen had had when she married the young King. She spoke of her first husband, Louis and how she had been desperate to leave him.

It was at that point that I interjected, "And yet you would run to him rather than your husband."

She turned to me with a cold look upon her face, "I go to my sons. I am a mother."

She turned away from me as though I was summarily dismissed. It was at that moment that I knew I could never be my father. I had tried to emulate him but my early years had meant I had wasted too much time. I would have to see if I could make my son a model of his grandfather. England needed a Warlord. King Henry had shown me that. A king with absolute power, as King Henry had become, was a dangerous man. I saw now that my father had been the reins guiding the King. Now that my father was at the end of his life those reins were slipping and I was not the man to grasp them. I could not do what my father did. The last sixty miles were instructive. I learned much about my father and about the

The Princes' Revolt

Queen. More, I learned about the King and the hidden bond between him and my father. It was stronger than the bond we shared. It was remarkable.

By the time we reached Rouen news had reached us of King Henry's reaction to the invasion of his Duchy. He had sent for more men from England, attacked and defeated the Flemish and, when we arrived, he was ready to repulse King Louis and the Young Henry who were attacking from the east.

The King himself greeted us inside his castle. He was gracious, almost intimate with his wife. "My Queen, I am pleased that my noble knights were able to bring you safely to me so that we can endure this assault together."

Eleanor was cold, "It is our sons we are talking about Henry!"

He put his arm around her and led her away, "Then let us talk of our family in private. My lords, I will return shortly. Make yourselves comfortable. I am in your debt."

His steward took us to the Great Hall. There we saw many of the loyal Norman barons. All were dressed in war gear. This was not a court full of politicians. This was a counsel of war of warriors. As soon as we were recognised we were descended upon for news. My father was the centre of attention. He was the King's talisman. If the Warlord was here then King Henry would not lose. My father wore the responsibility like a rock around his neck.

The King was not away for long. We did not see the Queen again and I know not where he put her. King Henry was a man of decisive moves. Ignoring his other barons and counts he led us to one side. He spoke urgently, "King Louis brings an army from the east. Young Henry is with him. I have had reports of rebels coming from Brittany."

My father nodded, "You have a plan?"

He nodded, "I will send William d'Aubigny, the Earl of Arundel and the men of Anjou who accompanied you. He has a force of men he brought from Cornwall. They will deal with the Bretons. Anjou is solid and with Aquitaine neutralized we can apply all of our force towards Louis. I would have the two of you come with me when we go to meet him."

"King Henry, what of our home? This is an opportunity that King William will not spurn."

"I know Earl William, you are right. My spies tell me that he is gathering an army even as we speak."

The Princes' Revolt

"Then we should go home and defend my land."

"You and your father are two men. If your knights, the Bishop of Durham and the Sheriff cannot hold off the Scots then it is a sad day for England. We are talking of the Scots!"

I struggled to control my temper, "King Henry, they have been probing us for some time. They know our strengths and they know our weaknesses."

He shook his head. "First we deal with the French and then you can go home! I am King and that is my command!"

That was the end of the debate.

The Princes' Revolt

Chapter 15

When we headed east we were just behind the vanguard with the King. He showed genuine concern about my father's health. That did little to appease me. Sir James now rode behind us. Since we had come to France he had changed. He now acted and behaved as a knight. I trusted him. Had he wished harm to come to us then he had had ample opportunity to do so and he had not. My father and I were very familiar with the land through which we travelled. We had fought there under Old King Henry as well as Geoffrey of Anjou and the Empress Maud.

Louis was coming from Chartres. Perhaps he hoped to cut us from the loyal men of Anjou. The rebel Norman knights along the Flemish border would be another enemy we had to deal with. We had, I suspected, a smaller army than the French. We had sent a third of our men to Brittany. Ultimately, I was confident in the quality of the men under our command. The barons who led the knights, men at arms and archers had fought in Ireland, Scotland and Wales. War was their trade and they were masters of it. I had assigned Thomas to help Simon to watch over and protect my father. Thomas had grown in the three years he had been with me. Sir Philip, his father, would be proud of him for he had become a man. Thanks to his father's physique, he was an archer, he had a broad chest and continued to grow. When he swung a sword and connected his sparring partner knew it. Ralph had the bruises to show for it. With no banner to carry Ralph would be riding as my bodyguard. I was happy about that for I would be knighting him in the next year. He would be a worthy knight.

The knights who lived in the Vexin, D'Aubigny and the others had sent their scouts out ahead. They knew this land. Louis did not. Thus it was that they found the French before they found us. That was important. It meant that we could select the battlefield.

The Princes' Revolt

There was a huge forest which extended many miles east of La Hauteville. To the north was the smaller forest of Grandchamp. La Hauteville was small and, more importantly, it was French. King Henry did not need to appease the French. Our men drove the villagers towards the east. They would tell the French of our position. With a forest behind and around us it would appear, to the French as though we had trapped ourselves. Nothing could be further from the truth. We had a hundred archers with us. Not as good as the men I had left in England they were still better than anything the French could field. With another one hundred of our best men at arms they would wait in the forest to the east. The French would see just our knights and mounted men at arms along with the one hundred crossbowmen we had brought. We were a lure to make the French and Young Henry's men, attack us. When we counterattacked it would be the archers and me at arms in the forest who would determine the battle.

The plan was all my father's. He had an eye for terrain. He had noticed how the wood and the forest were both higher than the road and the fields over which the battle would be fought. We would be charging downhill and the French uphill. The land closest to La Hauteville was common grazing land while the land over which the French would be charging was ploughed fields. I was in awe of my father. He had given us every advantage which could be had. It would still come down to the mettle of our men but all of us were confident in that.

The men at arms and archers camped deep in the woods so that their movement into position would not be noticed. We waited in La Hauteville. The French arrived at dusk and camped just a mile from us. Both armies had pickets out but neither of us risked a night time attack. We rose before dawn for we had heard the French moving around. Ralph helped me to don my mail. He had a spare spear for me and my sword was freshly sharpened. We had so few men that the four servants were given helmets and given the duty of helping Simon and Thomas to guard the Warlord. Everyone else would be fighting.

As dawn broke, we saw their serried ranks. King Louis intended to batter us out of his way. His foot guarded his camp while his crossbows formed a crude skirmish line in front of his three hundred mailed knights. They were backed by another one hundred men at arms. With just one hundred and eighty knights we were seriously outnumbered. I recognised the banners of Leicester and Norfolk. The English traitors had joined the French. I would be fighting Englishmen.

The Princes' Revolt

I was in the front rank with the King. My father with his guards were safe and close to the barrage. The other leaders he had brought from England, as well as his nobles from Normandy, were there with us. It was a bold statement. It was a lure to draw in the French. If they could wipe out our front rank then the war would be over in one battle. Young King Henry had already been crowned. I had no doubt that the King of France's support had been bought with the Vexin.

We waited as the French ponderously formed their lines. The men hidden in the forest had been given clear instructions not to attack until the French were committed. We would have to wait until the French attacked before we could counterattack. My helmet hung from my cantle and Ralph held my spear.

King Henry said, "I did not see my son in the front rank."

I peered at them but I saw no sign of any of his sons. "Neither do I see King Louis nor the Prince of France, Philip."

The King sniffed, "Then they are cowards all. My son wants the kingdom handed to him on a platter of other men's blood. Tell me I was not like that, William."

"From what my father told me he had to restrain you from reckless acts."

He laughed, "Aye I was trying to win a kingdom. What kind of sons have I produced from my loins?"

"They are young. When I was young I was not the man I am today."

He looked at me and nodded, "You are right. Then there is hope that they may change."

William d'Aubigny said, "Majesty, they are preparing to charge."

"About time too." He spurred his horse and rode twenty paces from us so that we could all see him as he turned around. "Today, English and Norman unite to fight traitors and Frenchmen. Those who survive I promise you the castles of those traitors who fight against us this day!"

I smiled. He was using bribery to ensure victory. Often that was as effective as an appeal to honour.

He returned to our lines and his squire handed him his helmet. I donned mine and my world shrank as my face mask was lowered to protect the upper half of my face. The holes through which I peered were large but I still preferred the old nasal helmet worn by my squires and James de Puiset. He was behind me next to Ralph. Ralph nudged his horse forward and handed me my spear.

The Princes' Revolt

As he did so I said, "No foolish heroics today. If I fall I want you to take my sword back to my son Samuel."

He laughed, "You will be there with me, lord, of that I am certain."

A French horn sounded and the crossbowmen began to run towards us. They would have to be within two hundred paces for their weapons to be effective. The horsemen were ordered forward by a herald with the French fleur de lys. They walked. The ploughed fields over which the French moved was little problem for their horses but the men on foot found it hard. I watched as they glanced over their shoulders. Their own horsemen were closing rapidly.

"Squire, sound the advance."

King Henry's squire gave one blast on the horn and I spurred my horse. As soon as the horn sounded and the line moved forward the crossbowmen stopped. They were three hundred paces from us but they knew how quickly we could move forward. They dropped to their knees and each loaded a bolt. King Henry did not intend to charge too quickly. He wanted to strike them when we were on firm ground and they were in the ploughed field. He wanted to hit them when our archers released their arrows and our men at arms attacked their flanks. The men with crossbows did not know that and they feared we were about to gallop through them. We were two hundred and fifty paces from them when they released. Many bolts flew high, some struck shields, mail and helmet. Two hit horses but did little damage. It is hard to reload a crossbow quickly and the French knights behind were now galloping. The men with crossbows fled. Some did not escape the hooves of the knights who were anxious to get to us. The bodies of the men who had been trampled and the discarded crossbows broke up the second and third lines.

We were a hundred paces from them when King Henry shouted, "Charge!" I lowered my spear. Many of the French were using lances. I thought a lance too heavy and unwieldy. Used well it was a knight killer but a knight had to be well trained to use one. The French knight who aimed his lance at me struggled to keep it level. It wavered up and down. I rested my spear on the cantle of my saddle. As we neared each other my horse began to open his legs. The French horses were doing the same. Ridley's gait made even my spear waver. Rather than thrusting up I changed to an overhand grip. As his lance punched towards my chest I stabbed down at his middle. His lance glanced off the side of my helmet and my spear struck him in the right side. As the spear was torn from my

The Princes' Revolt

grip it ripped open a hole in his side. Even as he tumbled from his saddle I was drawing my sword.

I had managed to get ahead of King Henry, who had slain his opponent. I saw the second knight pull back his lance ready to impale the King. I pulled my reins to the left and smashed my shield into his. He began to overbalance and King Henry rammed his spear into the mouth of the French knight. Gradually we began to tear a hole in the centre of the French lines and the flanks began to surround us. The archers in the woods began to loose their arrows and our men at arms raced towards the knights and French men at arms who were at the rear of the column of mailed men. The effect was devastating. The French to my left and the King's left almost disintegrated.

The flaw in my father's plan now became obvious. As the French right fell away and we turned their line so the pressure on our right mounted and knights broke through. Suddenly Ralph shouted, "Lord, they are heading for the Warlord!"

"Ralph, James, go to his aid!"

I could do nothing for two French knights had closed with me. Sir Leofric had told me that the horse I rode, Ridley, had been trained for the tourney. I used that now to my advantage. Rather than using my shield to block the knight to my left I stood in my stirrups and pulled back on the reins with my left hand as I swept my sword across the head of the knight to my right. Ridley did what he was trained to do he reared and flailed with his mighty hooves. The skull of the other French knight was crushed.

I turned and saw there was a race between six knights and Sir James, Ralph and James' squire, Henry. I would not reach the knights before they struck my father, his protective squires and servants. I prayed that James and the two squires would be able to hold them. I spurred Ridley. Although we were galloping uphill he was a powerful beast. His legs began to eat up the ground. I saw that James had cleverly decided to try to break up the French attack. He led his two squires at the side of the knights. It meant that at least two would reach my father but the other four would be attacked by James and his two brave squires.

"Come on Ridley!"

I held my sword behind me and almost lay flat against my horse's mane. Ridley seemed to fly. James and his two squires clattered into the side of the four French knights. James' spear scored a lucky hit and went under the arm of one knight. He rose from the saddle and fell. The spear was lost and James drew his sword. I pulled back my arm for I was close enough now to swing. Even as I swung at the last of the knights I saw my father, Simon and Thomas hit by the two knights. Simon and Thomas took the force of the strike. Then I could see nothing for my sword had hacked into the side of the French knight. I had hit so hard that I had bitten through to the spine of the knight. His falling body hid the tableau from me. Pushing his body from my sword, I galloped at the knight who was about to skewer Ralph. My squire had protected James' squire with his horse but it meant he was exposed. I almost launched myself from my saddle as I lunged at the knight whose arm was raised to take my squire's head. My sword went up through his armpit and emerged on the other side of his body. I discarded his body and spurred my horse towards the Warlord. I left James, his squire and Ralph to deal with the last knight and I rode at the two who were trying to get at my father. Thomas was on the ground but he held a spear before him. My father and Simon lay awkwardly on the earth. I could not tell if they were alive or dead.

I saw Thomas lunge at one of the knights with his spear. The other pulled back on his reins and I knew that he intended to make his horse rear and crush my squire. I threw my sword like a throwing knife. It impaled the knight in the back. His falling body pulled on the reins and his horse crushed whatever life was left in him. I kicked my feet from my stirrups and, with my shield before me threw myself bodily at the last knight. He tumbled from the saddle with me on top of him. He landed first and I had the wind knocked from me as I fell upon him. Even though I could barely breathe I forced myself to my feet. He had been rendered unconscious.

I turned and, throwing my shield to the ground ran to my father and Simon. I saw that Simon had been impaled on a spear. He was dead but my father appeared to have no wound. I took his helmet from his head. I put my ear to his mouth. He was alive.

"Thomas, go and find a healer." As I looked around I saw that the four servants had fought off the knight's squires. Four squires lay dead but Osbert and Brian had fought their last fight. I raised my arm, "Whatever is on the dead squires is yours."

"Thank you, lord. We will see to our dead first."

James, Ralph of Piercebridge and Henry of Auckland, blood-spattered, rode towards me. Beyond them, I saw that the French were in flight. We had won but I wondered at the cost. Thomas returned with a healer.

"Priest, see to the Warlord."

"Aye lord."

"What happened, Thomas?"

"We saw the knights approaching and Simon said to present spears. The Warlord said that we need not fear, you would reach us. He took out his sword. As they neared us we held our spears before us. One made his horse rear and when Simon flinched he was speared. The horse's hoof caught the Warlord on the helmet and he fell. I just tried to hold them off lord. I am sorry that I failed Simon."

"You did not. Today you became a man." I saw that the priest, with his bag of potions, had arrived, "Priest, look to my father's head!"

James and the others dismounted, "Thank you, James de Puiset. I am grateful."

"Lord, I am just sorry that I could not reach him in time." He was looking at Simon.

"He was a brave squire. I am just sad that he was not knighted. He deserved it, and you, Ralph, you shall be knighted when we reach England. Thomas here has proved that he is ready to be my sole squire. And Thomas know this, should I have a grandson then I would want him named him after you. You have a courage beyond your years. You defended the Warlord and Simon despite the fact that you thought you were going to die. That is true courage."

My father opened his eyes. "I am well." He saw Simon and took his squire's hand. "He was the bravest squire I ever had and he died for me. I will have no more squires and I go to war no more. I grow weary of watching those I love, die."

By the time the King returned we had cleaned up my father and the bodies of our dead. King Henry was ebullient. "A great victory and it was your plan Warlord. What would I do without you?"

My father stood. "You will soon find out for this is my last battle. I have seen my squire die and could nothing about it. I have made you king, Henry FitzEmpress. I have helped you hold onto a kingdom and make it larger. I have fulfilled my oath to your grandfather and your mother. Ask no more for I am done. I have a family and they will now be my sole occupation." He turned and, leaning on Thomas walked to his horse.

The King looked pale, "He cannot mean it. He is my lucky talisman. He inspired this victory. We have won. The French fly back to Paris."

"Does not the Warlord deserve a life, lord?" Henry said nothing. "We will return to England for I fear mischief from the Scots. I will ever serve you but I will not leave England again." I waved my hand at the lords whom we had led to victory. "Here are your new Warlords. Make peace with your sons. Speak with your wife. You have a great empire. I beg you to hold on to it."

We had Simon's body escorted to La Flèche. Sir Leofric had been Simon's father's greatest friend. He would tend to the burial and ensure that the grave was tended. We looked after our own.

Chapter 16

By the time we reached Rouen word had reached us that Leicester and Norfolk had ridden north to Flanders. Archers captured some of their men who, after torture, told us that the two lords were intent on starting a rebellion in England. We also heard that King William had been sent a chest of coins to begin war in the north. There had been another time when my father had been delayed on the King's business and that had cost him Sir Edward and the valley had been ravaged. That could not happen again! We had to reach home as quickly as possible. The King had realised how much he owed us. We took a chest of gold back with us but it meant nothing for we had lost two servants who were as close as family and Simon. His was a life undone. Young men are supposed to sow wild oats. Simon would never have that chance. We were a sombre group who boarded the ship to take us to the Tees.

The journey became even more fraught when my father became unwell. He was a good sailor and we knew it was nothing to do with the voyage. It was something more sinister. He had dizzy spells and then his sight became blurred. With no healer on the ship we had to do the best that we could. I prayed for fast winds but they never came. That was when I doubted God for the first time. I wondered if it was the blow he had taken to the head. There had been little blood. We had thought that was a good sign. Now it appeared to be a bad one.

I insisted that the captain take advantage of the high tide and sail up the Tees at night. He would have argued with me but he heard the steel in my voice. The wind was from the east and aided us. My squires acted as extra lookouts. We made Stockton as the first hint of light was in the east. As soon as we landed I sent for Brother Peter. Since I had taken him as my priest and healer, warrior, he had never let me down. My son must have been told of my ship's arrival for he had crossed the ferry to see what brought us back so early in the morn. While I spoke with my wife and son the warrior monk examined my father in my father's room.

"There has been no word of the Scots?"

Samuel shook his head, "Sir Harold and Sir John led our men at arms north to the New Castle as soon as Captain William brought us your message." Sir John would not know of his son's death until I met with him. I would break that news to him. It was my duty for my father was not going to leave Stockton until he was well.

"What of the rider I sent from London?"

Samuel looked at me blankly, "No messenger came from London."

"Then there are traitors further south. Send for all of my knights and my men at arms. Did Sir Harold take Aiden and Masood?"

"No, father, just Edward and Edgar."

"Then I would have them with us too."

He was about to leave and he asked, "What of grandfather? Is it his chest?"

"No. He received a blow to the head." He hesitated. "He is the Warlord. He is strong and we must be too. Time is a luxury we do not have. There are English rebels further south. I cannot believe that King William will wait too long before he takes advantage of us. And Simon is dead. He gave his life for his knight." Samuel's mouth opened and closed. "Go." As soon as he had gone I turned to James. "Now I need you to persuade your uncle to release all of his knights for me to command. This will not be a chevauchée by the Scots. This will be an invasion. We cannot have knights languishing at home. We need every warrior to stand with us. King William will lead this army. The traitors will have told him that my father and I were in Normandy. He will strike while he thinks we are disorganized."

My wife and I waited anxiously for Brother Peter and his verdict. His face was serious as he emerged from my father's chamber.

"Well?"

"He is a tough warrior. His hurts would have felled a younger man but he has heart. The blow broke his skull. The priest who tended him should have dealt with it there and then. Perhaps he was not experienced enough."

"Can you do anything?"

"I can shave his head and then try to repair the broken skull."

"Can that be done?"

"There were doctors in the east who did such things. I will ride to Durham. There is a library in the Bishop's palace. Perhaps there is something there that I can read which might help me. For the present, my lady, keep the Warlord in his room. I doubt that you will get much argument from him. He said that he is often unsteady on his feet."

"We ride to Durham tomorrow, Brother Peter, come with us." Aiden and Masood came to speak with me and I sent them north to scout. "This time they will not cross the Tweed at Norham, it will be further south. If you find Sir Harold then tell him that I come north and he should keep his patrol north of the wall."

"Aye lord."

Our early arrival meant that men began to arrive at the castle by noon. Once again, I left Sir Hugh at Barnard but I sent for his son. He was the last to arrive and my daughter, Ruth, came with him. She looked sadder than she had when last I had seen her. I wondered if it was because my father was unwell but Rebekah told me that Ruth had been with child and had lost it. Her sadness was exacerbated by the news that Eleanor, Samuel's wife, was with child. Once again, I cursed King Henry. He had taken my father and I away needlessly. My father had been grievously wounded and for what? Had we not brought Eleanor to him then the outcome of the battle would have been no different. I vowed to stay closer to home from now on.

My knights were all equally concerned about my father. They took it in turns to visit with him. When I went in he was scowling. "They think I am dying! I am not! Tell them to smile when they see me or do not come and visit. Their sour faces make me think that I am ill. I have had a blow to my head. Your monk will treat me and I will be well."

"They care for you, father. You trained most of them. You should know that they cannot ignore your hurts."

He forced a smile. I could see that he was bothered by a pain in his head, "You are right. You ride tomorrow to fight the Scots?"

"I do."

"The Tyne valley is where he will strike. You need to stop him taking the crossings and keep him north of the Tyne. The Romans had good reason to build their wall where they did. Use it."

He was ill but the Warlord still had a mind which I could only envy.

"One more thing, use the men of Stockton. They are better than any other that you will command. Ralph of Bowness and the old will be enough to defend Stockton. Ruth and Eleanor are both within these walls.

The Princes' Revolt

They will be safe. End this threat once and for all. If you capture the King then it will be over. War is often like chess and none more so than when you fight a King. Without King William, the Scots will crumble and fight amongst themselves."

I heeded those words as I headed north. We had not yet reached Durham when a rider came south to tell us that the Scots had crossed the border and they came in great numbers. It was not one of my scouts who brought the news but a messenger from Durham. Leaving Samuel to bring the rest of the men to Durham I spurred Goldie and, with Thomas, Ralph and Brother Peter by my side galloped to Durham.

I was gratified, when I arrived, to see that James had succeeded in impressing on his uncle the need for decisive action. The town and the surrounding area were filled with knights and their men. Brother Peter left me to head to the library. He would do his work and I would do mine. Both were equally important. Fitzwaller, Howden, the Bishop and James were gathered around a table when I entered.

The Princes' Revolt

"Thank God you have arrived, Earl. The Scottish King has crossed the Tweed. There are six armies which have crossed into our land."

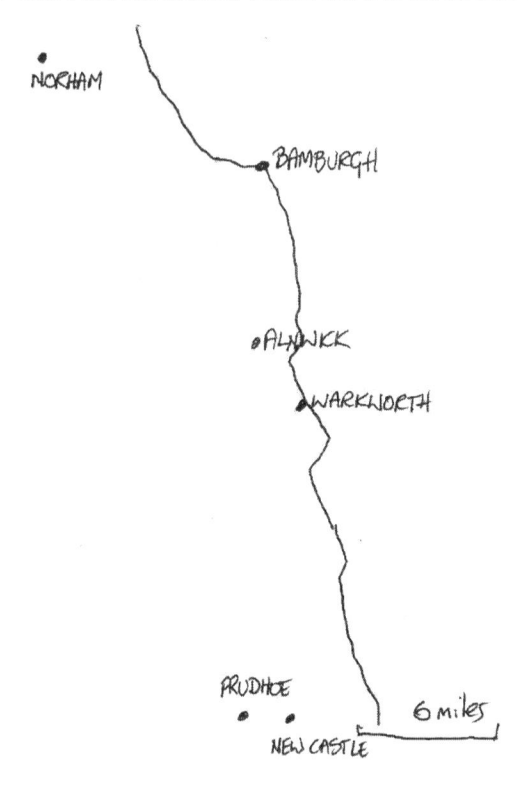

```
• NORHAM
       • BAMBURGH
       • ALNWICK
       • WARKWORTH

  PRUDHOE
  •   •         6 miles
    NEW CASTLE
```

"Six! They are small armies then?"

James had grown in confidence since he had first joined me, "No lord. The smallest has three thousand men. There are at least five hundred Flemish mercenaries with the Scottish King. Sir Harold is shadowing the one which is the furthest south. They have laid siege to Prudhoe and are marching towards the New Castle. The Sheriff has called out the fyrd and every castle is preparing for a siege. We just await you to lead us."

My father had been prescient. The only way to end this was to kill or capture the King. Obligingly he had placed himself within my grasp. He was with the southern army. "How many men with the King?"

"He has over five hundred knights with him and the whole army is more than five thousand men."

The Bishop shook his head. "We cannot match his numbers. I have sent for every knight and that will still give you only three hundred knights. With the rest of the knights north of the Tyne in their castles then how can we defeat such a large army?"

"We have God on our side, Bishop and we have better knights." I turned to James who was poring over the map. "Where are they now?"

The King is still with his army at Prudhoe. The vanguard is approaching the New Castle."

"And we hold the southern end of the bridge?"

"We do, lord."

I stared at the map. Prudhoe castle guarded the nearest crossing of the river. We would have to cross the bridge close to the New Castle. "And where is Sir Harold?"

"Your scouts reported him and Sir John to be south of Prudhoe."

I had my plans. "Begin the knights marching north to the New Castle. I will await my men."

For the first time since I had known him, Bishop de Puiset looked worried. Hitherto he had had an ally: the King of France, the Pope, for a time the King of Scotland, but this time he had to rely on me. My father and I had been his enemies for so many years and yet now I was his only hope. It was truly ironical. "You can defeat so many men, Earl?"

"It is not the size of an army which determines a battle. It is the quality of men. Your knights have become stronger in the last few years. I truly believe that we will win."

I left the castle to await my men on the road. They soon arrived. Like me, they recognised the enormity and urgency of our task. "Sir Philip, take Sir Ralph, Sir Tristan, Sir Padraig and Sir Gilles. Ride to Prudhoe. There Sir Harold and Sir John are shadowing the Scots. Your men at arms and archers will reinforce him. I will take the rest and the knights of Durham. We will try to force a battle with the King of Scotland."

"You divide your forces father, is this wise?" Samuel was not experienced enough to question me. Perhaps he wanted his friend, Sir Ralph, to go into battle with him.

"The King of Scotland has made a more serious mistake. He has divided his own, greater forces further. I am gambling that we can defeat him and then we can come to the aid of Prudhoe but Sir Harold needs to be a viable threat. With just two knights and a handful of warriors he is not. You will have more than sixty archers. The Scots respect our archers. Sir Philip, you will have forty men at arms as well as your knights. They will outnumber you but they will remember Gretna and Barnard. God willing, we can deflect King William and come to your aid. God speed."

"We will do our duty, lord. God be with you. If you and the rest can defeat King William then our task will be so much easier."

Samuel shouted, "Good luck, Sir Ralph!"

He laughed, "I need no luck for I will be with Sir Harold and Sir John!"

As I headed north, passing through the baggage of the knights of Durham, I began to doubt myself. Alnwick was under siege as well as Warkworth. His other armies were raiding the countryside north of the Tyne and south of the Tweed. The plans I had made with the Sheriff and the two constables would provide safe havens for the people but the land would still suffer. I had to somehow manage to defeat the King of Scotland. He would have more knights and a larger army.

I overtook the knights and reached the New Castle first. Goldie would need to be rested the next day. My horse was weary beyond words as was I. I was taken directly to the Sheriff.

"Thank God you are here. How many knights do you bring?"

"Not enough I fear. Just three hundred and twenty. How many do you have within your walls?"

"Barely a hundred."

"The King comes from Prudhoe. He does not have his full army. Tomorrow we sally forth and bring him to battle."

"That would be like risking all on one throw of the dice. You are gambling!"

"Of course I am. Our only hope is to defeat the King. He has not yet brought his full strength. If he had brought every warrior he has in his army then I would be truly gambling. He has had a clever plan. He is trying to take all of our strongholds. The cleverness of his plan is also its weakness for he is divided. I would strike before he can combine them." The Sheriff nodded his agreement. "Where is the Scottish camp?"

"North of the walls on the moor which bestrides the Ponteland road."

"And siege works?"

"The army arrived just two days since. They built a camp with a ditch is all."

The Princes' Revolt

I laughed, "They have learned from us then. Leave just the levy to guard your walls. We take our knights, men at arms and my archers to attack them. Their King will have arrived today. I would expect him to come and view your walls."

The Sheriff shook his head, "He came an hour since with Lord Dunbar and some mercenaries."

"Good, then tonight he will plan the assault. He will not know of our arrival for we came across the bridge he does not control. The last thing he will expect will be an attack from us."

There were so many knights, men at arms and archers that most were forced to camp by the river. The Scots had not encircled the town. The river prevented that but they had, instead, cut the town off from the north and the west. Perhaps the Scottish King hoped that the Bishop of Durham would be his normal obstructive self. Thanks to James he was not. I gathered the leaders with me in the Great Hall to give them my battle plan. My remaining knights attended too. Ranulf de Glanvill would lead the knights of the north. The Sheriff would remain in the castle in case things went awry.

"We will use the archers and my men at arms to attack the left flank of their camp. We have four hundred and twenty knights. That is not enough." I waved a hand towards my two squires who were busily scribing on wax tablets the words that I said. "My squires have shown that they have courage. All of our squires will ride as a reserve. It will make the Scots think that we have twice the number of knights that we do. Each will have a pennant on his spear. They will think they are knights."

Sir Ranulf de Glanvill said, "But Earl, is not that against our chivalric oaths?"

I smiled, "These are squires. They have sworn no oath save the one to serve their master. Sir Ranulf, the Scots are murderers and killers. They take slaves. They have no honour. This is my decision and I will not lose one moment's sleep over this." They nodded their agreement. If there was a sin then it would be mine alone. "This is like a game of chess. We have fewer pieces than our opponent and so we try to win the game by taking the King. We capture or kill the King and we have won."

I spent some time in the chapel when my knights left to make their preparations for the battle. I prayed more for my father than for our success. I hoped that Brother Peter had found the book he wanted and by the time I returned then we would know if he had succeeded or not. I had

The Princes' Revolt

to put him from my mind if I was to win the battle. If I failed then King William would win the ancient land of Northumbria and our enemies would be on our doorstep.

I heard a movement behind me and I turned. It was Ralph, my squire. "I am sorry, lord. I came to pray."

I stood, "I am done. The chapel is yours. Remember Ralph that when we are returned to Stockton you win your spurs." I smiled, "Try to win some good ones on the morrow eh?"

"I will lord. I owe it to Simon to become the best knight that I can be. We both wanted to be knights. He can never achieve that honour."

I slept but a little and, after rising, went to find Thomas who was preparing Volva. My armour was burnished as was my helmet. All of the squires now had a spear with a small pennant upon it. Some of the squires were young and they were small. They would be with the rear rank and I hoped that our serried ranks would disguise them. Our purpose was to achieve mastery of the battle field. If that involved using a trick then I would do so. "Thomas, tomorrow you will have to look like a knight but I pray that you do not have to fight as one. I would not lose another squire as we lost Simon. If the battle goes against us then I command you to lead the younger squires back to the castle. I would have you live."

"Lord, I could not desert the battlefield. When Sir Samuel led the squires at Gretna they helped you win the battle."

"Listen to me Thomas, this is not Gretna. Then we fought raiders. This day we fight an army. Obey me."

"Aye lord."

We left by the river gate. The men who had camped outside were ready. Roger of Bath and Aelric led the archers and the men at arms east. The Constable had told us of a path which led through the woods. It was an area known as Shieldfield. According to the locals it was some ancient name for a clearing in the forest. Although most of the forest had gone the wood remained and it would provide cover. We hoped that the arrival of our knights would distract the Scots and allow our men to close with their left flank.

The land rose towards the moor. It was a flat piece of ground with few trees on it. The locals used it for grazing. We were able to approach it in a column of knights fifty men wide. That helped to disguise the squires at the rear. We were seen when we were less than a mile away. The alarm was sounded. Scottish horns and drums roused the camp. This time the King was with them. I saw his lion standard. When we reached a point half a mile from them they were beginning to array in their battle formation. I had the horn sounded, I had retained Thomas with my banner, and we formed three lines of one hundred and thirty knights. I gave no speech. I did not rouse the men. If they did not know what they were fighting for by now then a few words from me would not help.

The knights on the two ends of my line raised their spears when all was ready and I had Thomas sound the advance. "Now ride to the squires and God be with you, Thomas! Remember my command!"

I rode next to my son and Sir James of Forcett. Both were young but had proven themselves more than enough. With spears held vertically we trotted towards the Scots who were still trying to get in some sort of formation. The woods of the Shieldfield had disguised the movement of our men on foot. They would be seen as soon as they emerged from the woods but by then the Scottish would have made their dispositions. As usual the Scots who were not nobles were vociferous in their battle lines. They jeered, cheered and chanted. Some dropped their breeks and bared their backsides at us and that suited us for it meant their attention was not on our slow and steady approach. The Scottish knights were vying for the honour of the centre of the Scottish line so that they could face the son of the Warlord.

I waved my spear forward and spurred Volva so that we began to canter. Our line was now a little uneven; the rising and scrubby ground did not help us but we were largely boot to boot. Suddenly I heard a shout from the Scottish lines and men on the extreme left began to point towards the woods of the Shieldfield. My men at arms and archers had been spotted. Indecision can lose a battle. The King vacillated. I saw him point to his right. He feared that we were trying the same on his right flank. All the time we advanced. We were less than a hundred and fifty paces from them and instead of arrows greeting us there was nothing.

Aelric and his archers sent their own arrows towards the left flank of the Scots and that initiated stones and arrows at us. I lowered my spear and spurred Volva. We were now less a hundred paces away and the Scottish horn belatedly sounded the charge. Their knights made a ragged attempt to counter charge us but they only had fifty paces in which to do so and it was not enough. I pulled back my spear and, sliding the shaft over my horse's neck, rammed it at the chest of a Scottish knight. His shield blocked it but he was not moving quickly enough and he was knocked from his horse. I pulled my arm back and stabbed at a knight to

The Princes' Revolt

my right. He had a lance he was trying to move around in order to unhorse me. My spear took him in the shoulder as his lance banged against my arm.

James of Forcett, James de Puiset and Samuel, my son were still with me. The blood on their spears showed that they had done their duty already. I spied the King and his household knights. I pointed my spear at him, "We take the King!" My knights and those behind cheered. As I lowered my spear I saw that, to my right the archers and men at arms had managed to drive the Scottish foot from the field. They were fleeing north.

King William shouted something and pointed at me with his sword. Ten knights immediately spurred their horses towards us. I did not look around for I knew that I would be supported. The knights who charged us had no lances. They charged us with swords, war hammers and axes. They did not have speed and we did. I still had my spear and that gave me the first strike. I aimed at the right side of the knight who had the golden lion on his surcoat. He tried to block it with his sword but failed. My spear tore through his mail and into his upper arm. Perhaps I ripped tendons, I know not but his sword fell. Pulling back my arm I switched to my left for a knight was swinging his war hammer at my shield. My father had suffered a serious wound after being hit by such a weapon on his shield. I braced myself for the impact as I stabbed almost blindly at the Scot. The blow made my shield and arm shiver but my spear struck mail and then flesh. It tore through the ventail and into his skull. He was dead before his body slipped from my spear.

It was then that two brave knights sacrificed themselves for their King. They rode across our line of charge. Our horses baulked. We lost momentum. Their shields faced us but our spears found gaps and the two of them died. They had given the King the chance to escape. His squire sounded the horn. He turned his horse and, surrounded by his household knights he headed north and west. The Scots were fleeing. Their King had gone and despite our lack of numbers we had struck harder than they had expected. My father was not with us but it was his plan which had worked.

The battle was not over for groups of knights and isolated bands of warriors fought on. The knights eventually surrendered. The ordinary warriors fought until they were killed. It all took time. By the time the battle was over there was no sign of the Scots who had fled. I took off my helmet to better view the field. I turned and saw that my household knights were still alive. In fact, I could see that we had lost few knights. To our right lay the largest number of bodies. The archers and men at arms had slaughtered the foot who had faced them.

"Search the tents and the baggage. Let us see what the King has left for us!"

I turned as I heard hooves behind me. It was Ralph my squire. He held in his hands a pair of spurs! Thomas was leading a warhorse upon which was a hauberk and sword. Ralph was ecstatic, "I killed a knight and I have his spurs, mail and warhorse!"

I nodded, "And you, Thomas heeded my words! Good!"

My plan had worked. The squires pretending to be knights had fooled the enemy. I was not sure we could use the same ruse a second time.

Samuel rode over and clapped my squire on the back, "Well done, Ralph and when you are knighted you shall have Thornaby!"

I was surprised, "You are sure, Samuel?"

He nodded, "Ruth lost her baby. Eleanor is with child and I would have my wife close to my mother. Stockton is my home; it is my castle. With grandfather there it seems right that I live there too. There will be three generations of knights. It is meant to be father."

"Aye You are right.

Chapter 17

Masood and Aiden rode in during the afternoon. Men were still being cleared from the battlefield. "Lord, we spotted the King. He and his men were heading to Prudhoe."

"Then he reinforces the siege."

"Aye lord and we saw that two of the warbands have combined and were heading for Alnwick."

This meant that the King had realised his mistake of dividing his army. He was combining. Speed was even more important now. I called an immediate war counsel. "We have to relieve Prudhoe's siege and then head for Alnwick."

The Sheriff and some of the Durham knights were not certain. "Earl William, this was a great victory. You said we had to drive the King hence and we have done so. Men are weary. They fought hard this day. Let us recover."

I shook my head. "The men of Prudhoe led by Odinel d'Umphraville and my knights do not have that luxury. We have not yet won. Appleby has fallen, Brough has fallen, Carlisle, Alnwick, Wark, Warkworth, all are under attack. If I had led this army to Prudhoe first to relieve the siege would you be happy for us to wait there and recover while you fought the Scots?"

My last argument worked and the next morning we headed west. I rode Lightning this time. I split the army into two. I led the one south of the Tyne and Sir Ranulf de Glanvill led the other. I divided the nights equally but I took my archers and men at arms. It would be a pincer movement intended to catch the Scots on two sides. It was just a twelve-mile ride and we heard the sound of battle as we approached. I had chosen the southern side because the rest of my knights, archers and men at arms were there. There was fighting on the southern side and that meant my men were involved. It spurred me on. Masson and Aiden rode ahead. They returned quickly.

"Lord our men are surrounded. They are making a last stand!"

"How far away are they?"

"A mile at most, lord. They are the other side of the stand of trees."

I turned, "Sound the charge!"

Samuel said, "But we are not yet in battle order!"

"It matters not. Our men will hear it and they will take heart!" Without waiting for a spear, I spurred Lightning and took off followed by Masood and Aiden. Both were fine archers. I glanced to my right and saw Samuel and James. To my left was Alf.

I could now hear the sound of battle. I prayed that our horn had steeled Sir Harold and my men. As we cleared the trees I saw that my men were gathered around their banners. They were fighting back to back. Archers, men at arms, squires and knights; all stood together. They were truly brothers in arms. There was a ring of bodies around them and the Scots were pressing hard. I waited for no one. Masood and Aiden leapt from their mounts and began to release arrow after arrow in the press of men around Sir Harold, Padraig and the others. I saw that Sir Harold was wounded but he and his son, Richard, held on to the standard. My men were dying. I roared with anger and spurred Lightning. I saw a Scottish lord on a horse try to make his horse rear and bring them to clatter down on the head of Stephen the Grim. Aiden's arrow smacked into his head and as he fell backwards he pulled the horse with it. Stephen the Grim had lost his shield and was using his sword two handed. I rode at the Scottish knight who was ordering his men forward and was the closest man to me. One of his men shouted a warning and he turned. He was too late and I tore my sword across his middle. I did not pause but stood in my stirrups to bring my blade down across the helmet of the man who had shouted a warning. Sir James de Puiset was next to me and he was doing terrible damage to the men on foot. He had learned to lean from his saddle and lay about him with his sword. Samuel too was cleaving heads but still our men fell. I saw Sir Harold disappear as the Scots surged forward.

I spurred Lighting and headed for the knot of Scottish warriors on foot who were trying to hack their way through my men at arms. I wondered what my archers were doing and then I saw that they were fighting with swords in their hands. I leaned forward and slashed down with my sword. My shield was still over my leg and I had to endure blows from swords as I passed men who had fled my horse. I struck first to the right and then, over my horse's head to the left. A spear was thrown at me and I barely had time to move my head. It clattered from my helmet. I saw that there were just three men between me and my warriors. I reined in Lightning and stood in the stirrups whilst pulling up his head. He reared and as he fell he killed two of the men. Stephen the Grim finished the third. I leapt from my horse and turned to face our foes. I blocked a war hammer with my shield and as the warrior had used it two handed was able to sink my sword deep into him. Our last attack had broken their spirits. They were fleeing as more of my men arrived. The knights of Durham, led by Robert of Howden pursued them to the walls of Prudhoe.

Sheathing my sword, I ran to Sir Harold. His son Richard, kneeling by his father, said, "My father said that you would come and when he heard the horn it gave us heart."

"How is he?"

"He lives lord but he has a serious wound."

"Fetch healers! Brave men need them!"

I looked around and Saw Sir John with a dented helmet but alive. Sir Padraig and Sir Tristan grinned at me. Sir Philip was nursing a bloody head but he was alive. I saw his son Thomas run up to him and begin to tend to his wound. Then I looked at where my men were gathered. I saw the bodies of Sir Ralph of Gainford and his squire. They both lay dead. My daughter was a widow. I saw that he had been cut by many weapons.

Stephen the Grim said, "Lord he stepped into the breach when James of Tewksbury and Peter fell. When he was struck his squire stepped before him. They took many Scottish lives before they were felled. "

I nodded. I was dumbstruck. I had been too late. Sir John of Fissebourne approached me. He had his helmet in his hand. "They died well lord but I am sorry for your loss. I was lucky. He held up his helmet."

I turned for I had bad news to give him. He must have seen it in my face, "The Warlord he is not…"

I shook my head, "He lives but he has another wound." I put my hand on his shoulder, "Your son, Simon, gave his life protecting him when he was felled. But for Thomas of Piercebridge then it might have been worse."

I saw his lips tighten. He nodded, "We all take risks and death is always a sword thrust away but a man should not outlive his children."

The Princes' Revolt

He suddenly realised what he had said, "I am sorry Earl. That was crass of me! Of course, you know and your bairns had less life on this earth than Simon. I am sorry."

"That was many years ago and it was God who took them."

"Where is Simon buried?"

"La Flèche. Leofric will tend his grave."

"We will visit the grave. My wife, Lady Edith, will need to grieve properly."

A knight galloped up. He was one of the knights from the New Castle. "My lord, the Sheriff and the Baron d'Umphraville wish to see you. The siege is relieved. The Scots have gone!"

Another victory but this one was the sourest one yet.

I handed my helmet to Ralph, soon to be Ralph of Thornaby. He shook his head, "I am sorry, lord for your loss. Sir Ralph was a valiant knight. Your son has taken it hard."

I had forgotten Samuel. I turned and saw him on his knees next to the body of his friend. He was openly weeping. He was not unmanned for they had been like brothers. This was another death I could lay at King Henry's door. If I had not been taken away from my home for what I considered an unnecessary task then Sir Harold and Sir John would not have had to do that which was my appointed task!

"A great victory Earl! You were right to come so quick."

"Aye Sheriff but obviously not quick enough. My daughter's husband died."

"I am sorry."

There was an uncomfortable silence. It was not their fault. "We rest for a day and then push on to Alnwick. This King William will pay for this!"

I saw the Sheriff shift from foot to foot, "Lord the men…"

"The men will do as I order!"

There were no more arguments.

We buried our dead by the church. The Scots were burned but our dead were treated with reverence and honour. We had lost men at arms and archers. I did not care that others had lost men. These were my men. Each one was precious to me for I had fought alongside them all. For Samuel this was his first grieving. This was personal and I saw a change in him from that day. He became more disciplined and a little colder. Both made him a better warrior. He also developed a hatred of the Scots.

He would become their nemesis. That was some years off. For the present he grieved, as we all did.

We had four hundred knights left and I devised a plan. I discussed it with my leading captains as well as my household knights. I saw that James de Puiset stood close to Samuel. He was aware of what was going through Samuel's mind. He had ridden with them when we had fought at Norham.

"I know that many of you think I am driving the army too hard. I am not. We have to finish this war quickly for the Earl of Leicester with the Earl of Norfolk and they are advancing from the south. There will be no reinforcements coming to aid us. Carlisle is under siege and the Earl of Chester forced to defend Chester. The enemy outnumbers us and their numbers will grow. We have one chance, we take their King. We cut the head from the hydra!" I saw nods. "Our men at arms and our archers have suffered losses. Our knights have barely been touched." I saw my son flash his eyes in my direction. "The ones we did lose will be avenged. I propose to ride with every knight that we have. We will be ahead of the main army. I will use my scouts to find the King's camp and we will attack him at dawn. Baron Prudhoe you will stay here and repair your castle. Sheriff you will lead the rest of the army."

Odinel d'Umphraville asked, "You would ride with, less than four hundred men into the enemy camp and try to take King William?" I nodded, "That is suicide."

"It is a risk I grant you but one worth taking. I have the two finest scouts in the land and they will find him. Once we have him then the army can protect us."

There were many more questions but none came from the knights I would be leading.

"The wounded men and knights who can ride will accompany the army. The rest will stay here in Prudhoe. It is fifty miles to Alnwick. Each knight will take two horses. One to reach Alnwick and one on which he will fight. We leave here in the afternoon so that we can travel during the night. They will not expect us then. You all have the night and the morning to rest."

Leaving them to discuss my plan I left and sought Masood and Aiden. Edward and Edgar had been with Sir Harold. Now I could use them too. "I need to know precisely where King William is camped. It will be close to Alnwick for that is the castle which is being besieged. He will not go west to Carlisle. It is too far. We will be following on the road. You must find him."

"Do not worry lord we will. It will be for Sir Ralph and the Lady Ruth."

I went to the horse lines with Ralph and Thomas. Both were more serious than they had been. Sir Ralph had been popular with everyone. "I will ride Goldie and take Volva."

"Do we bring the banner and accompany you, lord?"

"No Ralph. The squires will be the horsemen who ride with the army. You will all have a great responsibility. All the squires did well in the battle of the New Castle. You must behave as well tomorrow." The Sheriff would only have the squires if my plan failed.

As it was July the days were long and the nights were short. I did not sleep well. I was rehearsing how I would tell my daughter that her husband had lost his life and it was my fault. I had not kept him close to me with Samuel and I would have to live with that for the rest of my life.

It was a hot day. I did not ride in mail. I felt reckless and yet I also believed that there were no Scots between us and Alnwick. I was saving Goldie. All life was precious to me, even my horse. We did pass Scots but they were stragglers and deserters. They fled when they heard our horses. We had just ten men at arms with us. They would guard the horses. All were volunteers and all were my men.

Edward met us north of Warkworth. Warkworth Castle had not been defended. Roger Fitz Eustace was with us. His castle needed repairs and he had not defended it. As we had ridden through the village which nestled beneath the castle mound and walls Fitz Eustace regretted his decision. The villagers had been slaughtered. The church of St Lawrence in which many had taken refuge had been burned to the ground. The unburied bodies hardened the hearts of every knight. It hardened every heart against the Scots. They were savages.

"We have found them, lord. He is at Alnwick. There are three large camps around the castle and the King has a smaller one with sixty of his household knights. It is in a bend of the River Aln. We can ford the river, lord. The others watch it. I will lead you there."

Night fell and we continued north and west. When we reached the farm of Ledbury we halted. I had pushed the men hard. We needed to change into war gear and to mount our warhorses. I noticed that a fog had descended. Would that hinder or help us? Only God would know that. It took longer to prepare than I had expected. That was mainly because the knights had no squires and some had forgotten how to saddle a warhorse. Leaving the men at arms with the horses we mounted and followed Edward. The fog became thicker. It was hard to judge distances and to hear sounds. It was as though everything was muffled. I rode bareheaded but many of my knights had helmets upon their heads. They were in a grey tunnel.

Edgar met us in a wood. We had left the road at Ledbury. He spoke quietly. "Lord they are on the other side of the river. The fog is masking their sounds but Aiden and Masood can hear them. It is almost dawn and they are rising. Aiden says if you wish surprise you should strike quickly."

I nodded and signalled for men to prepare. I tightened the straps on my shield. I checked to see who would be rising close to me. Samuel, Sir Padraig, Sir Morgan; all my valley knights were there along with Sir James de Puiset. We would ride in together. To ensure that we all arrived together I had divided us up into ten groups of knights. Each would cross the river at a different point. The signal to advance would be when Volva stepped into the river.

I raised my spear and spurred my horse. Dawn was just breaking behind us and the fog was dissipating but it was a slow process. I leaned back in the saddle as Volva stepped down from the bank. The river was narrow but the water came up to my knees. I was just leaning forward as Volva climbed out when I heard a splash and a shout. One of the knights further along the river had fallen into the river. I heard the sound of a horn as the alarm was sounded. We would not have the surprise that I had hoped. I spurred Volva and shouted, "Death to the Scots!" The cry was taken up along the river as my men also spurred their horses.

As soon as we broke through the trees which grew along the river we were in the open but there was still fog lying like a blanket on the ground. I had to trust that there were no stakes hidden beneath the grey fog. I was aware of knights to my left and right. The sun came up, suddenly, behind me. It must have cleared the trees. I saw the royal tents and, beyond them King William and his knights. This time he did not flee. He was going to charge us. The fog had aided us. He would not see our true numbers. For the first time that I could remember we outnumbered our enemy. Both lines were ragged but we were prepared for war and the Scots had woken to it.

The first knight who reached our line had the misfortune to meet me. As a royal knight, he was skilled but I was vengeful. I pulled back my spear and rammed it hard towards his right side. It went under his sword and came up to strike his mail shirt. My punch was hard and I drove the spearhead into his body. I twisted and pulled. It looked like I had pulled snakes from his body. I veered Volva to the left and caught a Scottish knight by surprise. He had seen a chance to attack me on my left when suddenly he found my spear lunging at his throat. As he tumbled backwards his dying body he pulled the spear from my grasp.

As I drew my sword I saw Padraig charge at King William. Sir Morgan was on his shoulder. The two of them were obeying my orders. They were trying to kill the King. Padraig's spear took the King's horse. That saved the King's life for Alf's spear hit the shield of the King as he fell from his mount. As soon as he was down the Scottish knights behaved as a King would hope they would. They dismounted and made a shield wall around him. "The knights with spears attack!"

The sun had now cleared the trees and the fog was disappearing quickly. Already half of the Scots had died and, so far as I could see, we had lost not a man. When the knights with spears began to stab and skewer the Scottish knights the circle of Scottish knights shrank. I nudged my horse forward.

"King William you are surrounded. These are brave men! Do not let them die needlessly for they will die!" As if to make the point one Scottish knight ran at Samuel with his long sword held in two hands. My son deftly pirouetted his horse and as the Scot struck fresh air my son's sword bit through the back of his neck and took his head.

King William shouted, "Enough! We yield! Curse you, son of the Warlord!"

Sir Samuel laughed, "King William your curses are about as effective as your plans. The war is over and Sir Ralph is avenged."

My household knights all chorused, "Amen!"

We could go home and I could see if Brother Peter had managed to help my father.

The Princes' Revolt

The Warlord

Epilogue

My son had, once more, made me proud. It was six months since the battle of Alnwick and it had been as complete a victory as one could wish. King William had been taken, first to the New Castle and thence to Falaise. We had heard that as part of the treaty King William had sworn to acknowledge King Henry as his liege lord. The Scots would have to give up their claims to the land of the north. Armies were coming from the south to occupy Roxburgh, Berwick, Jedburgh, Edinburgh and Stirling. The Scots were finished and it had been in my lifetime. My work was done. I had saved England from King Stephen and my son had saved the north from the Scots.

The sad news of Ruth's husband's death had cast a pallor over the castle and the valley which stopped us enjoying the victory. Ruth grieved and entered a dark place. That gloom was lifted when Eleanor bore Samuel a son. He was named Thomas and he was a healthy boy. I had a great grandson. The blood of Ridley the Housecarl would flow once more in the veins of a warrior who would defend England.

While all that had been going on I had been fighting my own battle. I had fought it alongside a warrior monk from the east. Brother Peter had shaved my head and I was given drugged wine to make me sleep. When I had awoken my head had been bathed in bandages. Brother Peter had had a serious look on his face when I recovered from the drugged wine.

"You could not heal me?"

"I have mended the broken skull, lord but..."

"Brother Peter, I am a man and I have lived seventy years. Whatever you tell me I can take." He nodded. "And whatever you tell me is like the confessional; it does not leave this chamber." He looked at me. Questions were in his eyes. "I would have you swear. You are an honourable man and a priest."

"I swear." He sighed. "I fear that your life will be measured in months not years. I saw something inside your skull. It should not have been there. This is beyond my limited skills. I can do nothing about it. You may have less pain but..."

I had smiled and put my hand on the old crusader. "Then I will enjoy what time I have left. Remember your oath. I would have you check me each month. Let me know when my time is nigh. I will then make preparations for the end."

He had kept his word. My son had returned when the bandages had been removed and just the raw scars remained. The stubble on my head had begun to hide them. When Ruth had been given the news, she had come to me and laid next to me sobbing. I had cradled her head in my arms. If I could have exchanged places with her dead husband it would not have needed a moment's thought. I had not been there. My days of war were over.

"When she had finished crying she had said, "Thank you, grandfather. Somehow your silence helped. I felt your thoughts." She looked at me. "Is that blasphemous? Am I a witch?"

"No, my love, you are of my blood. I know what you feel."

"Then know this I shall never marry another. I could not replace the love of my life." She shook her head. "I was not meant to have children. I lost one bairn before he could be born. I swear that when my brother's wife has a child then I will care for that as though it was my own."

"But the child will have a mother."

"Then I shall be the best aunt. And I can also make certain that the people of Stockton are protected. I will do good works. There are poor here. I have money left by Ralph. I will use that. Do not worry, grandfather, my life will not be wasted. There is a purpose to it. There must be. I had Ralph for such a short time but I lived for those few years."

And when Thomas was born Ruth was as happy as her brother and his wife. My son and his wife beamed and I felt complete. My blood had been passed on. In my heart I knew that Thomas would be as I had been, as his father was, he would be a Warlord. He would be the bane of the Scots and he would defend this land with his life. Wulfstan had once said that the world was a circle and held together by webs we did not understand. He had told me of hidden threads that bound together men born long apart. When I held Thomas' hand, I felt such a thread. I looked into his clear blue eyes and it was like looking into a mirrored pool; my land would be safe in Thomas' tiny hand.

The End

Glossary

Aldeneby - Alston (Cumbria)
Al-Andalus- Spain
Angevin- the people of Anjou, especially the ruling family
Arthuret -Longtown in Cumbria (This is the Brythionic name)
Bannau Brycheiniog – Brecon Beacons
Battle- a formation in war (a modern battalion)
Booth Castle – Bewcastle north of Hadrian's Wall
Bachelor knight- an unattached knight
Banneret- a single knight
Burn- stream (Scottish)
Butts- targets for archers
Cadge- the frame upon which hunting birds are carried (by a codger- hence the phrase old codger being the old man who carries the frame)
Caerdyf- Cardiff
Caparison- a surcoat for a horse; often padded for protection
Captain- a leader of archers
Chausses - mail leggings. (They were separate- imagine lady's stockings rather than tights!)
Chevauchée- a raid by mounted men
Coningestun- Coniston
Conroi- A group of knights fighting together. The smallest unit of the period
Corebricg – Corbridge
Cuneceastra- Chester-Le-Street
Demesne- estate
Destrier- warhorse
Doxy- prostitute
Dyflin- Dublin
Dùn Èideann- Edinburgh
Fissebourne- Fishburn County Durham
Fess- a horizontal line in heraldry
Galloglass- Irish mercenaries
Gambeson- a padded tunic worn underneath mail. When worn by an archer they came to the waist. It was more of a quilted jacket but I have used the term freely
Gonfanon- A standard used in medieval times (Also known as a Gonfalon in Italy)

Hartness- the manor which became Hartlepool
Hautwesel- Haltwhistle
Hulle- Rhyl (North Wales)
Liedeberge- Ledbury
Lusitania- Portugal
Mansio- staging houses along Roman Roads
Mare anglicum – English Channel
Maredudd ap Bleddyn- King of Powys
Martinmas- 11th November
Mêlée- a medieval fight between knights
Morthpath- Morpeth (Northumbria)
Moravians- the men of Moray
Mormaer- A Scottish lord and leader
Mummer- an actor from a medieval tableau
Musselmen- Muslims
Nithing- A man without honour (Saxon)
Nomismata- a gold coin equivalent to an aureus
Novo Burgus -Newport (Gwent)
Outremer- the kingdoms of the Holy Land
Owain ap Gruffudd- Son of Gruffudd ap Cynan and King of Gwynedd from 1137
Palfrey- a riding horse
Poitevin- the language of Aquitaine
Prestetone- Prestatyn- North Wales
Pyx- a box containing a holy relic (Shakespeare's Pax from Henry V)
Refuge- a safe area for squires and captives (tournaments)
Sauve qui peut – Every man for himself (French)
Serengford- Shellingford Oxfordshire
Sergeant-a leader of a company of men at arms
Striguil- Chepstow (Gwent)
Surcoat- a tunic worn over mail or armour
Sumpter- packhorse
Theophany- the feast which is on the 6th of January
Ventail   a piece of mail which covered the neck and the lower face
Veðrafjǫrðr -Waterford (Ireland)
Veisafjǫrðr- Wexford (Ireland)
Witenestaple- Whitstable (Kent)
Wulfestun- Wolviston (Durham)

ID# The Princes' Revolt

Historical Notes

The wars with the French

The Vexin was the parcel of land controlled by King Henry and close to the French capital. The French wanted it back and it formed the core of many disputes which lasted long after King Henry died. Despite always being defeated the Irish, Welsh and Scots constantly tried to defeat the Anglo-Normans and allied with the French at every opportunity.

Long-running tensions between Henry and Louis VII continued during the 1160s, the French king slowly becoming more vigorous in opposing Henry's increasing power in Europe. In 1160 Louis strengthened his alliances in central France with the Count of Champagne and Odo II, the Duke of Burgundy. Three years later the new Count of Flanders, Philip, concerned about Henry's growing power, openly allied himself with the French king. Louis' wife Adèle gave birth to a male heir, Philip Augustus, in 1165, and Louis was more confident of his own position than for many years previously. As a result, relations between Henry and Louis deteriorated again in the mid-1160s.

Meanwhile, Henry had begun to alter his policy of indirect rule in Brittany and started to exert more direct control. In 1164 Henry intervened to seize lands along the border of Brittany and Normandy, and in 1166 invaded Brittany to punish the local barons. Henry then forced Conan to abdicate as duke and to give Brittany to his daughter Constance; Constance was handed over and betrothed to Henry's son Geoffrey. This arrangement was quite unusual in terms of medieval law, as Conan might have had sons who could have legitimately inherited the duchy. Elsewhere in France, Henry attempted to seize the Auvergne, much to the anger of the French king. Further south Henry continued to apply pressure on Raymond of Toulouse: the King campaigned there personally in 1161, sent the Archbishop of Bordeaux against Raymond in 1164 and encouraged Alfonso II of Aragon in his attacks. In 1165 Raymond divorced Louis's sister and attempted to ally himself with Henry instead.

These growing tensions between Henry and Louis finally spilt over into open war in 1167, triggered by a trivial argument over how money destined for the Crusader states of the Levant should be collected. Louis allied himself with the Welsh, Scots and Bretons, and the French king attacked Normandy. Henry responded by attacking Chaumont-sur-Epte, where Louis kept his main military arsenal, burning the town to the ground and forcing Louis to abandon his allies and make a private truce. Henry was then free to move against the rebel barons in Brittany, where feelings about his seizure of the duchy were still running high.

As the decade progressed, Henry increasingly wanted to resolve the question of the inheritance. He decided that he would divide up his empire after his death, with Young Henry receiving England and Normandy, Richard being given the Duchy of Aquitaine, and Geoffrey acquiring Brittany. This would require the consent of Louis as king of France, and accordingly, Henry and Louis held fresh peace talks in 1169 at Montmirail. The talks were wide-ranging, culminating with Henry's sons giving homage to Louis for their future inheritances in France, and with Richard being betrothed to Louis' daughter Alice.

If the agreements at Montmirail had been followed up, the acts of homage could potentially have confirmed Louis' position as king, while undermining the legitimacy of any rebellious barons within Henry's territories and the potential for an alliance between them and Louis. In practice, however, Louis perceived himself to have gained a temporary advantage, and immediately after the conference he began to encourage tensions between Henry's sons. Meanwhile, Henry's position in the south of France continued to improve, and by 1173 he had agreed to an alliance with Humbert, the Count of Savoy, which betrothed Henry's son John and Humbert's daughter Alicia. Henry's daughter Eleanor was married to Alfonso VIII of Castile in 1170, enlisting an additional ally in the south. In February 1173, Raymond finally gave in and publicly gave homage for Toulouse to Henry and his heirs.

Thomas Becket and the Archbishop of York

The incident with William FitzEmpress and Thomas Becket happened the way I wrote it. The new Archbishop of Canterbury chose to deny William his happiness. He fled England for France when King Henry brought him to book for his refusal to confirm Henry's choice of priests. I made up his collusion with France. However, I am not a fan of Becket. In my view he was self-serving and sought power. I have no evidence that he wished to be Pope but it suits my story.

Roger de Pont L'Évêque was probably born around 1115 and was a native of Pont-L'Évêque in Normandy. His only known relative was a nephew, Geoffrey, to whom Roger gave the offices of the provost of Beverley Minster and archdeacon of York. Roger was a clerk of Archbishop Theobald's before being named Archdeacon of Canterbury,

The Princes' Revolt

sometime after March 1148. When Becket joined Theobald's household, their contemporary William Fitz Stephen recorded that Roger disliked the new clerk, and twice drove Thomas away before the archbishop's brother Walter arranged Thomas' return.

In June 1170, Roger de Pont L'Évêque, the archbishop of York, along with Gilbert Foliot, the Bishop of London, and Josceline de Bohon, the Bishop of Salisbury, crowned the heir apparent, Henry the Young King, at York. This was a breach of Canterbury's privilege of coronation, and in November 1170 Becket excommunicated all three. While the three clergymen fled to the king in Normandy, Becket continued to excommunicate his opponents in the church, the news of which also reached Henry II, Henry the Young King's father.

Upon hearing reports of Becket's actions, Henry is said to have uttered words that were interpreted by his men as wishing Becket killed. The king's exact words are in doubt and several versions have been reported. The most commonly quoted, as handed down by oral tradition, is "Will no one rid me of this turbulent priest?" but according to historian Simon Schama this is incorrect: he accepts the account of the contemporary biographer Edward Grim, writing in Latin, who gives us "What miserable drones and traitors have I nourished and brought up in my household, who let their lord be treated with such shameful contempt by a low-born cleric?" Many variations have found their way into popular culture.

Whatever Henry said, it was interpreted as a royal command, and four knights, Reginald FitzUrse, Hugh de Morville, William de Tracy and Richard le Breton, set out to confront the Archbishop of Canterbury.

On 29 December 1170, they arrived at Canterbury. According to accounts left by the monk Gervase of Canterbury and eyewitness Edward Grim, they placed their weapons under a tree outside the cathedral and hid their mail armour under cloaks before entering to challenge Becket. The knights informed Becket he was to go to Winchester to give an account of his actions, but Becket refused. It was not until Becket refused their demands to submit to the king's will that they retrieved their weapons and rushed back inside for the killing. Becket, meanwhile, proceeded to the main hall for vespers. The four knights, wielding drawn swords, caught up with him in a spot near a door to the monastic cloister, the stairs into the crypt, and the stairs leading up into the quire of the cathedral, where the monks were chanting vespers.

Several contemporary accounts of what happened next exist; of particular note is that of Edward Grim, who was wounded in the attack. This is part of the account from Edward Grim:

'The wicked knight leapt suddenly upon him, cutting off the top of the crown which the unction of sacred chrism had dedicated to God. Next, he received a second blow on the head, but still, he stood firm and immovable. At the third blow he fell on his knees and elbows, offering himself a living sacrifice, and saying in a low voice, "For the name of Jesus and the protection of the Church, I am ready to embrace death." But the third knight inflicted a terrible wound as he lay prostrate. By this stroke, the crown of his head was separated from the head in such a way that the blood white with the brain, and the brain no less red from the blood, dyed the floor of the cathedral. The same clerk who had entered with the knights placed his foot on the neck of the holy priest and precious martyr, and, horrible to relate, scattered the brains and blood about the pavements, crying to the others, 'Let us away, knights; this fellow will arise no more.'

After Becket's death

Following Becket's death, the monks prepared his body for burial. According to some accounts, it was discovered that Becket had worn a hair shirt under his archbishop's garments—a sign of penance. Soon after, the faithful throughout Europe began venerating Becket as a martyr, and on 21 February 1173—little more than two years after his death—he was canonised by Pope Alexander III in St Peter's Church in Segni. In 1173, Becket's sister Mary was appointed Abbess of Barking as reparation for the murder of her brother. On 12 July 1174, in the midst of the Revolt of 1173–74, Henry humbled himself with public penance at Becket's tomb as well as at the church of St. Dunstan's, which became one of the most popular pilgrimage sites in England.

Becket's assassins fled north to Knaresborough Castle, which was held by Hugh de Morville, where they remained for about a year. De Morville held property in Cumbria and this may also have provided a convenient bolt-hole, as the men prepared for a longer stay in the separate kingdom of Scotland. They were not arrested and neither did Henry confiscate their lands, but he failed to help them when they sought his advice in August 1171. Pope Alexander excommunicated all four. Seeking forgiveness, the assassins travelled to Rome and were ordered by the Pope to serve as knights in the Holy Lands for a period of fourteen years.

Bamburgh Castle

I have used this castle in many books from the Saxon ones onward. I had made up a story about a tunnel from the castle leading to the sea. Imagine my surprise when, on a visit in 2016 a guide told me that there was such a tunnel which was accessed through the well. The last person who had been down had gone there 30 years ago. Sadly, the entrance and exit have now been blocked for health and safety. It is a magnificent castle and although it has many later additions the site must have remained the same for millennia. It is well worth a visit and, to my mind, superior to the much more popular Alnwick Castle.

Bamburgh Castle (author's collection)

Norham Castle

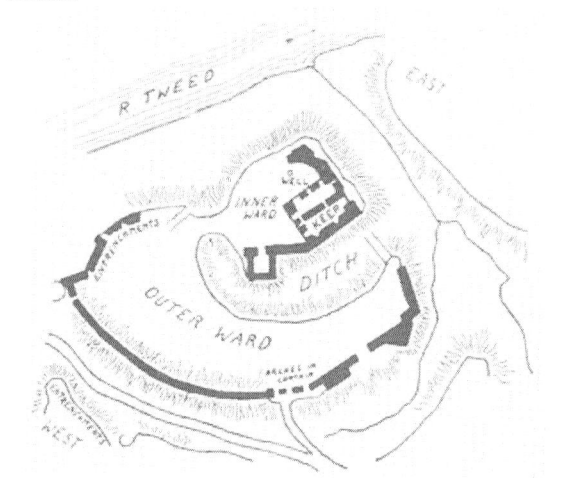

The Great Revolt
The Princes' rebellion happened almost exactly the way it was written. Young King Henry fled to Louis' court followed by his brothers. The Queen tried to flee but was captured and taken to Henry. King Henry gathered his loyal knights and they defeated first the Flemish then they destroyed Louis and his son's army. Finally, they routed the Bretons. The Earl of Leicester then returned to England to begin a rebellion there while Henry was still in Normandy. King William of Scotland took advantage of the King's absence to invade the north. The revolt was futile. King Henry emerged even stronger. By the Treaty of Falaise King William acknowledged that King Henry was his liege lord. The King and his sons agreed a peace. It was an uneasy one and it lasted just a short time.

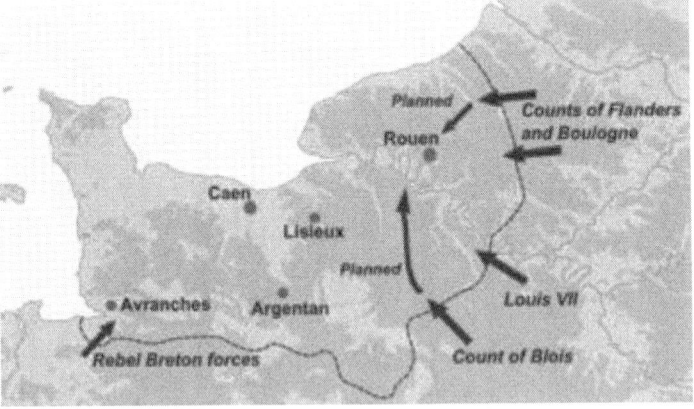

The rebellion of 1173-74 and the planned attacks.
William of Scotland
William had inherited the title of Earl of Northumbria in 1152. However, he had to give up this title to King Henry II of England in 1157. He spent much of his reign trying to regain his lost territory. In 1173, whilst Henry II was occupied in fighting against his sons in the Revolt of 1173–1174, William saw his opportunity and invaded Northumbria. He advanced on Newcastle but found the partly built stone castle too strong to allow him to take the town. He also attacked Prudhoe Castle but found the defences too strong. Unwilling to undertake a lengthy siege, William returned to Scotland. In 1174, William again invaded Northumbria with an even larger army that included a contingent of Flemish mercenaries. The army was said to have numbered eighty thousand men, but this is almost certainly an exaggeration. This time he

The Princes' Revolt

avoided Newcastle but attacked Prudhoe Castle again. The castle had been strengthened since the previous year and after a siege of three days, William moved north to besiege Alnwick. William divided his army into three columns and one of these, under the command of Duncan, Earl of Fife, attacked Warkworth and set fire to the church of St Lawrence with a large number of refugees inside.

The battle

William made the fatal error of allowing his army to spread out, instead of concentrating them around his base at Alnwick. On the night of 11 July, a party of about four hundred mounted knights, led by Ranulf de Glanvill, set out from Newcastle and headed towards Alnwick. This small fighting force contained several seasoned knights, who had fought against the Scots before. They reached Alnwick shortly after dawn after becoming lost in a heavy fog. There they found William's encampment, where the Scottish king was only protected by a bodyguard of perhaps sixty fighting men. At the sound of alarm, William rushed from his tent and hurriedly prepared to fight. The English force charged and the Scottish king and his bodyguard met the charge head on. The fighting did not last long. William's horse was killed beneath him and he was captured. Those of his followers who had not been killed surrendered.

Aftermath

William was brought back to Newcastle as a captive. His army found itself leaderless and wandered back to Scotland. William was held at Newcastle for a time but it was not considered strong enough, and he was finally moved to Falaise in Normandy. Whilst he was there, Henry sent an army to occupy part of Scotland, with its five strongest castles: Roxburgh, Berwick, Jedburgh, Edinburgh and Stirling. To obtain his freedom, William was forced to sign the Treaty of Falaise, under which he swore an oath of allegiance to the English king and agreed to the garrisoning of the captured castles by English soldiers at Scottish expense. When William was released, after signing the treaty, he travelled back to Scotland via Newcastle, and was attacked by a mob; such was the antipathy of the local people towards Scottish invaders.

This is a novel and as such fiction. I have condensed the two attacks into one and poor Ranulf de Glanvill has been replaced by Earl William. Apologies to his descendants.

This is the penultimate book in the series. It ends in 1174 and the series ends in 1180. The story does continue with Thomas but that is in the Border Knight series. The last book is called **Earl Marshal**.

Books used in the research:

- Chronicles of the age of chivalry- Elizabeth Hallam
- The Varangian Guard- 988-1453 Raffael D'Amato
- Saxon Viking and Norman- Terence Wise
- The Walls of Constantinople AD 324-1453-Stephen Turnbull
- Byzantine Armies- 886-1118- Ian Heath
- The Age of Charlemagne-David Nicolle
- The Normans- David Nicolle
- Norman Knight AD 950-1204- Christopher Gravett
- The Norman Conquest of the North- William A Kappelle
- The Knight in History- Francis Gies
- The Norman Achievement- Richard F Cassady
- Knights- Constance Brittain Bouchard
- Knight Templar 1120-1312 -Helen Nicholson
- Feudal England: Historical Studies on the Eleventh and Twelfth Centuries- J. H. Round
- Armies of the Crusades- Helen Nicholson
- Knight of Outremer 1187- 1344 - David Nicholle
- Crusader Castles in the Holy Land- David Nicholle
- The Crusades- David Nicholle
- Bamburgh Castle Heritage group
- Warkworth Castle- English Heritage Guide
- The Times Atlas of World History
- Old Series Ordnance Survey Maps #93 Middlesbrough
- Old Series Ordnance Survey Maps #81 Alnwick and Morpeth
- Old Series Ordnance Survey Maps #92 Barnard Castle

For those who like authentic maps, the last two maps are part of a series now available. They are the first Government produced maps of the British Isles. Great Britain, apart from the larger conurbations, was the same as it had been 800 years earlier.

I also discovered a good website http://orbis.stanford.edu/. This allows a reader to plot any two places in the Roman world and if you input the mode of transport you wish to use and the time of year it will calculate how long it would take you to travel the route. I have used it for all of my books up to the eighteenth century as the transportation system was roughly the same. The Romans would have been quicker! I used it in this book and according to Orbis the journey from London to Rouen would have taken 2.7 days! In summer it would have been 3.1! it is an impressive resource. It explains why Henry get to and from Normandy so quickly.

Griff Hosker
April 2018

Other books by Griff Hosker

If you enjoyed reading this book, then why not read another one by the author?

Ancient History

The Sword of Cartimandua Series
(Germania and Britannia 50 A.D. – 128 A.D.)
Ulpius Felix- Roman Warrior (prequel)
The Sword of Cartimandua
The Horse Warriors
Invasion Caledonia
Roman Retreat
Revolt of the Red Witch
Druid's Gold
Trajan's Hunters
The Last Frontier
Hero of Rome
Roman Hawk
Roman Treachery
Roman Wall
Roman Courage

The Wolf Warrior series
(Britain in the late 6th Century)
Saxon Dawn
Saxon Revenge
Saxon England
Saxon Blood
Saxon Slayer
Saxon Slaughter
Saxon Bane
Saxon Fall: Rise of the Warlord
Saxon Throne
Saxon Sword

Medieval History

The Dragon Heart Series
Viking Slave
Viking Warrior
Viking Jarl
Viking Kingdom
Viking Wolf
Viking War
Viking Sword
Viking Wrath
Viking Raid
Viking Legend
Viking Vengeance
Viking Dragon
Viking Treasure
Viking Enemy
Viking Witch
Viking Blood
Viking Weregeld
Viking Storm
Viking Warband
Viking Shadow
Viking Legacy
Viking Clan
Viking Bravery

The Norman Genesis Series
Hrolf the Viking
Horseman
The Battle for a Home
Revenge of the Franks
The Land of the Northmen
Ragnvald Hrolfsson
Brothers in Blood
Lord of Rouen
Drekar in the Seine
Duke of Normandy
The Duke and the King

The Princes' Revolt

New World Series
Blood on the Blade
Across the Seas
The Savage Wilderness
The Bear and the Wolf

The Vengeance Trail

The Reconquista Chronicles
Castilian Knight
El Campeador
The Lord of Valencia

The Aelfraed Series
(Britain and Byzantium 1050 A.D. - 1085 A.D.)
Housecarl
Outlaw
Varangian

The Anarchy Series England 1120-1180
English Knight
Knight of the Empress
Northern Knight
Baron of the North
Earl
King Henry's Champion
The King is Dead
Warlord of the North
Enemy at the Gate
The Fallen Crown
Warlord's War
Kingmaker
Henry II
Crusader
The Welsh Marches
Irish War
Poisonous Plots

The Princes' Revolt
Earl Marshal

Border Knight
1182-1300
Sword for Hire
Return of the Knight
Baron's War
Magna Carta
Welsh Wars
Henry III
The Bloody Border
Baron's Crusade
Sentinel of the North
War in the West

Sir John Hawkwood Series
France and Italy 1339- 1387
Crécy: The Age of the Archer
Man At Arms

Lord Edward's Archer
Lord Edward's Archer
King in Waiting
An Archer's Crusade

Struggle for a Crown
1360- 1485
Blood on the Crown
To Murder A King
The Throne
King Henry IV
The Road to Agincourt
St Crispin's Day

Tales from the Sword

Conquistador
England and America in the 16th Century

The Princes' Revolt

Conquistador (Coming in 2021)

Modern History

The Napoleonic Horseman Series
Chasseur à Cheval
Napoleon's Guard
British Light Dragoon
Soldier Spy
1808: The Road to Coruña
Talavera
The Lines of Torres Vedras
Bloody Badajoz
The Road to France

The Lucky Jack American Civil War series
Rebel Raiders
Confederate Rangers
The Road to Gettysburg

The British Ace Series
1914
1915 Fokker Scourge
1916 Angels over the Somme
1917 Eagles Fall
1918 We will remember them
From Arctic Snow to Desert Sand
Wings over Persia

Combined Operations series 1940-1945
Commando
Raider
Behind Enemy Lines
Dieppe
Toehold in Europe
Sword Beach
Breakout

The Princes' Revolt

The Battle for Antwerp
King Tiger
Beyond the Rhine
Korea
Korean Winter

Other Books
Great Granny's Ghost (Aimed at 9-14-year-old young people)

For more information on all of the books then please visit the author's web site at www.griffhosker.com where there is a link to contact him or visit his Facebook page: GriffHosker at Sword Books

Printed in Great Britain
by Amazon